ARI

Hope N

MICHAEL
STEPHEN
FUCHS

ARISEN

RAIDERS

VOLUME 2
TRIBES

# ARISEN
# RAIDERS

*VOLUME 2*
*TRIBES*

# MICHAEL
# STEPHEN
# FUCHS

First published 2020 by Complete & Total Asskicking Books
London, UK

Copyright © Michael Stephen Fuchs

ISBN: 9798486843631 (hardcover)

*For Alex (it's been a while).*

# ABOUT THE AUTHOR

**MICHAEL STEPHEN FUCHS** is co-author of the first eight books of the bestselling *ARISEN* series, and solo author of Books Nine through Fourteen (the climax and conclusion of the series), as well as the stand-alone prequels *ARISEN*: Genesis, *ARISEN*: Nemesis, *ARISEN*: Odyssey, and *ARISEN*: Last Stand – which have repeatedly been Amazon #1 bestsellers in Post-Apocalyptic Science Fiction, #1 in Dystopian Science Fiction, #1 in Military Science Fiction, #1 in War Fiction, and #1 in War & Military Action Fiction, as well as Amazon overall Top 100 bestsellers. The series as a whole has sold over a half-million copies. The audiobook editions, performed by R.C. Bray, have generated over $3 million in revenue. He is also author of the D-BOYS series of high-tech special-operations military adventure novels, which include *D-Boys, Counter-Assault,* and *Close Quarters Battle* (coming in 2021); as well as the existential cyberthrillers *The Manuscript* and *Pandora's Sisters,* both published worldwide by Macmillan in hardback, paperback and all e-book formats (and in translation). He lives in London and at www.michaelstephenfuchs.com, and blogs at www.michaelfuchs.org/razorsedge. You can follow him on Facebook (facebook.com/michaelstephenfuchs), Twitter (@michaelstephenf), Instagram (@michaelstephenfuchs), or by e-mail (michaelstephenfuchs.com/alerts).

# ABOUT THE
# *ARISEN* SERIES

The eighteen books in the bestselling, top-ranked, and fan-favorite *ARISEN* series have repeatedly been ranked #1 in five different Amazon category bestseller lists, as well as in the Top 100 across all of Amazon. Collectively, they have earned over 5,000 reviews averaging 4.7 stars out of 5.0 (Including a 4.9-star average for each of the last two books in the main series, *The Siege* and *ENDGAME*.)
Readers call ARISEN:

**"thoroughly engrossing, taking you on a wild ride through utter devastation" … "the best post-apocalyptic military fiction there is" … "Wall to wall adrenaline – edge of your seat unputdownable**

until the very last page" … "the most amazing and intense battle scenes you've ever experienced" … "rolls along like an out of control freight train" … "They grab you on the first page and kick your ass through the entire series" … "insane propulsive storytelling" … "You feel like the explosions are going off beside your head" … "you never know what the hell is coming at you next" … "Every time I think it cannot get any better, BAM!" … "Blows World War Z out of the water" … "The Game of Thrones of the Zombie Apocalypse" … "Like a Michael Bay movie on steroids" … "like trying to ride a bronco in a tornado" … "roars out of the gate at 200mph and just keeps going" … "If you haven't read these you need to reevaluate your life" … "dials the volume to the point of annihilating the sound system" … "A superb ending to an absolutely mesmerizing and phenomenal series. This was an experience I'll never forget."

# LET'S GO HOME

*USS Rainier – Sick Bay*

*Blackness. Rest, peace – safety and care.*

*Voices – muffled, and distant. But also close.*

*"Do you think he can hear us?"*

*"No, probably not. But you never know. It definitely doesn't hurt having you here. The sound of human voices. His teammates."*

*"Okay, Doc. What about his prognosis?"*

*"We're keeping him sedated until the brain swelling goes down, and obviously treating it as a TBI. There's the severe concussion, of course, but imaging also shows a contusion on the right side of his pSTS – the posterior superior temporal sulcus."*

*"Afraid I don't that know that one, Commander."*

*"Well, an injury there shouldn't impact his ability to do his job – if anything, it'll turn him into one of your Marines."*

*"What does that mean?"*

*"Hey, just a joke. Sorry. The pSTS is the part of the brain that mediates social interactions. It processes social information, cooperation and competition – hey, don't look so glum, Gunny. The brain has a lot of plasticity, and the ability to heal itself, or else route around damage. I wish I had a neurologist on staff, or at least an MRI or CT scanner to shoot better film of his brain. But most modern medicine honestly comes down to giving the body enough time to heal itself. That goes double for the brain, which we don't understand well enough to do a lot of fiddling. There's every chance he'll have a full recovery, with no lingering effects from the injury. Or just minor ones."*

*"Okay."*

*"We just have to give him time – to heal."*

*** 

*"Jesus, Gunny. You look like shit hammered with a rock. You been sleeping in here? Fuck me, Wyoming looks worse. Oh, yeah, I mean, Wisconsin. Whatever. What? Don't look at me like that. It's not like he can hear us. Oh, Doc Walker – hey."*

*"Master Guns, could you kindly get the hell out of my improvised half-assed bullshit welfare hospital ward?"*

*"Hey, what I do?"*

*"I think you just got out-Ficked is what."*

*"What you have done is you've already annoyed me in your first five seconds in here. And if you and your devil dogs do turn into flesh-eating freaks in quarantine, I don't want you to be the freak who eats me."*

*"Don't tempt me, Doc. 'Cause you are one long tall drink of... whatever it is you're a long tall drink of. Okay, okay, I'm going... Just tell me one thing. Yaz gonna be okay?"*

*"God loves corpsmen, Master Guns. Marines and medics."*

*** 

*"Doc."*

*"Doc."*

*"What do you need, Milam? And how's the hand?"*

*"Hand's fine. Little stiff. Just wanted to check on him."*

*"If what you mean is you wanted to check if there's anything you can do I haven't already done, the answer's no."*

*"Yeah. I know that."*

*"And if you what you mean is, Is there anything you could have*

2

*done to prevent this, the answer is also no. If you're really intent on lacerating yourself because you didn't stay behind to help your Marines fight their way out of there, be my guest. But there's less than no point. And it's because you went back on the casevac bird, looking after the wounded, that Flynn was still breathing when he landed on the flat-top."*

"Yeah. I know. I really just wanted to check on him."

"Okay. His chart's there. Be my guest."

\* \* \*

*"How's he doing?"*

*"Ice Cube, you should not be hobbling around on that thing."*

*"Eh, it's basically healed. I have been instructed not to compete in the 400-meter hurdles anytime soon, and I also feel a little violated, having had Yaz's fist all the way up my pelvis. You can't unremember that shi— Hey, did his eyes just open?"*

*"Maybe. He's also smiling. Guess he had a good time, too."*

*"Yaz, hey. I just want you to know, without you... I..."*

*"I think he's out again, Brandon. And he knows."*

*"Yeah. Okay. I guess I'll, uh... I'll speak to him later."*

*"Go lie down, brother. Two weeks shouldn't be too long for you to take it easy, with a severed and reconstructed artery. The plane hitting that bridge tried to take you out."*

*"But I'm too fast, too pretty..."*

*"You're too something. Now go lie down."*

\* \* \*

"Well, your timing's pretty damned uncanny."

Yaz's mouth felt like he'd been chewing on a glue stick from the beginning of time to the end of the world. He was afraid to speak because of what his breath must smell like.

Every part of his body felt stiff as old tree stumps, and achy as a boxer the morning after a twelve-round title fight. He tried twisting his neck to the right, which made his head pound. But it also allowed him to see Gunnery Sergeant Blane, sitting on a folding chair by his bedside, bare forearms resting on his knees. He wore MCCUUs – the Marine Corps Combat Utility Uniform, more commonly known as cammies – with the sleeves rolled up to his elbows.

But no rifle, vest, or combat gear.

So they must have made it back alive.

Another blurry look around showed Yaz they were in a small and rudimentary sick bay, which had been somewhat tricked out. X-ray and ultrasound machines sat crammed against a counter, and of the three hospital beds in there, one was surrounded with elaborate ICU equipment.

That was the one Yaz lay on.

"Where are we?" he croaked.

Blane smiled down at him, the look on his square, dark, and handsome face suggesting he was very happy indeed to see Yaz awake. "We're on the *Rainier*. Our ammunition, oiler, and supply ship. Also now our plague ship."

"Plague ship? That sounds pretty cool." Yaz blinked several times, his eyes feeling almost as sticky as his mouth.

Blane laughed. "Yeah, it kind of does. But it was really just the most backwater place in the strike group to quarantine us. They've cordoned off several frames on 01 Deck, a dozen compartments including the sick bay. With two sets of dogged hatches and armed guards at either end."

"What kind of armed guards?"

"NSF."

"Huh." Yaz worked his glue-stuck mouth, then saw a glass of water on the bedside table – with a folded paper napkin wrapped around it. He decided for the moment to not ask who did that, but drank half the water before speaking again. "Anybody think NSF'll stop you if you want to get out?"

"Stop *us*, you mean." Yaz noticed the emphasis. Blane was making something clear – that Yaz was one of them now. And that meant everything. "No, I don't suppose they could stop us. Not if we're still alive, anyway. But that's the point of quarantine. Keep us getting out if we're dead. Mainly, the guards just pass us our meal trays three times a day."

With this, a female officer entered, stopped just inside the hatch, and put her hand on her hip. She wore a crisp khaki uniform with a Flight Surgeon Badge on her chest and a service side arm on her hip. Her nametape read *Walker*, and she had a commanding presence, owning the room instantly. "Thought I heard you two yakking it up in here."

She stepped over to a wall dispenser, pulled out a pair of examination gloves, and pulled them on as she approached Yaz's bedside. "Good morning, Corpsman. I'm Lieutenant Commander Walker, CO of the hospital on the *Kennedy*. How are you feeling today?"

"Good," Yaz said. "Little stiff. All this trouble for me?"

Walker ignored the question as she started to palpate Yaz's body parts, as well as bend his limbs around.

Blane said, "Doc Walker just spent two weeks here in quarantine – to look after you."

Yaz didn't respond to this. He didn't know how to.

Walker pulled out a penlight and peered into Yaz's eyes, checking pupil dilation response, and intracranial pressure. "I'm here to look after all of you. Anyway, it got me out of the office, and away from my staff for a while. Ever have a whole department reporting to you? Have kids instead. They can at least amuse themselves for a while."

She then tested and examined Yaz's motor functions, reflexes, sensory systems, and coordination – including the old finger-to-nose test. She must have liked what she saw, because she straightened up and said:

"Okay. You ready to get the hell out of here, or what?"

Looking at Blane, Yaz said, "I thought we were quarantined."

"We were," Blane said, checking his watch. "Until seventy minutes ago, which is when our mandated two weeks came to an end. That's why I said your timing was good."

Yaz looked back to Walker. "Am I discharged?"

"Only from this taco stand. I can keep a better eye on you on the *Kennedy*."

"And while we all appreciated being allowed back in the strike group at all," Blane added, "this place is kind of grim. Like sitting around inside a rundown oil refinery."

Sitting up, Yaz said, "Is the rest of the team going back?"

"You kidding?" Blane said, crossing the room to open a drawer. "They left sixty-nine and a half minutes ago. We're the stragglers." From the drawer, Blane retrieved not the fatigues Yaz had worn on the mission, but a fresh set of cammies. Yaz knew when he put these on, he'd be visually indistinguishable from the Marines he served with.

And also the men he served.

Yaz said, "I presume nobody turned into… well, turned."

Blane said, "No, none of us. But it wasn't just us in here."

"Who else?"

"As soon as Drake got this place set up, he backfilled it with everyone who'd been ashore – all those shore patrolmen and other sailors who came back before us."

"And?"

"And it was a damned good thing he did."

"Shit. Wait – we were all locked up in here with them? What the hell was that like?"

"Like that scene from *The Thing*, or one of the *Alien* movies, when people are locked up in a cell with one of them, screaming at the others to let them the fuck out."

"Jesus Christ."

"Yeah, well, everyone was screaming but Doc Walker here. And that side arm of hers isn't just for show."

Yaz nodded his respect. "All of us are okay?"

"Yeah," Blane said. "Everyone's good. And Coulson's recovering nicely – thanks to you."

Yaz threw the thin blanket off, slowly swung his legs over the edge of the bed, and then untied and removed his hospital gown. Looking down, he could see his abs, and obliques. It looked like two weeks of IV feeding had gotten the last body fat off. As he pulled on the crisp new fatigues, something tickled the back of his brain. Something about the mission, and casualties.

"Wait – Flynn. How's Flynn doing?"

Blane's expression sagged. "He didn't make it."

Her expression kind, Walker said, "There was nothing anybody could've done, Corpsman. Not outside a Level-5 trauma center. His vital organs were too torn up. But what you did for him gave him the best chance he was going to get."

She and Blane reached out steadying hands as Yaz stood up and wobbled.

"Come on," Blane said. "Let's go home."

Yaz liked the sound of that.

Perhaps more than anyone would ever know.

# BUTT PIRATES

*Pacific Ocean*

The brilliant sunshine, pristine air, and salt breeze were the best sensory experiences Yaz could remember having.

Then again, all his memories were from a different world.

Right now, he and Blane rode on the outside of a little 10-meter utility craft, piloted by a single enlisted sailor in a helmet and life vest, while LCDR Walker sat inside the small cabin, dealing with someone on her cell phone. This was one of the *Rainier*'s two launches, used for moving personnel and supplies around the strike group, or back and forth to shore.

But there was absolutely no shore visible now.

Only trackless ocean, on all sides.

And it was also a fair distance from where the *Rainier* sat at anchor to where the rest of the strike group lay in rows.

"They sure kept us at arm's length," Yaz said to Blane.

"Yep. It's almost enough to make you feel toxic. Or infected."

Yaz scanned the bare and featureless horizon in all directions, through the spray the boat was kicking up, visibility good enough that he could see the curvature of the Earth, where dark blue ocean met brilliant blue sky. He didn't know how far from San Francisco they were. But it was far enough that this was basically open ocean.

"Where are we?" Yaz asked.

"About two hundred miles off the West Coast."

"Has there been any contact from Mattis? His team?"

Blane just shook his head sadly.

Yaz figured that meant they were assuming the worst. And they sure wouldn't be mounting another rescue mission. Not now. He turned around and looked off into the distance behind them, in the direction of America.

"What happened?" he asked.

"It's over," Blane said. "And we lost."

* * *

The two of them stood on the rear dock of the *Kennedy* for a few minutes, just watching the launch burble away again.

Walker had practically leapt off the boat, heading back to her duty station, though not before making Yaz promise he'd come by the hospital every day to get checked out, until she told him to stop. But the sunlight and fresh air were too delicious for Blane and Yaz to give up again so soon, before disappearing into the bowels of the supercarrier.

"How long did Flynn last?" Yaz asked.

Blane shook his head. "You can't think about that. Anyway, it was my fault. I hung him up in that shooting gallery."

Yaz looked over. "You were trying to keep him safe."

"So much for that plan."

"I didn't save him, either, Gunny."

"No one could have saved him, Doc. Not after that."

They both just stood there with the sunlight on their faces, feeling the clean breeze on their skin. Washing it all away.

"When's your briefing?" Yaz asked.

Blane checked his G-Shock, at the end of one bare forearm. "I've got a little time. Come on."

They turned and climbed one of the two ladders that led

up from the dock to the recessed fantail deck. Judging from the armed sailors posted there, the Force Protection Condition (FPCON) throughout the strike group must have been set at least to Charlie, the second highest level. But no one asked for their shipboard security cards, which was good because Yaz didn't have one yet.

He was in the weird position of having deployed on one of the most dramatic and lethal shore missions ever conducted by any embarked Marines, while having taken fewer than 20 steps on the vessel they were embarked to.

And he'd never yet been belowdecks.

Yaz already knew, at least in theory, that the USS *John F. Kennedy* was a giant, floating, self-sufficient city. Over 1,100 feet long and 250 feet both high and wide, she consisted of a billion individual parts, making up over 3,000 individual compartments, stretching across 25 decks. And she was home to nearly 5,000 personnel, working across 16 departments, some which would be medium-sized private companies.

As Yaz and Blane traversed the twisting ladders and passageways, making their way from one of the lowest decks, at the very stern, toward someplace in the middle, the boat made a soothing *Enterprise*-like hum that seemed to surround them on all sides. Part of this might have been the nuclear reactors, and ship's engines, Yaz wasn't sure. At the same time, legions of sailors went by, as individuals or groups small and large, ducking around Yaz and Blane like they weren't there at all.

This city was alive, and life here went on.

Perhaps most bizarrely, everything looked and smelled clean and brand-new. Was there such a thing as that new aircraft carrier smell? Yaz didn't really know. The only other one he'd ever been on, and then just long enough to switch aircraft on the flight deck, was a *Nimitz*-class boat, the *Carl Vinson*. And she had been forty years old, and both looked and smelled it. An old, salt-worn, floating scrapyard.

But this was like being aboard a floating city of the gods.

After nearly twenty minutes of walking and climbing, Yaz and Blane arrived at their destination.

The Raiders' inner sanctum.

Also, Yaz figured, his next test.

\* \* \*

"Welcome to the Team Room," Blane said, holding open the hatch, then pulling it shut behind them.

Inside, Yaz could see two couches and a couple of upholstered chairs in an open lounge area to the right, and a single desk with a laptop and desk speakers in a sort of office area to the left. In the middle and all around, mainly stacked up against the periphery, sat piles of boxes and crates, and shelves stacked with supplies.

In the lounge, facing one of the couches, a flat-screen TV hung on the bulkhead, the cabinet beneath holding a streaming set-top box, a media player with hard-drive, and also a gaming console – an Xbox One X, if Yaz wasn't mistaken, the same pricey model they'd had at FOB Chapman in Afghanistan. And all of it looked brand-new, like it had just been unboxed or taken out from under plastic.

But mainly what Yaz saw in this room was… a dozen pairs of eyes looking up at him. Again.

The last time he'd seen those faces, they'd been framed by identical helmets, and nearly identical uniforms, weapons, and gear. Now, suddenly, they were individuals. Clothing was a mix of cammies, PT gear, and "utes and boots," as Marines called utility trousers, t-shirts, and combat boots — but also a lot of casual wear: jeans, khakis, shorts and t-shirts. As for haircuts, there were no ponytails or Mohawks, but still some shagginess, MARSOC obviously allowing a fair bit of latitude around the standard Marine high-and-tight.

Only about half of them were particularly well shaven.

Virtually all were head-down in their phones, and when they looked up at Yaz's entrance, it was over the top of them.

And what Yaz mainly got from them was: a vibe of intelligence, and restless energy. He knew shipboard life almost always involved a lot of downtime — eating, sleeping, and lifting — but Marines didn't get into MARSOC by being passive or content. They were after something.

And Yaz could feel it in the air of the room.

"Hey," Blane said, raising his voice to get the others' attention. And when he spoke, it was with profound understatement. "Since we didn't get a chance to do this before, everyone meet Team Two's new SARC — Tom Yaskiewicz... Doc Yaz."

A single beat of silence passed.

And then every Marine in the room, all of whom had been sitting or lounging on couches or chairs, or down on the deck with their backs up against crates, stood up as one. Those wearing hats — a watch cap, one utility cover, a couple of baseball caps — took them off, as soon as the first one did. And they all just nodded, wordlessly. Nodding their respect.

Yaz nodded back, trying not to fuck it up by smiling.

Maybe he'd passed this test.

* * *

Squinting and cocking his head, Yaz realized he could detect something else underneath the intelligence and energy, or maybe overlaying it. And then he realized it was the elephant absent from the room. It was Captain Day.

These men had just lost their unit commander – their most senior Marine. They'd also lost Team 2's most junior one.

Yaz knew they'd be a long time recovering from that, resolving their issues around it, both as a team and as individuals. But then, with a cold shock of horror, he also remembered these guys had lost much more than that, as had everyone else left alive – in the fall of human civilization. It was probably too much to face or engage with right now. Dealing with it all might take a lifetime.

And suddenly Yaz realized what they had all been doing on their phones. Trying to contact their loved ones.

Probably trying to contact anyone.

Then, just as Yaz was getting lost in his own head, Master Gunnery Sergeant Fick, hidden in back, hunched over the laptop and facing away, straightened up, twisted at the waist, and said, "Well if you're all gonna suck the Doc's dick, I suggest you form an orderly queue, and get to it."

They all sat down again amid laughter and shaken heads.

"What?" Fick said, looking around. "What I say? I mean, I understand the Corps lets in people of all sexual orientations and gender identities now. I get it. It's fine." He lowered his voice and turned back to the laptop screen. "But I still don't want to see anyone tongue-punching fart-boxes in my bay…"

Blane shook his head and gave Yaz a look like, *You see what I have to put up with?* Then he pointed out and named each of the dozen Marines in the room, most of whom Yaz knew at least by sight, from his first mission out with them.

Blane said, "We don't all fit in here at once, so the idea was we'd sort of time-share between the two teams. While one's slacking off in here playing *Apex Legends*, the other's sleeping or eating – maybe, on a good day, working, working out, or training. Also, if it's too much of a mob in here, you can use any of the other lounges on this deck. Trouble is…"

"It's not just us in them," Yaz said.

"Exactly. As you can see, these are all Team One guys." He nodded over at the desk on the left. "Well, except Fick, of course. Who always does whatever the hell he wants."

Blane led the two of them in that direction, stepping over people and crap, then spoke to Fick's back. "Trust you're hard at work updating the spreadsheets with our ammunition and stores manifests?"

"Fuck, no," Fick said, not turning around. "I'm downloading all my playlists, while Spotify's still up and running. Manifests are the LT's job. And spreadsheets are the number-one reason, on a list as long as my cock, that I'm not an officer."

Yaz saw Fick had a gigantic mug of coffee on the desk beside him. Hilariously, it had a picture of his own face, puffing on a cigar, above the words, *20 Years Of Running on Caffeine and Hate*. Yaz guessed it had been a gift from his Marines, when he finished his twenty. If he was still in after that, they were going to have to carry him out.

Blane said to Fick's back, "Well, since you didn't manage to get him killed in San Francisco, I'm sure you'll now make yourself available to help our new SARC settle in."

"Sure," Fick said, twisting around in his chair. "We fucking love swabbies. Why else would we maroon ourselves in a floating tin can with five thousand of them? I mean, we have to be pretty careful about dropping the soap in the shower, with so many of you butt pirates lurking around. But otherwise."

"Don't worry," Blane said. "This Neanderthal hazing shit is how you know you're being accepted. All part of the process."

Yaz did know it. It was part of becoming a member of this tribe. So he was happy to take as much as they dished out.

"Anyway," Blane said to Fick, "you won't be laughing when you're bleeding out in the dirt and Yaz is the only thing between you and radical exsanguination."

"At least then I'll be spared you and your five-dollar words, Gunny. But, yeah, you're right. Yaz took a fucking girder to the head keeping Coulson alive. And I fucking like Coulson." He looked back to Yaz. "So you're okay by me, Wisconsin. But you're the only sailor we're gonna let in the clubhouse."

Yaz looked around again at the Marines in there, and tried to think who else, other than Day, was missing from Team One. And then it hit him – the one other sailor, and his counterpart. "Where's Doc Milam?" he asked.

Blane said, "He tends to keep to himself. But you're bunking with him, so you'll see him." He moved back toward the hatch.

"Come on, that's our next stop."

# REMEMBERING HOW
# TO BREATHE

*JFK – 02 Deck*

"NSF ops room is that way," Blane said, pointing down a intersecting passageway as they crossed it. "It's basically like a small-town police station." He turned and pointed the other way. "Our own armory's up there. Where we keep all the fun stuff, under lock and key. I'll give you a tour at some point."

They carried on another 30 meters down the main passageway for 02 deck, turned left, then came to a stop outside one hatch in an identical row of them.

"This is you," he said, unlocking the hatch by waving a keycard, then handing it over. "When you get a ship's ID card, it'll be keyed to open your berthing compartment, and anywhere on the boat you need to go, and are authorized to."

Inside, the first thing Yaz saw wasn't the other SARC. It wasn't even the nice appointments – desk, chair, two double bunkbeds, four lockers, four footlockers, all clean and new. There was even enough room to swing a cat, which was a lot of room belowdecks on a warship, even the world's largest one.

No, the first thing Yaz saw was his own rifle, propped up in a corner, along with his vest and belt, all of his combat kit – and even his big deployment ruck. Not only had someone made sure all his belongings made it back here safely.

Someone had cleaned all of it.

He rubbed a finger down one pristine strap of the ruck, and looked up when Blane said, "We had a lot of time on our hands in quarantine. Plus, you know, the infection risk."

Yaz sensed it wasn't just about the infection risk.

Blane checked his watch. "Okay. That's me. Anything else you need?"

"I'm all squared away."

"Good. Make yourself to home. I'll see you later."

As they finally parted, Yaz felt some words rising in the back of his throat. He wanted to say: "Thanks – for carrying my unconscious ass out of there. For not leaving me behind." But they sounded stupid even in his head. He knew Blane would find them absurd, or at best unnecessary.

For him, it went without saying.

\* \* \*

When the hatch opened again, about twenty minutes later, it had Milam standing behind it. When he entered, Yaz was sitting on one of the lower bunks, just staring off into the distance, reflecting on it all. Trying to get his head around it.

When he glanced up, he saw Milam looked much the same off duty as on – desert camo bandana disguising however he wore his hair, and the same wispy mustache. Cammies, but no combat gear or med ruck. Obviously.

"Hey," Milam said. "How you feeling?"

"Hundred percent," Yaz said, maybe a little too eagerly. If there was one person he couldn't bullshit about the speed of his recovery, it was the other corpsman in the room.

"You get shown around? Settling in?"

Yaz nodded. "Saw the Team Room, and here."

"Mess is next. Then you're squared away. Hungry?"

"No. Not yet."

Milam took a seat at the desk, facing Yaz on the bunk.

Yaz nodded at the double bunkbed opposite, which also had packs and vests hanging from it. "Who we bunking with?"

"Jeschke and Chesney," Milam said. He had a slow, level, and matter-of-fact way of speaking. "RTOs for the two teams. They're okay. Young, but well behaved. Reasonably."

They both smiled. SARCs tended to be a little older, both because of the long and arduous training pipeline, and the seriousness of the job. Yaz said, "I didn't know MARSOC went out with radio operators."

"No, the MSOTs don't normally have them. But there was an expectation we'd be operating pretty far inland."

Yaz'd had precious little briefing about this assignment before taking it. He'd been so desperate to land somewhere after his last attachment went south, and so grateful when he did, that he hadn't asked too many questions. After that, he'd been frantically trying to make his way here before the strike group sailed. And he figured they'd explain everything he needed to know when he got here. But "pretty far inland" could mean all kinds of things. Syria? Iran? North Korea?

"So what is our job on this boat, actually?"

Milam nodded. "Kind of fluid during the sea trials. Someone at Fleet wanted MARSOC integrated with the strike group – finding its place alongside SEALs in the surface fleet, like they've been doing beside the other units in SOCOM. I think the idea was we were going to run covert amphibious insertion exercises. I'm guessing that's on hold now."

"Where do they post the training schedule?" Yaz knew

enough to know that, when they were at sea, and not out on ops, it was going to be training and more training.

"Outside the Team Room. But there's not one up right now."

"Okay, so nothing operational going on, and no training. What the hell's everyone doing?"

Milam exhaled. "Remembering how to breathe, mainly. After our little Mattis misadventure in San Francisco, with the casualties we took, and then the quarantine, I think command's giving us a few days just to lick our wounds."

"Huh. Speaking of which, how's your hand?"

Milam held up his shot-through right hand, still wrapped in a bandage, but not blood-soaked this time, and wiggled his trigger finger. "Hundred percent."

Yaz smiled. Then again, wound-licking didn't sound like the Marines he had known, never mind Recon or MARSOC guys. But he kept this to himself. The last thing he needed to do was show up on day one and try to tell these guys how to be Marines. Also, they'd just lost two men, including their commander, a man who had seemed unkillable. But Yaz had seen him die right in front of him, and heard his last words:

*"Give me five minutes."*

But he hadn't had five minutes left. How much time did the rest of them have? Too much, maybe. Or not enough.

Yaz's heart sank as he thought of the other Marine who died – the young corporal, Flynn, who'd gotten drilled full of holes standing right beside him. And who, ultimately, Yaz had failed to save. Given that was his whole job with this team, the death of Flynn wasn't a great start.

And definitely not a good omen.

Hell, everyone in that Tactical Element, 2/1, was supposed to be unkillable. So much for that.

Arguably, it was Yaz who had fucked it up.

Part of why he'd chosen a fleet-deployed unit was embarked Marines on board ship were said to be extremely tight-knit. They were physically cut off from the rest of the Corps, separated by thousands of miles of ocean. But they also weren't integrated with the sailors or the life of the ship. They mostly kept to their own areas, and their own training and operational activities. It was said to be the closest thing to combat, in terms of unit cohesion – the closest thing to a family. Or a tribe. And this was what Yaz was desperately looking for.

A place where he could belong.

"Hey, you okay?"

He looked up and realized he'd disappeared into his own head again – a known problem with him, and which he knew sometimes made him seem weird. That was pretty much the opposite of how he wanted to come off right now, trying to fit in. But, looking up at Milam, he remembered again that he wasn't a Marine. As an attached SARC, he sometimes felt like the family dog – not aware he wasn't human. But at least here, in the kennel, he was in the right place to talk about it.

"What's life here like?" he asked.

Milam shrugged. "I only got here six weeks before you did. But you know how it is. We're in it, but not quite of it. And it's like everything else. What you make it."

"I wonder how everyone else is coping."

"As far as I can tell, everyone on this boat is mainly burning through their thumb pads trying to call home."

"God, I bet," Yaz said, remembering everything all over again. He suddenly realized that every day, perhaps for the rest of his life, might be like this — waking up into a bad dream. Remembering what had happened, and the world they now lived in, the one after the end of the world. "What's the news?"

"Either bad, or nonexistent. Broadcasts and online news sites are disappearing as fast as you click, or flip the channel."

"Fleet Forces Command?"

Milam just shook his head.

"Jesus," Yaz said, "I need to make some calls."

"You and the other five thousand people on this tub. The phone bays are a zoo, ditto the computer rooms. If you want to try email or messaging, your best bet is your own cell or laptop. I can get you on the Wi-Fi for this deck. If you do want to try a phone-call type phone call, not Internet calling, the team has two sat-phones. Either of the ops sergeants can hook you up."

"Thanks," Yaz said. He fished his laptop out of his ruck, but didn't power it on right away.

He was terrified of what he would find.

* * *

Two hours later, he'd worked out what all the *JFK*'s Marines and sailors, and everyone across the strike group, had.

There was nobody out there.

Somehow, the entire country, possibly the entire world, had fallen — faster and more catastrophically than anyone imagined possible. Though, with Yaz's deployment up in the Hindu Kush, followed by a multi-stage journey circling half the globe, he'd gotten even less warning, fewer updates, and poorer information than most.

But from conversations in the Team Room, in one of the

lounges, and just roaming the halls, he learned pretty much everyone was as stunned and shell-shocked as he was.

No one could believe it.

Of the news sites Yaz was able to load, the majority hadn't been updated in days, with the most recent articles still sitting on the front page, like yellowing newspapers in musty drawers. And the articles he did read suggested most people went down before they had any idea what was going on, or what to be afraid of.

A few of the guys Yaz talked to had got through to buddies, friends from previous units, many stationed overseas – in bases now besieged by the dead. But no one had been able to reach loved ones, not anywhere in the civilian world. Maybe it was communications, or maybe people were holed up, or on the run, or had made it to remote bugout locations.

But aside from that faint and fading hope…

It looked like the outside world was gone.

# GET SOME

Yaz looked down, at his last hope for this.

In his hand was the sleek black shape of an Iridium sat phone, one of two they had in their loadout. Gunny Blane had given it to him, and told him to take as long as he needed.

Looking up from the phone, Yaz saw the endless expanse of wind-whipped and sparkling ocean. He was up top, out on the great expanse of the carrier's flight deck. And he wasn't the only one. From where he stood at the prow, he could look back and see men and women – enlisted ratings, chiefs, officers of all ranks – walking around the 6.5 acres, talking in small groups, or, like Yaz, just standing alone, staring out at the sea, trying to make some kind of sense of it all.

Obviously, flight ops had been suspended for the moment, or maybe for the duration. Perhaps just long enough to let people come out and have this moment to themselves, where they could enjoy the solace of sea and sky, rather than the claustrophobic quarters and low overheads below.

Yaz looked up, and then out again, where the sun was still climbing a blue sky with a thin scattering of white cirrus clouds. But a cold wind on his face was blowing in something more ominous, from the south Pacific. He could already see the low bank of storm clouds crowding the ocean's surface, probably a low pressure front. He even thought he heard faint rumbling, and definitely felt the temperature drop.

He took his own cell phone out of his pocket, and when he unlocked it, the number was already on the screen – her number. He felt weirdly ashamed to have never learned it. But nobody really knew anyone's phone number anymore – except their own cell, and their mother's landline.

The latter of which he had already tried.

Somehow this one was going to be more painful. He dialed the number into the sat phone, then pressed the green key to initiate the call. It rang twelve times, Yaz's heart climbing higher into his throat with each ring, before going to voicemail.

*"Hi, this is Vicky. I'm not available right now, or at least not available to YOU right now…"*

Yaz listened to the greeting, both the voice and those words so familiar, then left a simple message, just telling her to call him. To let him know she was okay. As his finger hovered over the red button to end the call, he had to fight the impulse to tell her the other thing.

That he still loved her.

Somehow the end of the world made resentment, regret, bad feelings of any kind, seem small and stupid. Only one emotion, and one act, seemed equal to the enormity of the events that had befallen them.

And those were love… and forgiveness.

As Yaz fought the tears that welled up and tried to overflow his eyes, he heard the first definite rumble of thunder, and the sun overhead began to dim. He didn't even know if the tears were for her, or for everything else he had lost. Or maybe just for all the general loss and devastation, the sadness and fear that seemed to be rolling in over them like those storm clouds.

Perhaps it was just the shock, the extremity, of all this transformation – too much change, too fast, and all at once. New unit. New duty station. All-new teammates, men who had been strangers to him a few days ago. Somehow surviving that insane mission, launched literally seconds after arriving. And, on top of it all, not just the end of the world – but the loss of perhaps everyone he used to know.

Including the woman he used to love. And whom he only realized now he still did. After everything.

It was too much to process, or even to accept.

He turned and scanned around again, boggling at the dozens of other survivors who surrounded him, never mind the oddity of just standing on an airport built on top of a warship, all of them floating out in the middle of the ocean, one soon to be lashed by a severe squall.

He faced forward again and looked out at the endless expanse of ocean, and the handful of other ships around them, tiny cocoons of life floating on the vast, trackless, and empty ocean. And he couldn't help but think of *Battlestar Galactica*, in the opening miniseries – when the survivors in the fleet realized everyone they knew and loved back in the colonies was gone.

And it was just them.

He shook his head again. *Jesus, that's us now…*

Looking up again, he figured the open ocean was as good a metaphor as any for the cold, empty, and uncaring cosmos they inhabited. And the Earth itself, perhaps the only cocoon of life in the universe, with its thin and fragile film of air and water, floating on a rock through an empty and godless void. Would this rock, too, soon be as devoid of life as the barren space that surrounded it, for billions of miles in every direction?

But he was going to talk himself into jumping off the flight deck this way, if he sat around marinating in his dark thoughts. He had to get some kind of structure back, take some positive action. As the first fat cold raindrops hit the deck around him, he finally started moving back belowdecks. Back toward the closest thing he had now to familiarity. And what he had to believe would be his new home.

*This had better be the place for me, he thought.*

Because there was nowhere else left to go.

\* \* \*

When he stepped back inside the Team Room, the shift had changed, and now it was all Team 2 guys there. His team. And they all seemed genuinely and profoundly glad to see him – Brady and Reyes, Meyer and Kemp, Graybeard having taken Fick's place at the laptop, doing something unrelated to Spotify… and especially Coulson, who limped over and gave Yaz a big smile, handshake, and crushing bear hug.

All of which was exactly what he needed right now.

He looked over at the rec area to the right, where Brady had just finished grinding coffee beans and started brewing the result in a fancy-looking cafetiere, looking up to give him a big smile and nod. Then Yaz proceeded to just shoot the shit with his teammates – small talk, gossip and scuttlebutt, asking after injuries, getting told where shit was, and what shit to look out for. He saw Reyes on the couch, but he was face down in his phone, headphones in. On the screen, Yaz could see a Skype call ringing, and just make out the face of the intended recipient, a dark-eyed little girl.

But she wasn't picking up.

Taking care to give Reyes plenty of space, Yaz spent a few minutes just watching the younger guys, Meyer and Kemp, play *Doom Eternal* on the Xbox, apparently because no one was showing up for *Apex Legends* or *Call of Duty: Warzone* online anymore.

They took turns in the single-player campaign mode, cheering each other on as they rocketed and plasma-gunned Arch-Viles and Cyberdemons at frenetic speed. The sounds of shotgun blasts, demon screams, and the pounding metal soundtrack were set at dorm-room volume.

Yaz only looked up from the game when Brady finished brewing his coffee, poured two cups, and handed one off to Yaz. He then got busy doing something that at first seemed odd. He starting packing small weights, little 5-pound steel plates, into the pouches of a tactical vest.

Once it was fully loaded, he hefted it up and shrugged into it, his delts and biceps swelling under his t-shirt as he tested the weight. Below that, he wore utility trousers and boots, classic utes and boots. He grabbed a gas mask and put it on top of his head. Then he grabbed his weapon, a SCAR-L, which most of them carried, but without a mag seated. He pulled the charging handle to clear the chamber, then hefted it with one hand under the magazine well.

Finally, he looked around the room. And, seemingly casual, but loud enough not to be ignored, he said:

"Okay. Who's coming?"

"Coming where?" Yaz asked Meyer, who sat beside him.

"Wind sprints," Meyer said. "Out on deck. He does this."

"Does he know there's a category-four storm blowing in?"

"That's exactly why he's going now."

"Come on, you pussies," Brady said. "Who's coming?"

Yaz stepped forward. "I'm in."

With this, Graybeard pulled his head out of the laptop and said, "Hey, Yaskiewicz, that a good idea?"

"Yeah," Reyes said, pulling an earbud out. "You do know you were unconscious in intensive care – this morning?"

Yaz shrugged. "I got signed off."

"By who?" Reyes said. "Yourself?"

Some of the others looked at Yaz like he had three assholes in his forehead — but underneath that was obvious and not-so-grudging respect. Maybe he was a total fucking maniac to go out running on the edge of a carrier flight deck in a gale, the day he woke up from an induced coma. But Marines, especially Raiders, loved fucking maniacs. Being a maniac was awesome. It was a big deal.

From Yaz's point of view, he wasn't trying to impress anyone, or not mainly trying to impress them. It was just the Navy, and especially SEALs, had drilled into him the swim-buddy ethos. You never let anybody go anywhere alone.

He headed toward the hatch and nodded at Brady. "Gimme two minutes to grab my weapon and plate carrier."

"Good man," Brady said, following him out.

As they disappeared, a few of the Marines hooted after them: "Yeah! Get some!"

And Meyer said: "I love you, Fruity Rudy!"

# FACE PALM

Blane already had his elbow on the conference room table, and went ahead and put his forehead down in his palm.

*The good ole face-palm maneuver, he thought.*

They were well into the second hour of a senior leadership meeting, all 16 of the ship's department heads, as well as the Captain, the XO, and a few other officers in critical roles, crammed into the briefing room that let off the back of the Flag Bridge. With his head facing the tabletop, Blane could see the page-long printed agenda that sat there.

*At least there is an agenda*, he thought. He knew from hard experience that a meeting without one was just a bunch of people bullshitting in a room for an arbitrary length of time, usually ending when they'd exhausted one another.

As to why Blane himself was there, that was a bit of a mystery. As commander of the embarked MARSOC element, the LT's presence made perfect sense. And Blane even understood why Drake had brought Fick in – because he was the most experienced Marine on the boat.

And the LT was one of the least.

Blane didn't particularly agree with the decision. But he didn't have to agree with it. As far as his own presence went, yes, he was Operations Sergeant – but for a team of 15 guys, not a warship of 5,000. But he gathered he must have said something smart to Commander Drake one time or another, and the XO had pegged him as some kind of steadying force, or mensch, or rising star.

Plus they all knew the LT was in over his head.

And Drake had probably figured out, sooner than most, that these embarked Marines were about to become one of the most critical components of strike group operations – critical to any of them surviving for long.

Right now, the XO was trying to keep them on topic, which was like herding cats. Toward a bathtub. Blane looked over at the Captain, and realized he hadn't said anything in a while. He actually looked like he had somewhere else to be.

The main topic of today's meeting was the strike group's stores, supplies, fuel, and general sustainability – cut off, as they were, from access to any of the port facilities they depended on for replenishment of all those things.

"Okay, look," Drake said. "I'm going to recap. The good news is every boat in the strike group – every surviving boat – is nearly fully fueled, since our shakeout cruise didn't even stretch to a hundred nautical miles. The *Rainier* is topped as well, two million gallons of diesel, and two-point-six of JP5. That's a lot of ocean we can cover, and a lot of air ops and top cover we can run. Our ammo situation is almost as good. Ship's Magazine is fully loaded with SeaSparrow and Rolling Airframe missiles, plus auto-cannon shells for the Phalanx guns. Ship's Armory is almost as good – full of belted fifty-cal for the M2s, plus small-arms rounds and grenades."

"Yeah," Fick said. "We kind of got into that a little bit."

"Already?" Drake sighed. "You have your own armory."

Fick just shrugged. "Which kind of got a depleted a little, in that dumb-ass suicide mission you sent us on out in the city of brotherly bullshit."

Drake and Fick now undertook a staring contest.

Just due to having invited him here, Drake must have forgiven Fick for what he said about his sister during that near-debacle in San Francisco. Then again, as he'd basically been leaving them there to die, anyone would forgive it.

"Hey," Fick said. "We don't like being light on ammo. And I promise you don't want us being light on ammo, either."

Drake sighed. Blane and the LT just looked away.

It had already been touched on, and everyone there knew, that the Marines were going to be the *Kennedy's* indispensable lifeline. They were almost certainly the only ones who could go ashore to scavenge for food and other resources, and have a prayer of coming back alive.

And maybe even uninfected.

Which meant the 7,500 personnel across the eight ships of the strike group were going to be nearly totally dependent on these 28 surviving Marine Raiders. The fact that they'd lost 6.67% of their strength on the first day of the apocalypse was not a fantastic start. And not reassuring.

*Okay, fuck it*, Drake thought, just giving Fick that one.

"Right," he said. "Moving on. We know the desalination plants, and the nuclear reactors, are the key to everything for us. So I want full readiness reports and updated maintenance histories from both sections, as a priority tasking."

The heads of the nuclear reactor section and the ship's life-support systems – which included heating, ventilation, electrical, and sewage, as well as fresh water – both reported in to the head of the Engineering Department. But Drake had instructed both subordinates to attend anyway.

"Sir," the Reactor Officer said. "I can report that our twin A1B reactors are brand-new, fully fueled, and good for fifteen to twenty years' uninterrupted use."

"Great," Drake said. "But I need to know – is it fifteen or twenty?"

The officer looked like that question had never come up before. Sounding a little flustered, she said, "How long do you think this is all going to last?"

"I think we'd better assume this is it."

"It, sir?"

"This is our world now. And if we want to survive in it, we'd all better look lively and start jumping through our asses to stay alive." He looked over at the life-support guy. "If those desal plants stop turning 600,000 gallons of seawater a day into drinkable fresh water, we all stop breathing in about a week."

The man visibly gulped. "There's bottled water, sir."

Fick grunted. "Yeah, sure, you wade ashore and pick up a liter a day for each one of 7,500 thirsty motherfuckers."

Drake just glared at Fick, his meaning obvious.

"And that brings us to the bad news – food supplies. Big John," Drake said, using the *Kennedy*'s nickname, "left port with substantially less than our maximum load of seventy days' provisions – exactly twenty days' worth, in fact. Fleet's big idea for the sea trials was to stage a dry run of large-scale at-sea replenishment of food stores."

He scanned the unsmiling faces in the room.

"Yeah, I know, just past the nick of time. But, like it or not, and fate being a son of a bitch, we started this thing with less than three weeks' worth of grub. And we've been going through it at the rate of 17,300 meals a day. That's not going to stop, or even slow down much."

Blane remembered the old rule of thumb that people will riot after three days without food, which meant humanity was always nine meals away from anarchy. He dared to hope military personnel would hold it together a little longer. But he didn't volunteer an opinion on this one way or the other.

Drake said, "The other ships vary from three to eight weeks of food storage. We can even out the stores across the strike group, and that's being done. But we're just passing two weeks into this shit storm, and the fresh stuff is already running out or going bad. In another six days, we're going to be fly-fishing off the flight deck. Or eating each other. The wolf's nearly at the door. And we're not gonna wait for it."

Drake looked around the room, where he saw a lot of disbelief. Even more than two weeks into their exile, many of them were still having trouble getting their heads around all this, never mind accepting it. It was probably no different for anyone on the boat, actually – all of them grappling with the shock, the magnitude of what had befallen them.

Lieutenant Commander Cole, the Commander of the Air Group (CAG), rapped the table and said "I can't believe every single U.S. and allied port facility is closed to us."

Drake looked up. "We already covered this. Believe me, we're hailing everything and everyone nonstop – every other surface vessel, sub, CSG, port, base, shore facility, Fleet Forces Command…"

"And you're telling us there's no one out there."

Drake just returned his stare. He hadn't told them that. But he also hadn't told them, or anyone else not required to know, that the few responses they were getting, and the status of the facilities and personnel they managed to reach, were no cause for celebration. Everyone still alive out there was beleaguered, surrounded by the dead, and looked like going down soon. And the more they hailed, the fewer stations they reached.

The lights were going out.

It was early days yet. But Drake for some reason already had a strong sense that morale was going to become their most indispensable resource.

*Not even morale, he thought. Hope.*

And he didn't want to start squandering it out of the gate.

"Full readiness reports," he said. "And a tiger-team drawn from the Engineering, Supply, and Deck departments, putting together a detailed, long-term, sustainable plan for water distribution. Also, I'm going to want an updated, triple-checked manifest of fuel, food, and other stores from the *Rainier*. Like I said, her being fully loaded is the good news. The bad news is she slows us all down to her top speed of twenty-six knots."

"Slows us down… on our way to where?"

Everyone stopped and looked up. It was the Captain. This was the first thing he'd said in a while.

And it was an excellent question.

# BATTLE BUDDY

"So," Drake said. "Naval Station Pearl Harbor."

Blane shrugged. This is what he got for volunteering an opinion. Now he'd be on the hook if it all went to hell.

"You three follow me," Drake said.

"What," Fick said. "Out into that? Speaking of shit storms."

They'd all exited the eternal meeting, leaving the briefing room at the back, out into the unmanned Flag Bridge. Like the Bridge, it had a little observation deck outside, sticking off the island itself.

"Yeah," Drake said. "Out into that. I need some air."

"You mean you need a fucking swim," Fick said.

Nonetheless he, Blane, and the LT followed the XO outside. The observation deck was covered, but the rain was being blown around more than it was falling, in what was turning into a proper squall. Blane resigned himself to it, and figured this would at least put a time limit on their post-meeting meeting.

"Talk," Drake said, squinting into the mist.

Blane exhaled. "Well, as you said, sir, there's no reason to think any West Coast port, or any place in CONNUS for that matter, is going to be any better than San Francisco was."

Fick grunted. "Which was more fucked up than a one-legged nun doing power squats in a cucumber patch."

Drake just shook his head, and didn't bother glaring at him this time. "But there's also a reason Fleet wanted an at-sea replenishment exercise – because it's damned tricky. Particularly with the quantities of food we're going to need."

The LT said, "How is it done normally, sir?"

Drake suddenly remembered how new this young officer was. And it was clearly his first shipboard posting. He said, "In port, we just lower one of the aircraft elevators to the level of the dock, and they roll hundreds of tons of fresh food and dry goods right into the belly of the boat on forklift trucks. And actual trucks."

"And while at sea?"

Drake sighed. The answer was that at sea it was done by a combination of Underway Replenishment (UNREP) by supply ships, Carrier Onboard Delivery (COD) with fixed-wing aircraft landing on the flight deck, and sling-load delivery (VERTREP) by helicopter squadrons. Each method had its drawbacks and dangers. The flight deck of an aircraft carrier on pitching seas was a dangerous place at the best of times, without adding tons of swinging cargo and 70-foot spinning blades to the equation. All of which Drake knew Fick and Blane already knew, and which he didn't feel like explaining to the new guy.

So he just said, "Very carefully. But our question today is how it's done from shore – but without docking the ship, and without the active support of a replenishment base."

Blane said, "Not a question that's ever come up before."

"Exactly. And the answer is going to be one gigantic planning job, and then a major logistics and supply exercise."

"Not an exercise," Fick said, "An operation. One which we're gonna have to conduct under fire."

Drake wasn't sure that was the right expression. Getting eaten was arguably worse than getting shot. In any case, Fick was right – they were going to have to secure the supplies along with whatever hostile area they were stored in, before moving it all across overrun ground and out onto the water. This would be an assault, clearing and holding ground, then providing security for the supply train from source to ship.

Drake sighed. "It's also a gigantic logistical pain in my ass, organizing the large-scale movement of goods, vehicles, and people." He shook his head.

This was all brand-new, and it sucked.

"Okay," he said, shifting gears. "Just assuming we go with Gunny Blane's bright idea, at the top speed of our slowest vessel, it's still only eighty hours from here to Hawaii."

"That's some good news," the LT said.

"Not for you. Because that's all the time you ground-pounders are going to have to plan the military side of this caper. It's also all the time my staff has got to plan the rest of it. And a lot of this planning totally depends."

The LT said, "Depends on what, sir?"

Blane said, "On what we find when we get there."

"Exactly," Drake said. "Like I said, the little intel we have is confused and conflicting. But it seems possible Hawaii didn't fall as hard or fast as the continental US. The population density's also lower, so maybe that slowed transmission. Anyway, we're going to send up aerial ISR as soon as we're close enough. That will tell much of the tale."

The LT said, "Sounds like you've made up your mind."

Drake shrugged, and looked at Blane. "I think your Ops Sergeant nailed it. We know food is going to be the critical-path resource – we're going to run out of that first. So we need to get this figured out, sooner rather than later."

He paused and squinted out into the increasingly raging storm, then down at the flight deck below. Following his gaze through the sheets of rain and mist, the three Marines saw what he was looking at – two figures hauling ass around the perimeter of the deck. Carrying weapons. And probably doing 5.5-minute miles, at the pace they were keeping up.

Also, one of them was wearing a gas mask.

Drake squinted at them. "Who the fuck is that?"

"Two fucking maniacs," Fick said. "Obviously."

Blane shook his head. "I can tell you who one is – Staff Sergeant Brady, Two-One's Assistant Element Leader."

Drake looked over at him. "Should we be letting him do that? They're gonna get blown overboard in this storm."

"You try and stop him," Fick said.

"Who's the other one?" Drake asked.

Fick said, "That's a battle buddy, is who that is. You know what a battle buddy is? A true battle buddy is somebody who'll go into town, get two blowjobs, and bring one back for you."

Neither Drake nor the LT had any response to this.

But Blane just smiled cryptically. "No. That's a guy who woke up from a two-week coma and asked me what happened. I said it was over, and we lost. But try telling these guys that."

The others remained silent, impressed.

Then they heard some kind of primal shouting from below, and looked down to see Brady hefting his weapon at them, pumping it up and down in the rain-lashed air, bellowing into the storm. Seeing this, Fick couldn't resist – though it seemed to Drake he didn't resist much – and stepped up to the railing, the slashing rain buffeting his chest, and shouted back at them through the raging gale.

*"Yeah! GET SOME!"*

# PRETTY FUCKING GUCCI

*JFK – 02 Deck, Stern Head*

Yaz woke up slumped in the bottom of a shower stall.

He didn't know how long he'd been out – only that it must be at least a minute, since that's how long the shower-head would keep flowing without pumping the button. He checked himself out for injuries, aided by his nakedness. There were none evident. Then again, blacking out, for a guy who'd recently sustained a serious head injury, wasn't a great sign.

Maybe he shouldn't have gone for that run. But he already knew he wouldn't trade it. Not for anything.

Hauling ass around the flight deck of a nuclear supercarrier with Brady – a teammate who seemed to both like and respect him – the two of them pumping their fists and shouting into the raging storm, was already one of the highlight-reel experiences of his military career.

He climbed to his feet, finished rinsing off, grabbed his towel, and tried not to worry about his body betraying him. After all, it had just completed a five-mile run, ten times around the perimeter of the flight deck, probably faster than he'd ever run that distance before. Sure, he felt a little dizzy.

But he also felt fucking great.

He brushed his teeth then ran his fingers through his hair, while looking at himself in the small and slightly steamed mirror. Then he grabbed his shower kit and headed back to his cabin.

Feeling alive.

* * *

Dried off and dressed, he grabbed his weapon from his cabin and headed out toward the Team Room, where he'd seen weapon cleaning kits earlier. Having soaked the rifle on his hurricane fun-run with Brady, now he wanted to disassemble, clean, and especially oil it.

He greeted a few of the other Marines inside, not quite the same group as before, and saw the LT was now at the laptop in the office area. No longer padded out with vest, helmet, and radio, he looked even more like a teenage boy playing at war. Also, judging from his despairing expression, he was either in mourning for Captain Day – or else pitying himself for being the poor asshole who now had to deal with all the spreadsheets Day used to maintain.

Probably a bit of both, Yaz figured.

He found a cleaning kit and sat down on a couch to get to work. He'd just flipped the rifle's upper receiver away from the lower when he heard a low whistle.

"That's pretty fucking Gucci."

Looking up, he saw it was Staff Sergeant Gifford, Assistant Ops Sergeant on Team 2, who Yaz didn't really know yet. As a senior NCO and one of the team leaders, Gifford was arguably the final person Yaz needed to impress, and develop a working relationship with. Everyone else above him in the chain of command – the LT, Fick, and Blane – already knew and at least seemed to like him. Trying not to think too much about sucking up, Yaz just smiled and nodded in response.

But after a few seconds of staring at him, Gifford got up,

came over, and sat on the other end of the couch. He was a rough-looking man in his mid-thirties, with red chin stubble, a sandy buzzcut, and a nose that had been broken at least once somewhere along the line.

"Huh," Gifford said, leaning in closer. "Beretta ARX200 battle rifle – chambered in six-point-five Creedmoor." He sounded either impressed or contemptuous, Yaz couldn't tell which. But he decided to assume the former, as it was a beautiful weapon. He was surprised no one had commented on it during the mission. But then again it was black and roughly AR-shaped, and everyone had been pretty busy.

"Gucci" referred to any flashy or expensive weapons or gear. But in this case it might have been righter than Gifford knew, as it literally referred to an Italian luxury brand. The ARX200, developed by Beretta for the Italian Army's *Soldato Futuro* program, and issued only to their Special Forces units, was constructed from a lightweight polymer with a matte-black finish, and had a 12-inch barrel in a heat-dissipating stock, with Picatinny rails on three sides, ambidextrous everything, and a folding telescopic stock. It was said to be impervious to heat and cold, salt water, sand, dust, and mud.

It was without question lighter and more accurate than the SOF Combat Assault Rifle the Marines carried. Yaz's was fitted with an Elcan Spectre 4x sight, underneath a ruggedized Trijicon mini-reflex sight, for CQB and quick target acquisition – neither of which were particularly cheap either.

"Okay, I'll say it," Gifford said, leaning back and draping his arm on the couch. "Who paid for that thing? That's like a three-thousand-dollar fucking weapon."

Still breaking it down, Yaz said, "Something like that."

"SARCs get a weapon allowance?"

"I wish."

"So you paid for this yourself. You rich? Trust-fund kid?"

"No. Nothing like that. I used to do okay, before the military. And I knew when I signed up that my life might depend on my weapon. So it seemed like a good investment."

Gifford whistled again. "Three... thousand... dollars..."

Graybeard looked over from where he sat in a chair with his feet up, reading a dog-eared copy of *The Old Man and the Sea* by Ernest Hemingway. He was about the only dude on either team not on his phone half the time. He said, "That's roughly your porn budget for the year, ain't it, Gifford?"

Yaz tried not to smile, and eyed the Master Sergeant rank insignia on Graybeard's blouse – E-8 to Gifford's E-6. Not that rank meant all that much in special operations. Still, E-8s were generally not to be fucked with.

Gifford squinted at Graybeard's book and said, "Isn't that kind of a fucking obvious reading choice for you?"

Yaz saw his point – a little too on the nose.

"It was either that or this." Steepling the first book against his chest, Graybeard reached over, grabbed another paperback, and held it up. It was *I Am Legend* – the first ever post-apocalyptic horror novel about a world-ending pandemic.

Gifford just grunted in response, then reached over and picked up one of the textured, boxy, 24-round mags Yaz had brought in with him. "Yeah, pretty fucking tacti-cool."

Yaz had to face the fact he was being hazed again. And it was all about how he reacted to it – or, rather, didn't react.

"Hope you don't have to do much shooting," Gifford said.

"Oh?" Yaz said, running a rag down his barrel. "Why not?"

Gifford stared into Yaz's eyes with his piercing pale-blue

ones. "How much ammo for that thing you think you're gonna find lying around or stockpiled out there?"

"They kept a lot on hand in my previous unit."

"Which was what?" Gifford asked.

Yaz paused a beat. "Naval Special Warfare."

Gifford squinted deeper at him when he didn't elaborate – then looked up as two of the younger guys wandered over, attracted by the surprise high-end gun show. One was Meyer, who Yaz already knew and liked. The other looked even younger, and his nametape read *Chesney*. Yaz already knew he was their RTO, not to mention his bunkmate. Checking out Yaz's weapon, he said, "When are we getting M5s?"

Meyer shook his head. "Never, dude. You know how long command took agreeing to standardize on the SCAR?"

Yaz refrained from pointing out the obvious – that, given current events, none of them might be getting issued new weapons or gear of any sort… ever again.

Gifford pressed down the follower of Yaz's mag and peered inside. "I'm not sold on the six-five Creedmoor round."

"Why not?" Meyer said. "Everyone says it shoots great."

"Maybe. But when the shit comes down, I want to be able to pull rifle mags from dead soldiers, dead sailors, dead airmen. Dead fucking Coast Guardsman. Pick up ejected rounds off the ground. Keep fighting. Doc Hollywood here will be SOL."

"Nah," Graybeard said, not bothering to look up from his book this time. "Every caliber of rifle works the same when you're beating someone to death with it."

Gifford tossed the mag. "He should get a five-five-six."

Still not looking up, Graybeard said, "Well, to borrow a line from the great Sergeant Major Basil Plumley – as played by the greatly mustachioed Sam Elliott – if the time comes when he needs one, there'll be plenty lying on the ground."

"Great line."

The others looked up to see this was Gunny Blane, who'd slipped in without anyone noticing. Looking down at Yaz, who was snapping his upper back into place, then zipping up the cleaning kit, he said, "You must be hungry by now."

"I guess so," Yaz said, standing up. "See you all later."

As he exited with Blane, Gifford tracked him with his slitted eyes, and waited until the hatch closed behind him. "I don't like that he can just go around strapped with whatever the fuck he feels like. It's against regs."

"You know it's a gray area," Graybeard said.

"Gray how? Like you? He's under our fucking command."

"True. But he's not a Marine. Anyway, you also know big boy rules apply. Look at Fick's weapon. Common sense works."

Gifford shook his head and stood up. "Big boy rules don't mean we're not still fucking squared-away Marines."

"Hey," Meyer said, plopping down on the couch beside Chesney. "At least they loosened up the grooming standard."

Chesney responded in a high-pitched, rednecky, sing-song voice: "*Grooom-ingggg… staaan-dard…!*"

"Fucking Sixta," Meyer said, shaking his head.

# TRIBES

"There's a mess on almost every deck," Blane said, as he and Yaz walked down the main 02 Deck passageway again, but in the opposite direction this time. "There are actually seven galleys scattered across this beast, but four are for officers. Anyway, there's no point in climbing stairs just for fun."

"Any damned fool can be uncomfortable," Yaz said.

"Right." Blane looked over. "Don't let Gifford get to you."

"It's fine. He won't."

"And you know what?" Blane said. "I come from a well-off family myself. I don't exactly advertise the fact. But there's no shame in it." He paused to hold open the double hatch to the 02 Deck Mess and let Yaz in first. They grabbed trays and cutlery and got in the food line.

"Define well off," Yaz said.

"My dad was an engineer for Intel, then test manager, then director, and finally VP. Good career. Some stock options."

"How'd he feel about you making a career of the military?"

"Just fine. Because his dad, my grandfather, was career military. Fought in Korea with the 24th Infantry Regiment."

Yaz squinted. "That one of the desegregated units?"

Blane nodded. "In theory, they were all desegregated by that point. The reality was slower coming. The 24th was a historically black regiment. They served when they were second-class citizens, subject to overt racism. Served when they were equal in theory, but still discriminated against. And they served in Iraq and Afghanistan, when history caught up with, you know, basic decency. Now, in the Corps, there are people of color at every level. And there are no black Marines, Hispanic Marines – just Marines. The younger guys will just give you a weird look if you try to say anything different."

"Nice," Yaz said. "But in special operations…"

"Yeah, you got me there. Still pretty white."

Yaz smiled. "Well, at least you're in a leadership role."

Blane smiled back. "We'll see how that works out."

"Though I thought Team Ops Sergeants were all E-8s?"

"Yeah," Blane laughed. "You missed the silent P after Gunnery Sergeant. I've been on the promotion list a while. And if we're ever not deployed for five minutes in a row, I'll get that pinned on…" He trailed off, remembering the current likelihood that their deployment would ever end, or that anyone would be seeing to the promotion list anymore.

Yaz said, "I've also seen some E-4s, and even an E-3." Corporals and a lance corporal. "I thought you couldn't even apply for MARSOC Selection unless you were already an E-4. And, by the end of training, everyone was E-5." Sergeant.

Blane nodded. "Ordinarily. But they expanded the ranks pretty rapidly not long ago – to have two MSOTs deployed to each of the new carrier strike groups, the *Ford* and the *JFK*. So they opened Selection up to Marines with extraordinary records and high potential. All the guys you've seen below E-5 are either up for promotion, or on the list." Blane smiled slightly. "In fact, the way they created us was to peel open one experienced MSOT and make two new ones, dividing up the senior guys, and slotting the junior ones in."

"So you're saying our two teams used to be one?"

"Exactly. So we've got more unit cohesion than any other two MSOTs thrown together, even from the same MSOB."

Yaz liked the sound of that.

As they reached the front of the line, they stopped talking to request entrees and sides by pointing them out to mess staff, who wore gloves, hair nets – and face masks. Yaz guessed the masks were a recent addition. As they took their trays and moved to the salad bar, Yaz said, "God, it's like the whole coronavirus fiasco all ever again. Except, obviously, worse."

"I don't know," Blane said. "Maybe it's better. At least for us."

Yaz got engrossed in heaping his plate with a variety of fresh salads, impressed with the offerings. The SEALs ate well, but you could only ship so much fresh food up to 18,000 feet. He also had a sense what they had here wasn't going to last, so he may as well enjoy it now.

"How could this possibly be better?"

"Well, for starters, we're all together. Rather than isolating in lockdown."

"Fair point," Yaz said.

When they'd both loaded up and got drinks, they sat down on an empty bench at a nearby table. As Yaz started firing food down, Blane picked up his knife and fork, put his forearms on the table, and looked Yaz in the eye.

"In past disasters or periods of hardship – the Great Depression, 9/11, the Blitz – people were all in it together. Rates of depression and suicide actually went down. Because we were forced to band together and cooperate to survive. Arguably what we were designed for in the first place."

Yaz nodded and kept shoveling. His appetite had come back with a vengeance. As Blane started eating, Yaz chewed in silence, while he chewed on these ideas.

Blane looked up. "Sorry, you didn't sign up for the history lecture. Never mind evolutionary psychology."

"No, go ahead," Yaz said. "I'm interested."

Blane shrugged. "Basically, for ninety-nine percent of human evolution, we lived in small nomadic bands, maybe a hundred or a hundred-and-fifty people. You knew everyone. You worked together, played together, intermarried, raised kids together, hunted and gathered as a team. When you went out to take down a mastodon, it was with guys you knew your whole life."

Yaz nodded. "And who would have to explain it to your mother if you got stomped into a hunter-gatherer pancake."

"Exactly. We're built for cooperation. We're built for each other, and to have our people around us. But look at modern life, for most people. You live one place, commute to work in another, drive some more to hang out in bars mostly filled with strangers. You keep in touch with loved ones and lifelong friends on Skype or Zoom – or, worse, as little text scrawls on your messaging app. You work with people you'll never see again after the layoffs. You live in a single-family home, where it's just the atomic family, all on your own for everything. Maybe you can afford childcare – from strangers. Or, like more and more people, you live completely alone. In a modern city or suburb, you can go all day, even a whole life, encountering no one but strangers. How do you think a hominid, evolved on the African Savannah in tribal units, is gonna react to strangers?"

"Probably by freaking the fuck out."

"Exactly. And we haven't evolved any in the last ten thousand years, since civilization started. Our great-ape brains have no hardwiring to deal with anonymous crowds, high-speed transport, industrial society, information-age virtual existence. So we're pretty much always in a low-grade freak-out."

"What the hell was your major, anyway?"

Blane smiled – he'd been found out, as a college boy. "Psychology. UC Santa Barbara."

"Ha," Yaz said. "Why didn't you go in as an officer?"

"Like my dad, I guess. Like to work my way up. Also, I had no time for ROTC – too busy surfing and chasing girls. But I did get bumped straight to E-2 after Basic. Yippee."

They both smiled. It was little enough.

"So are you saying our genes control us?"

"No." Blane nodded around them. "Obviously our genetic programming can't make an aircraft carrier. Or most of what humans have made. But there's still a lot of primal human behavior that's impossible to make sense of without understanding the environment it was designed for – by evolution. And, in the modern world, which looks nothing like that environment, it can be hard to just keep it together."

Yaz considered this. "Maybe that's why most people are on antidepressants and everyone drinks a lot."

"Exactly. Or dying from opioid abuse. Depression and anxiety are modern epidemics. And a predictable outcome."

"Predictable outcome of what?"

Blane paused a beat. "Of having disbanded our tribes."

Yaz whistled. Gunny Blane had just nailed it. Then he pointed out the elephant in the mess. "Maybe that's why people join the military. To get back into one."

"Yep. Pretty much."

Yaz shook his head, and started cleaning up his plate. "Anyway, depression and anxiety *were* modern-day epidemics. I think we've got a worse one now. And terror may be the new dominant emotion."

"Yeah," Blane said, forking over some green beans on his

plate. "I guess I can't argue with that. Still, I'm gonna say there are some advantages to the current unpleasantness."

Yaz just looked up and listened.

"For those of us left alive, anyway. Sure, now we're isolated in this giant tin can, floating on the ocean, wondering if there's anyone else out there. But we're all in the same situation, facing the same trials. We're all in it together."

Yaz got it. And he realized this was definitely why people joined the military. To be part of something bigger than themselves. It was sure why he had.

"I'm glad you made it," Blane said. "Before we sailed."

"I'm glad I made it out of San Francisco. Which was only thanks to you and the others."

Blane waved this off. Yaz had been right – Blane found the sentiment unnecessary. It went without saying.

Yaz put his fork down. "You know what, I actually don't."

Blane looked up. "Don't what?"

"Come from a well-off family. I mean, we were basically middle-class. But there wasn't a lot of money."

"Okay," Blane said. "So where'd yours come from – the money for that Beretta?"

"From my first career."

"Which was?"

"Wall Street asshole."

Blane laughed out loud. "Hey, no shame in that, either."

"Yeah. There kind of was. We fucked millions of people out of their nest eggs, retirement funds, kids' college savings…"

"That why you enlisted? To atone?"

"Not really."

"What, then?"

"Like I said. To be part of something."

"Didn't find that in your finance career? In New York?"

"God," Yaz said. "Investment banking would be like a school of sharks in a feeding frenzy – if the sharks ate each other. It was the exact opposite of a team. Nobody gave a shit about anyone else."

"And New York?"

"Probably the loneliest city in the world."

Blane also took a guess. "And what was your major?"

"Econ. University of Virginia."

"So how come you didn't go in as an officer?"

"Got direct enlistment to the SARC program. I guess I wanted to do something that mattered. And be part of a team – not be responsible for one."

Blane squinted. "Yet you picked an MOS where you get farmed out and attached to other people's teams."

"Yeah. I kind of fucked that up."

They both grinned. "Given current events, I don't think you need to worry about getting TDY'd again anytime soon."

Yaz grinned. "No. I guess not. Here for the duration."

Blane nodded. "I thought I was gonna do this for four years, then get out and go to the private sector."

"What happened? Get addicted to the action?"

"Maybe I just like the food."

Yaz smiled and looked around. "I guess the good news is we're back to being a nomadic tribe."

"Kicking it old school." Blane rose and picked up his tray.

"Oh, good, you're leaving." This was Fick, swooping in with his own full tray, along with Graybeard, to take their seats. "LT's called a leadership meeting in the Team Room for fourteen-hundred. Start getting into the weeds on planning this next FUBAR mission."

"Roger that," Blane said.

Sitting down and squaring up his tray, Fick looked up at Yaz, then Blane, and said, "Nomadic tribe, huh? The Gunny here is a proper fucking intellectual, ain't he?"

Blane just clapped Fick on the back and smiled.

Digging in to his food, and talking with his mouth full, Fick looked up at Yaz, and said, "So what kind of rarefied academic bullshit is he subjecting you to today?"

Blane said, "The same kind of academic bullshit that would probably use the word 'rarefied'. But nice try playing the working class-hero, Master Guns."

"Foiled again," Fick said, rolling his shoulder. He looked up at Yaz. "Hey, speaking of people who don't work for a living, I heard you used to roll with Tier-1 guys – a certain naval special warfare unit that doesn't exist."

Graybeard looked up and said, "So what made you want to come slum it with us vanilla SOCOM guys, down in the muck and bilge of the surface fleet?"

But Yaz was saved from having to answer when the tumult of conversations in the mess got cut by a two-tone whistle, the prelude to an announcement on the 1MC, the ship-wide public address system.

*"All hands, all hands. The ship will make way at fifteen-hundred hours. Make all preparations for getting underway. Set the special sea and anchor detail. Set Condition X-Ray. Repeat, the flat-top and all support ships will be getting underway one hour from now. All hands make ready to be underway."*

Yaz locked eyes with Blane. And he wondered if they were leaving behind the whole world they'd known, perhaps forever. He didn't know where they were going.

All he knew was they were going there together.

Maybe that was enough.

# ACT OF GOD

*USS John F. Kennedy – Bridge*

"The Commander's out on the observation deck, gentlemen."

Once again, the LT, Fick, and Blane were back on the Bridge, up in the sky near the top of the island. And once again, Blane wasn't 100% sure why he'd been dragged along for this. But that was the trouble with saying smart things and not griping too much.

It made you seem sane, and people rallied to you.

The LT nodded at the bridge officer directing them, and they all threaded through stations to the exterior hatch. When they stepped outside, they found the storm had finally died down, and the rain nearly stopped. You could really miss a major change in the weather, being belowdecks for long stretches on a ship so heavy it practically made its own weather.

A stiff breeze moved the sodden gray air, though some of that was due to the carrier making 26 knots, as it had been for most of the day. The *Kennedy*'s support ships were visible behind them and off to both sides, the flotilla even more impressive underway than lying at anchor.

Less impressive was the carrier's XO, Commander Drake – leaning on the railing with his forehead in one palm.

*That doesn't look good*, Blane thought, but kept silent.

"Commander," the LT said. "Reporting as ordered."

Drake straightened up and turned, revealing a tablet in his left hand, and returning the LT's salute with the other.

The LT squinted. "Haven't seen the Captain in a while."

Drake nodded toward the interior of the Bridge, and the little hatch at the back of it. "He's in his Ready Room." He didn't add, *Again*. But he wasn't the only one thinking it.

"Sir," the LT said, presenting his own tablet. "We've developed a concept of operations for the military operation in Honolulu. Just an initial draft. But given the timeline, we wanted to get it in your hands."

"Fantastic," Drake said. "But it doesn't matter now."

"Sir?" The LT looked crestfallen. Blane had a steadier keel. And Fick had seen it all, and was surprised by nothing.

Drake raised his own tablet and tapped the screen. "After that endless briefing yesterday, we somehow missed the elephant in the room. Or rather, the absence of elephant."

"Yes, sir," the LT said. He obviously had no idea what Drake was talking about. And was determined to be okay with that.

"I ran the numbers. And we don't have the lift capacity for this mission. Or anything like it. Our MH-60 Seahawk helos have a rated external lift capability of nine thousand pounds. In a pinch we could push that to ten or twelve."

"Yeah," Fick said, "if you wanna pinch your way to disaster."

"Call it five tons max per sling-load." Drake spun the tablet around, then pointed out numbers on it. "This figure is the tonnage of food required per day to feed everyone in the strike group. And here's the number of round trips required to transport seventy days' worth, enough to top up all our galleys, using just the Seahawks."

"Jesus Johnnycake Asscrack Christ," Fick said. "We'll be defending that HLZ until the undead cows come home."

"Yeah," Drake said, sounding weary. "We'd be there for days."

Blane glanced at the Marines' own tablet, with the mission concept they'd developed, which was now totally moot. "So, basically, getting out the supplies we need, with the rotary-wing air assets we have, is impractical."

"If by that," Fick said, "you mean impossible, then yeah."

"Suppose we added the surviving Defiant?" the LT said.

Drake shook his head. "Aside from the fact it's your team's ride in and out of there? And already inadequate for that task? And doesn't have a belly hook to take a sling-load?"

"What's our alternative?" Blane asked. "Ground transport?"

"Yeah," Fick said. "No. Getting that many tons of shit across miles of overrun ground isn't real appealing, either."

"Plus," Drake said, "it requires a port facility that can tie up a supercarrier. Or else going out and finding something like a heavy-lift hovercraft to move it all across the water."

"Having one of those would be kick-ass," Fick said.

"Maybe, but finding and stealing one," Drake said, "plus tying it to a ground convoy operation, would be an order of magnitude more complex than defending a single marshaling point and HLZ."

"Yeah," Blane said, "and also orders of magnitude more labor-intensive, ammo-intensive, and dangerous."

"So," Fick said, "I guess we get busy starving to death."

The LT shook his head. "Wish we'd hung onto one of those heavy-lift helos from the supply runs back in San Fran."

"Yeah," Fick said. "It's like how mice wish they had grenade launchers. You can bet cats wouldn't fuck with them."

Drake eyed Fick, trying not to laugh. This guy was going to take some getting used to. But he definitely made life on the carrier more colorful. "That actually would make a difference. The external lift capacity of those King Stallions is 35,000 pounds.

They're freaking huge. We could also use it to transport the shore teams, without making a half-dozen trips."

"So then we go steal one of those," Blane said.

Drake sighed. "Which is still a whole new mission. To a military base, with all those attendant risks." They'd already discussed, and rejected, the idea of scavenging a military base, identifying a thousand reasons it was a bad idea.

The LT said, "And it also brings us back to the drawing board, planning a whole new mission before we can do the food-scavenging mission."

Drake exhaled. "Maybe that's going to have to be it. It's either that, or sit around waiting for an act of God."

"God's pretty unreliable in my experience," Blane said.

Fick grunted. "He's definitely gotten me out of a couple of bad scrapes. Only real explanation for me still being here."

With that the group fell into glum silence.

And then the 1MC, including the tannoy speakers on the island and out on the flight deck, burbled to life.

*"All hands, all hands. Priority aircraft inbound. Repeat, aircraft inbound, rotary-wing, clear the helicopter landing area for air recovery ops. All shift-one helicopter LSE personnel report to stations. Repeat, clear the deck for aircraft recovery."*

The Commander and three Marines stared down wordlessly at the flight deck below, as it began to swarm with green-shirted flight deck personnel. Drake was the first to look up and see a buzzing speck approaching, then swelling, off the stern of the ship. He only turned again when a bridge officer stuck his head out and called his name.

"Sir, we went ahead and cleared them for HLZ Three."

"You didn't maybe want to run it by me first?"

"They were already cleared to land sixteen days ago, and

their secure transponder shows aircraft ID is the same. They check out. But, uh, mainly, they're pretty much out of fuel." He started to withdraw, but Drake snapped his fingers.

"Same as what?"

"See for yourself, sir."

Drake turned and saw the incoming helo was now close enough to visually identify. Then again, it didn't have to be all that close, because it was gigantic. It was a hulking, bulbous, dishwater-gray Sikorsky CH-53K King Stallion.

The LT shook his head. "That the same one that brought in the last of our gear? In San Francisco?"

Blane boggled as well. "And also brought our new SARC."

"Well, I'll be fucked," Drake said.

"Me, too," Fick said. "Also – fuck yeah, go God!"

Drake was already hopping down the first flight of stairs toward the flight deck, the others following.

No one wanted to miss this.

* * *

Seconds after the hulking aircraft settled on its fat tires, and the flight deck crew chocked and chained it, both pilot and co-pilot were out on the deck, pulling their helmets off.

"Where the hell did you come from?" Drake asked.

"Yeah," Blane said. "Last time I saw you, you were hauling ass to get off this boat."

The pilot had the insignia of a captain, and his nametape read *Freeman*. He smiled and said, "Turned out getting our asses out of here was exactly the wrong idea."

"Worst idea you ever had," said the co-pilot, a lieutenant named Pless. "Things were a lot more hairy back on shore."

Drake shook his head. "How'd you fly out this far?"

"Two words," Pless said. "Auxiliary fucking fuel tanks."

"And where have you been for two-plus weeks?"

"Base-hopping," Freeman said. "First MCAS Miramar, our home station. Then we tried Edwards AFB."

"What happened to those facilities?" Drake asked.

"Brother," Pless said, "you do not even want to know. Both times we just got out with our asses intact."

"Last place we tried was Coast Guard Island," Freeman said. "Nearly right back where we started. Thought it might last a little longer, what with being an island and all."

"And?" Drake asked.

"We just had time to top both sponson tanks, and fill all three auxiliary internal ones," Pless said. "Before getting out with our lives again, dead swarming over the airfield."

Freeman said, "But the auxiliary tanks doubled our ferry range. Which we hoped might give us a prayer of pulling off our last hail Mary. Which is making it out to you guys."

"And we did!" Pless said. "And you're alive!" He looked like he wanted to hug somebody, and went ahead and did it, to the LT, who looked most cuddly and least likely to react violently.

Freeman shook his head. "Also, that doubled range is how far across the Pacific you guys got before we caught you."

Pless let go of the LT, who was gently patting him on the back. "It was definitely gonna be a one-way trip, whether we caught you or not."

Drake smiled. "How close was it?"

Freeman shrugged. "Oh, I expect if you stick your head in the tanks you'll still smell a good solid fume or two."

Drake belatedly shook both their hands. And he said:

"Gentlemen. You are most welcome."

*One damned stroke of good luck*, he thought. *Maybe that's all we need.* Then he turned to the Marines, all of whom were wearing side arms. "Now if you could please escort these gentlemen to quarantine over on the *Rainier*."

Everyone looked slightly stunned, not least the pilots.

The LT said, "Who's gonna fly this thing for our mission?"

But Drake was already turning to leave, back to the Bridge. "We'll figure it out."

# YOU DON'T HAVE
# TO LIKE IT

*JFK – 01 Deck Briefing Room*
*{Two Days Later}*

Yaz's eyes landed on her as soon as she walked in the hatch.

The surface fleet had been gender-integrated for 25 years, and nearly 20% of the crew of the *Kennedy* were female. Yaz had passed plenty of women roaming the passageways, working out in the gym, or running out on deck. But he hadn't talked to a single one in his time on the boat so far, never mind worked with one. If special operations was still overwhelmingly white, it was almost universally male.

Then again, it turned out there were going to be a lot more than just the Raiders in their first overseas shore mission. The shore team was going to be limited to the 28 in the two Marine teams, plus 55 others – the maximum number that could fit on the King Stallion, which had come back and found them like a lost puppy.

Right now, there were already more than that number thronging the briefing room – ops staff from CIC, aviation guys from the air wing, and a few other ratings Yaz didn't recognize. From her sleek flight suit, Yaz guessed the woman who drew his eye – with her pale skin and raven-black hair – was a pilot.

Which itself was intriguing.

He picked a seat at the edge of the Marines, but one row

behind her and to the side, where he could steal glances without getting caught. This put him next to Blane and Fick. There didn't seem to be any particular seating plan for the classroom-like space, which consisted of a lectern with a laptop up front, a whiteboard and digital displays on the wall behind it, and rows of bolted-down chairs facing forward and taking up most of the room.

Despite no assigned seating, departments were naturally clustering, in particular the Marines. And Yaz felt once again that they really were set apart from the rest of the ship. But, tomorrow, the survival of everyone on board…

Would depend on them.

\* \* \*

At the exact second of the scheduled briefing time, Commander Drake kicked things off. Yaz checked his watch. Like everyone else, he knew 0800 sharp meant 0745.

So he'd had a few minutes to regard that black hair.

"Good morning," Drake said, holding the lectern with both hands. He wore his usual khaki service uniform, short sleeves today, and his #1 haircut looked like it had been trimmed to its regulation 1/8th inch that morning. "I want to say thanks to all departments and personnel involved for jumping through their asses to get this operation planned in two days."

He took a breath, straightened up, and scanned faces.

"Obviously, this is going to be unlike any mission we've ever trained for. Then again, so was San Francisco. The difference this time is we know what we're facing."

He paused long enough for everyone to glance around and see how the other hundred or so people in the room were taking it.

"Make no mistake. Hawaii is gone. As far as we can tell, every place is gone." No one in the audience said anything, but there was a general murmuring and air of disbelief. "We are still in radio contact with a handful of far-flung military bases, a few deployed units, and some warships. But they are blinking out fast. And the ones we're still talking to don't sound like they're doing too well, or are going to be around a hell of a lot longer. Effectively… we're on our own."

One of the aviation guys raised his hand. Drake nodded.

"What about the other carrier strike groups?"

Drake just shook his head, chin angled low.

"Christ," the man said. He looked around the room, then back at Drake. "So how are we still here? The only ones left?"

"The quarantine ship."

It wasn't Drake who said this – it was Lieutenant Campbell, sitting in the front row, twisting at the waist to face the room. "That's the only reason we're still here." She nodded back up front toward the lectern. "By coming up with that little innovation…

"Commander Drake saved us all."

* * *

"Rest assured," said Campbell, now up front for her segment of the briefing. "The option of going into a Navy or other US military installation has been exhaustively explored."

She scanned the room before going on.

"There are two reasons we're not doing it that way. One, they've mostly gone black on comms. We're not assuming the worst." She didn't have to belabor what the worst would be – everyone dead, or undead. "But for now we are assuming anyone left alive inside military bases will be holed up, barricaded in, and armed to the teeth – and quicker to shoot unexpected visitors than ask questions. So it's too risky."

Yaz looked from her over to the Captain, sitting at the far right of the front row. He cut a respectable figure as the skipper of the flagship – mid-fifties, creased and lined face with a fresh shave, short-cropped white hair, also wearing a crisp khaki uniform, with a lot of rows of ribbon on his left breast. He had to have served both as naval aviator, then air wing commander, before getting this job.

They didn't let you be a carrier captain otherwise.

So he had to have something to contribute, at least about the air component of the operation. But he hadn't opened his mouth once. And he looked like he really wanted to be somewhere else. Maybe they all did.

Campbell went on. "The good news is our intel suggests everyone and everything in the AO we're looking at, the whole civilian world really, went down too hard and fast for the stores to get cleaned out. This was a pandemic without the hoarding. And their loss will be our gain." She called up some aerial imagery, from a drone flying ahead of the strike group. It showed a two-tone tan building – one the size of a small city. The parking lot out front was almost as big. Behind the building, parked in rows, was a small fleet of 18-wheelers.

Mounted above the front entrance to the building, in one corner, was a giant sign, blue and diamond-shaped.

"Fucking Sam's Club? Seriously?"

Yaz didn't see who said that.

It could have been anybody.

\* \* \*

63

"Right," said the Suppo – or Supply Officer, member of the Navy Supply Corps, and head of the ship's Supply Department, responsible for stores, galleys, and food service. "Obviously, we're not used to doing replenishment this way. Or working with this many departments. So bear with me."

The stout middle-aged officer looked around the room, clearly ill at ease briefing people from so many areas of ship's operations.

"But let me say it's an honor. And I know with all of us working together, this is going to go smoothly. On rails, even."

"Yeah," Fick grumbled, under his breath but loud enough for Yaz and the other Marines nearby to hear. "Whenever you hear that shit, it's time to start worrying."

"Start running, you mean." Yaz looked over his shoulder and saw Brady sitting in the row behind, along with Reyes and the rest of 2/1. The rest of it minus Flynn, anyway. His absence struck Yaz as a *memento mori* – a reminder of death. He just needed to not take it as an omen about the forthcoming mission.

The Suppo either didn't hear the Marines grumbling, or tactically chose to ignore it. "So I'm going to talk about what exactly we need to find and bring aboard to keep this show on the road – and everyone serving in it fed. Then I'm going to talk about the plan we've developed for moving approximately fifteen hundred tons of mainly dried goods from shore to ship. To set your expectations for what's to come, I've got two words for you: forklift trucks."

This raised a smattering of laughter.

"Also – hand carts. Okay four words. Oh – and sling-loads! Six words. Anyway. Moving on…"

\* \* \*

"Bodies." This was the head of the Administrative Department, responsible for a variety of boring things including personnel.

"This plan requires a lot of bodies to run smoothly. I've been tasked with pulling personnel to pad out team manifests for supply loading and handling. I'm also tasked with getting them on and offshore, utilizing a mix of rotary-wing air assets and motorized surface craft."

"Hey," Reyes hissed from behind, at Blane and Fick. "You did report up the chain that noise draws the dead, right?"

"Yeah," Blane whispered back. "They know."

"Just sayin'," Reyes said, leaning back again.

Now Brady leaned forward. "You tell 'em the other thing?"

"Staff Sergeant, shut it." This was the LT, leaning in from down the row. He'd evidently had it with his Marines disrupting the briefing. So whatever the other thing was, it would have to get discussed another time. But Yaz figured he had an idea, and it was something else they learned at Fort Point. That once the dead start coming…

They don't stop.

* * *

"Air." This was the officer in charge of the helicopter squadron for the carrier's deployed air wing. Or what was left of it. "For better and worse, we are not an ARG, nor an ESG. So we do not have LHAs, LHDs, LSDs, or LPDs, along with their well decks. If we did, we'd have an LCAC at our disposal."

Yaz let the acronym soup fly over his head, and just latched on to the last one: LCAC, or Landing Craft Air Cushion – a gigantic landing hovercraft with massive cargo transport capability.

"If we did have an LCAC, we could move sixty tons of

stores at a go. As it is we're limited to air transport by sling-load. I'm going to run through all the air assets being utilized, and their roles in each phase of the operation – from heavy-lift transport to extraction of the MARSOC element…"

Yaz zoned out again.

\* \* \*

"Obviously," said the MARSOC commander, the LT, taking his turn at the podium, "our team has our own mission briefs on the military component of this operation."

Yaz remembered that, however little combat experience he had, every junior officer was an expert at briefing.

"Right now, it's my job to make sure everyone involved has a reasonable idea of what we're going to be doing, and how we're going to ensure the safety of everyone going ashore. Hence, herewith, a quick high-level pass through our mission planning doc – which is based on the MDMP."

The never-popular Military Decision Making Process prob-ably accounted for the thousand-yard stares in the audience. The LT tapped the laptop and the lights went down.

"And, yes, that means death by Powerpoint."

He had to raise his voice to speak over the groans.

\* \* \*

And then the female aviator took the stage. But she wasn't the one speaking. That was left to a youthful man in a matching flight suit, who Yaz hadn't noticed sitting next to her.

"I'm Lieutenant Călinescu," he said. "Better and more eas-ily known by my call sign, Angel. Yes, it's from *Buffy*. Yes, it's because I'm from a place in Romania close to Transylvania." He nodded at the woman, standing beside and behind the lectern. "This is my back-seater and EWO, who I'm sure would like to be known only by her call sign, Rain. I'm actually pretty sure she'd prefer not to be up here at all."

This got a couple of laughs, but the pilot felt Drake's eyes burning his skin and got on with it.

"The two of us will be running top cover in our EA-18G Growler aircraft. Yes, it's an electronic warfare platform, whose primary job is to jam enemy communications and radar. But it's also a great ISR platform and comms relay. Yes, we could just send up a UAV. And you will also have high-altitude drone coverage. But command agrees with us that men on the ground appreciate having human beings overhead, watching over you, and actively working to keep you safe. No, we can't provide CAS. But I'm told you're unlikely to need it – and if close air support is required, I am assured there will be armed air assets on deck, ready to scramble."

"I am assured of this," Fick muttered under his breath.

"Honestly, I think we're only briefing for the same reason they're not just sending a drone – so you can see us in person, and put faces to the voices overhead. Okay, that's it. I'm sure it's the fighter jocks you really want to hear from, about the happy fun precision bombing phase of tomorrow's mission."

Rain never did speak.

But Yaz never stopped looking at her.

* * *

"Last item," Drake said, back at the lectern, closing the briefing. "This is the part some of you aren't going to like. But there's no requirement that you like it. Because it's happening. Be advised – everyone who sets one foot on shore will not be setting one foot back on this or any boat in the strike group before spending 168 hours, one full week, in quarantine on the *Rainier* – under armed guard and medical watch."

He paused, and looked around for any grumbling.

There wasn't any. They all got it.

"Dismissed."

\* \* \*

Or, anyway, they got the need to not gripe about it publicly.

"Shit, man," Brady said. "Another week sitting on our asses doing the five-knuckle shuffle."

Reyes grinned and said, "I'm sure Yaz here can hook you up with a week's supply of petroleum jelly."

Fick grunted. "Everything works with the proper application of violence and Vaseline."

"Man," said Graybeard. "I could have gone my whole life without that mental image."

Yaz said, "At least they brought it down from two weeks."

"Never mind the fucking quarantine," Fick said. "What I'm worried about is the plan for the mission before it."

"What's your concern?" the LT asked.

Fick traded a look with Graybeard. Both of them had been through the joint planning process more than once. "Too many moving parts. Too many friction points, way too many failure points, and too many goddamned unknowns. Mainly, too many kids on the jungle gym, most of them not Marines. Basically, a metric shit-ton of ways this can all go wrong."

There was a beat of silence while they all traded looks.

"And moreover," Fick concluded, "I don't fucking like it."

Blane smiled, trying to lighten the mood. "Yeah, well, as usual, you don't have to like it, Master Guns..."

"Yeah, yeah, I know," Fick said. "I just have to suck it."

"Exactly."

Yaz said, "I'm kind of surprised we're going into a civilian facility rather than a military one. I mean, I know military personnel will be armed, and probably twitchy. But this is just the usual problem of coming into friendly lines. You radio ahead, and make sure you move real slow."

Blane shook his head. "That's not the real reason."

"What then?"

"The problem's not them shooting us. It's us shooting them."

"What do you mean?"

The LT took over. "He means it's possible there are still military bases with survivors holed up. But virtually all the ones we've contacted have fallen, with everyone inside gone down to the virus."

Blane finished the rest. "And nobody's ready to start shooting American servicemen and women, even undead ones. Not yet. Nobody's ready for that."

Yaz nodded, sobered. "I've got to go."

He had one last tasking before he could step off.

# UNPLEASANT IN
# THE EXTREME

*JFK – Ship's Hospital*

"Tsk, tsk, Corpsman. You were supposed to see me yesterday."

"Sorry, Doc," Yaz said to LCDR Walker. "Mission prep."

She shook her head as she pulled on a pair of exam gloves. "And what's the tool you use for mission planning?"

"Powerpoint?"

"No. Your bruised and much-abused brain. I saw way too many undiagnosed TBIs in Iraq and Afghanistan. So if you think you're going to step off on this mission, without me signing you off first, you've— Ah. Of course. That's the only reason you're here now. To get signed off for the mission."

Yaz just gave her a wide-eyed look, all innocent.

"Have a seat," she said, nodding to the table in the tiny examination room, one of several in the *Kennedy*'s hospital, which was 20 times the size of the sick bay on the *Rainier*. Yaz had to walk through much of it to get here, and was already in awe of their facilities.

It had a fully-equipped ER, an 80-bed hospital ward, a 2-bed Intensive Care Unit, and two operating rooms for general surgery – plus a complete dental facility, physical therapy clinic, optometric services, pharmacy, radiology, and lab. It was staffed by six doctors, including one surgeon – LCDR Walker herself, who was also CO of the department – along with an anesthetist, nurses, PAs, and orderlies.

If the *JFK* was a floating city, this was its municipal hospital. And apparently Walker wasn't too high up on any org chart to pawn off one of her patients on an underling.

She said, "Start by telling me how you've been feeling."

"Good," he said. "Great."

She held up a blue hand. "Let me stop you right there – and urge you to remember your oath of enlistment. When you solemnly swore to obey the orders of the officers appointed over you. Which right now is me. And this is me ordering you to answer my questions truthfully."

"Yes, ma'am."

"Headaches?"

"Negative."

"Double vision? Nausea? Dizziness or confusion?"

"All negative."

She gave a him a look. Maybe he answered too quickly.

"Loss of balance, or memory? Flashes of light, or eye pain?"

He just shook his head.

She put her hand on her hip. "Are you just telling me whatever you have to to maintain your operational status?"

"Would I lie to you, Commander?"

"In my experience? Every single SOF guy alive would lie to his dying grandmother to not miss out on a mission."

"My grandmother's dead."

"So is everyone else's. This shit is worse than Covid was for the elderly." She paused to note his scandalized look. "Oh, come on. If you can't laugh about the death of almost everyone on the planet, what can you laugh about?"

"The Holocaust?"

"I'll ask one more time. Would you lie to maintain your operational status?"

"Of course."

"And have you been lying to me today?"

"Of course not."

She shook her head and mouthed, *Goddammit.*

"Okay," she said. "I'm going to physically examine you. Your body might reveal some of the truth. Then I'm going to shoot some more film of your brain, as some nice Nebraska farm boys have finally wrestled the X-Ray and MRI machines back over here. And X-Rays don't lie."

"That so?"

Walker sighed. "No. Actually, they conceal at least as much as they reveal."

Despite their adversarial relationship, and her gruff manner, Yaz really liked Walker, and had to respect her as a fellow medical professional. She was sharp, switched-on, committed, and obviously outstanding at her job.

So it was hard not to like her.

Though she obviously didn't care that much if you did.

\* \* \*

Yaz was out of the hospital in less than an hour.

Which left him an hour of personal time before the next and hopefully last round of mission planning and prep. He liked the idea of some air, and space, not to mention relative solitude – and an ocean view. But when he tried to climb up to the flight deck, he found his way blocked.

Air ops were back on.

Which made the flight deck a no-go. Yaz hadn't been here long, but he knew enough to know that 29,000 horsepower afterburning F-35 engines weren't the kind of thing you wanted to just accidentally wander out into.

But it turned out that, other than the flight deck, there weren't a hell of a lot of places on this boat to get outside, certainly not for an enlisted sailor who didn't work in the island. After wandering around fruitlessly for much of his free hour, he finally emerged onto the fantail deck.

This was the huge rectangular hole in the otherwise sheer wall that was the stern of the boat. It sat directly above the dock, and looked like a kind of giant oversized patio, with a long section of railing at its edge, which looked out over the water from two stories above it. Yaz was allowed out there by a very serious armed NSF guy, who told him he'd have to clear out 24 hours before mission launch – at which point, the ship would go into a combat posture, Condition Zebra, and this too would be a no-go zone for non-essential personnel.

Yaz didn't tell the guy that he was extremely essential personnel for the upcoming mission. He just counted his blessings and walked out to a free stretch of railing. He grabbed it, nodding to the sailors on either side, all of whom were doing the same thing he was, namely getting some air.

Then he leaned out and peered over. Two stories below, he could see the ship churning up massive volumes of ocean water into its Olympic-pool-sized wake. Yaz knew somewhere beneath that wake were four screw propellers, each 22 feet across and weighing 68,000 pounds, all pushing the 110,000 tons of warship forward at 26 knots, or 30mph.

"Don't do it, man. Life's still worth it."

He leaned back in and turned to see who'd said this – and it was her. The female EWO, or electronic warfare officer, from the briefing. Rain. He moved to make room for her, and she draped her arms across the railing, then looked across at him, brushing her hair behind her ear. She had black hair, fair skin, and fine lines around her mouth, and looked a little like Angelina Jolie, or some ice queen played by Angelina Jolie. Beautiful, but even more severe and striking.

Her piercing ice-blue eyes had a paralyzing effect.

At a guess she was a little older than Yaz, early thirties, and probably in excellent shape. *Or maybe not*, Yaz thought, as she produced and lit a Marlboro Light.

He said, "So what makes you think I'm gonna jump?"

"Maybe you think it's a faster and easier way of getting killed than going off and invading undead Hawaii."

"Sounds pretty good when you put it that way."

"Ah, but that's where you're wrong." She nodded down at the gigantic churning wake, her hair swinging in front of her eyes again. "You might think the propellers will chop you into chum. But before you make it down there, you've got to get through the wake. And most people trying to check out by drowning change their minds at the last second – survival instinct kicks in. It's the most primal thing, the need for air."

"So you think I'd try to swim for it?"

"Yeah, you'd try," she said, taking a drag of the cigarette. "But therein lies the problem. See all that foam? There's too much air in the water to hold you up – but too much water to catch a breath. You'll flail around trying to breath froth. For a little while."

"That sounds unpleasant."

She blew out a double lungful of smoke, which dissipated in the whipping air, from the 26 knots the carrier was making. "Didn't you get briefed on this? Shipboard health and safety, man."

"I came aboard at a strange time. Happened kinda fast."

She took another drag, then looked across at him, letting the smoke leak out. He coughed. "Sorry," she said.

"No problem. I'm used to it." Yaz's gaze went a little long, looking off into memory, and Rain must have read it.

"Girlfriend a smoker? Or wife?"

He looked back at her, impressed. "Girlfriend. Ex."

"My advice?"

He nodded.

"Let her go, man. Because she is definitely gone." She nodded out over the ocean, indicating the whole dead world behind them. Then she flicked the half-smoked cigarette over the railing, sending it tumbling and trailing sparks down into the wake. "Gotta get into preflight. See you when I see you."

As she disappeared again, Yaz realized this was literally true. Soon, she'd be looking straight down on him.

Like the weather.

*　*　*

When he got back to his cabin, Yaz found Milam, who tended to hang out there, but not Chesney or Jeschke, who didn't. They either liked being surrounded by other people, or else just really liked Xbox. Probably the latter.

But Yaz didn't expect to find Commander Drake there.

"Good timing," the XO said. "I won't be long."

Yaz nodded and stepped inside, moving to stand beside Milam in front of their bunks.

"Okay, here it is," Drake said. "When you two step off, you have a special responsibility as corpsmen."

Yaz nodded, his expression serious. Nobody took their

responsibilities more seriously than SARCs. It was drilled into them from day one of their two-year training pipeline.

But Drake shook his head. "You think you know what I'm talking about. But you don't." He stole a look at his watch, then went on. "Everything is different now. And we need to understand this sooner, not later – or there won't be a later. So listen to me. Anyone you encounter out there. Those are not sick people. They're dead. Everyone infected is gone."

Yaz and Milam both nodded, and glanced at each other.

"But, mainly, they are a lethal threat. Not just to you, and not just to your Marines. But to everyone still alive and healthy, aboard every vessel in this strike group. Every rank and rating, every station. Every one of us. You understand?"

He opened up his chest and put his hands on his hips.

"Your primary tasking, your overarching priority, is no longer keeping your Marines alive. It's keeping *everyone* alive. Everyone left. And that might entail… having to do something unpleasant in the extreme. Something you may not be prepared for. Do you get me? Or do I need to spell it out?"

He didn't. They got it.

The expeditionary medical corps had their orders.

# NOT RETARDED ENOUGH

*Honolulu – One Mile Offshore*

Three miles.

That was once again how far offshore the *JFK* carrier strike group had dropped anchor. Not off the edge of a mighty continent this time, but the island outpost of an empire. And so three miles was how much ocean the Marines had to cover in their insertion. But it wasn't the distance. It was the time.

Time for Yaz and the others to get into their heads.

The carrier's launch had a top speed of 30 knots, but they were only doing half that to keep the noise down. There were also complex operational timings to hit. The Marines were scheduled to insert one hour before BMNT, beginning of morning nautical twilight, a cumbersome military term for dawn.

So it was black and rolling ocean Yaz looked out upon.

But the ocean surface, and Yaz, and the other 29 hunched figures in the open-top boat, were also bathed in the light of the stars and the moon above. An ocean breeze – cool, clean, and strong – had blown in, sweeping the sky clear of the last clouds from the squall they had battled through three days ago. And it blew still.

"Where's my Team Chief?"

This was the LT, sitting up in the prow, speaking just loud enough to be heard over the engines and wind. They were practicing light discipline, the boat blacked out, but would only maintain strict noise discipline when they hit shore.

"Sir," Fick answered, from his spot in the stern.

"Any last words of wisdom for us?"

Fick cleared his throat. "Uh, yeah. The same I always tell Marines before going ashore: don't add to the population, or take away from the population."

That earned a laugh, rolling across the boat like a wave.

The LT shook his head in the dark. "I think what the Master Guns means is don't shoot any living people."

"Or fuck them," Graybeard added, under his breath.

"So we can fuck the dead people?" Brady asked, sounding a little too eager.

"No, dumbass," Reyes said. "Just shoot them."

"Okay, fine, I just want to be clear on all this."

Silence descended again, matching the darkness. From the prow of the boat, the minigunner and the LT behind him could now make out the distant smudge of land, a handful of lights still glimmering on shore to mark it.

The Marines had wanted to make the entire mission a night op. They were used to their advanced night-vision devices giving them a critical advantage over the enemy. So far, though, nobody knew how much the dead saw, even during the day, never mind at night. Some of them felt their experience in San Francisco suggested the dead relied mainly on sound, and maybe smell. But it was more gut instinct than hard data. And these were early days. So none of the shooters felt like taking the risk of operating in daylight.

However, every other department head had been adamant that trying to conduct the whole operation at night was madness – just asking for mishaps and injuries. Some of the others involved, aviators and flight deck crew, were trained to do their jobs under NVG conditions. But most weren't, and in any case none of this was going to be remotely like their normal jobs.

So a compromise had been reached. The Marines would take down "the target site" – calling it "Sam's Club" made everyone giggle, and kept them from taking it seriously – under cover of darkness. And then everyone else would be brought in to clean it out at first light.

Then they'd all get the hell out of Dodge.

\* \* \*

"And there it is – the ass crack of dawn. Motherfuckers."

All twenty-six Marines and their two SARCs were crouching down at the end of the slick wooden pier, exactly where they'd been for nearly an hour. The launch had cut its engines, glided in, and docked just long enough for them to hop off and take up security positions. But when the LT radioed to update CIC, he had been told to hold station.

There was some delay in getting their top cover launched.

"I knew it," Reyes hissed, pressing his head up beside Brady's. "I knew there'd be some fuck-up."

"Yeah," Brady said. "Going in at night wasn't retarded enough. Had to do it in daylight. Gotta like the weather, though."

Yaz, just able to hear this, smiled. They'd all basically just sailed into a tropical climate. Even now, they'd probably be too warm, squatting motionless in fatigues with full combat load, plus the tension of being on hostile ground. But that same clean breeze was still blowing, keeping them cool.

Brady nodded at the handful of masts that still lined the dock of the marina. "Well, however bad things get, at least we won't have to fucking swim for it this time."

The LT got off his radio and glared at Fick, his message clear – if the men were violating discipline, noise or any other kind, the Team Chief wasn't doing his job. Fick wheeled on the 2/1 guys, smushed their helmets together from either side, then pressed his own up against them, so he could hiss at full volume. This also caused Brady's helmet to skew down over his eyes, which he just had to live with for the moment.

"You two keep running your cock holsters, you'll regret it."

They both nodded in response, chastened.

Fick withdrew a few inches, then squinted at Brady. "Now straighten your helmet. Before I cum on your face."

Then he stared back at the LT, his own meaning clear.

*What in God's holy name is the hold-up?*

\* \* \*

Commander Drake kept himself up on the Bridge, but closely monitored radio traffic between the shore team and CIC.

*"Seven-Nine Combat, Reamer Actual, requesting updated sitrep, over."* This was the LT, commander on the ground, speaking in a whisper, but sounding none too patient. His voice was also clear and audible. During the cruise here, someone had finally figured out how to get the intra-station telephones piped to the wall speakers and ambient mics.

Lieutenant Campbell answered from CIC. *"Reamer, Seven-Nine Combat. Situation unchanged. They're still working the problem. We do already have drone coverage up. If you're comfortable going in without manned top cover, I'm going to say that's your call as ground commander."*

The LT hesitated before responding, and when he did, Drake could hear the lack of confidence in his voice. *"That's received, Combat. We're going to stick to the briefed plan."*

*"Copy that, Reamer. Your call. Hopefully we'll have this resolved shortly. Will keep you updated."*

Finally, Drake decided the tension and helplessness were getting to him, so he handed over the conn, exited, and took the stairs on the outside of the island down to the flight deck. As he descended through the glare of the working lights that illuminated the bow runway, he could see the Growler that had been parked there unmoving for the last hour. He could also make out the heads of the pilot and back-seater through the cowling, both with their helmets still on.

*That must suck,* he thought.

Lined up beside the Growler on the second bow runway was the newer, faster, meaner F-35C Lightning II, which wouldn't go up until after the Growler did. Every moving part in this op seemed to have five contingencies. And right now the part that refused to budge was the launch of the first manned aircraft.

A dozen personnel swarmed around the Growler in the glare and deep shadows, mostly flight deck guys identified by their colored jerseys. Half wore the yellow of aircraft handling and catapult officers, while a couple in green were maintenance personnel. Two wore the red of firefighting and damage-control, just observing, thank God.

For now.

One figure who didn't wear a colored shirt was hollering at the others. This was the Air Boss, down from his aerie of the gods up in PriFly at the top of the island. Shit must have really gone sideways if he had climbed all the way down here to shout at people to their faces. The Air Boss was a hearty and vigorous man, but he didn't have the physique of a guy who enjoyed climbing a lot of stairs.

As Drake approached, he saw the Boss screaming down at the surface of the flight deck, into the glass bubble of the catapult control pod, which protruded from the deck's surface between the two bow runways. Inside was the catapult officer, or "shooter", who ran the Electromagnetic Aircraft Launch System (EMALS), which had replaced the hydraulically powered catapults on the old *Nimitz* carriers.

Ironically, one of the great advantages of EMALS, aside from its greater precision and power, was it was supposed to be a hell of a lot more reliable. Then again, this was why they conducted sea trials – to work all the damned kinks out. They'd already tested these systems, including full interoperability, with deck-launch exercises hundreds of times. The only thing they hadn't tested was using them at sea – and when they were urgently needed.

Which is of course when they failed to work.

Drake only caught the end of the Air Boss's ass-chewing.

"—best get yourself unfucked, *right now*..."

But the ass-chewing worked. No sooner had Drake approached the plane than the Aircraft Director started shouting, waving, and even shoving people clear. He then took up his spot within view of the pilot, saluted, touched the deck at his feet, and pointed down the bow deck. The control lights at the deck edge went green, and the blast shield went up behind the plane, to keep its jet engine from barbecuing everything and everyone behind it. Only then did the single turbofan engine fire up to its full power, crescendoing to an ear-pummeling roar.

The holdback bar dropped, the towbar yanked forward, and the plane shrieked down the flight deck like something launched out of a catapult. It had so much thrust it was already climbing before it reached the end of the runway and the front edge of the ship.

It soared off into a sky glowing with the dawn.

* * *

"We're go," the LT whispered over the command net to his team leaders. "Patrol formation as briefed. Move out."

Most of the Marines grumbled, having to lift themselves up on cramped leg muscles they'd been squatting on for an hour, but they only griped inside their heads. They were mainly relieved just to get moving. Sitting in an exposed and static position wasn't something that made grunts happy, never mind special operators. They were often behind enemy lines, as now, and almost always badly outnumbered – definitely like now.

Moving fast and hitting hard was how they stayed alive.

*"Reamer Actual, this is God Six, comms check."*

At the head of the column as it moved out, the LT guessed the voice belonged to the female EWO from the briefing, Rain. Evidently she was in charge of comms with the ground team while the front-seater, Angel, flew the aircraft. "God Six, Reamer Actual, you're five by five, over."

*"Reamer, we've got eyes on your infil route, and show nothing moving ahead, and no heat signatures, over."*

As the pilot had predicted, it did feel good to have actual humans watching over them. The other good news was they hadn't spotted any movement or heat blooms. The bad news was no one had any idea if the dead moved around when there weren't living to chase.

And they definitely didn't have body heat.

The Marines' infil route, from insertion point at the water to target site, was just shy of a mile. But a mile was a long way when moving tactically, in patrol formation, and trying to maintain total silence plus situational awareness. The latter was necessary because they still had no great idea of what they were walking into. None of them had set foot on shore since their escape from the vortex of San Francisco. And the third of a million people who used to live in Honolulu had to be somewhere.

Near the back of the column, Yaz kept his rifle at low ready as he walked forward heel-toe, smooth but fast, covering his sector, making sure to keep his spacing with the others, and making sure to keep up. They were moving down the 40-meter pier, which had 16 berthings on each side, but only a half-dozen boats tied up. As he looked around, Yaz's boot slammed into a raised plank, making him stumble, and making a loud thump.

It was answered by another thump off to his right. He stopped and spun in that direction, but saw only a twin-hulled catamaran with a raised cabin in the middle. The banging noise from inside sounded again. Yaz couldn't visually identify any threat, and the door to the cabin was closed. But it banged again.

"You're fine, Doc. Keep moving."

This was Blane, beside and behind him, whispering and patting his shoulder. Yaz shook his head and got going again. They reached the end of the pier, which faced a boathouse, then turned right onto the main dock. At the end of it, they circled around the structure, crossed a road, and emerged into a big traffic circle, with some kind of hulking stone sculpture in it, along with a row of self-service rental bikes.

With no warning or buildup, Yaz heard the metallic clack of suppressed SCAR rifles from the front of the column. The suppressors they mounted greatly reduced the sound signature, but didn't eliminate it. Out here on this strange ground, in the silent dawn of a dead city, it sounded way too loud. When Yaz reached the other side of the circle, he saw three bodies on the ground, all leaking black fluid from head wounds. He stepped around them and stayed in formation.

If the noise of those shots drew more, the Marines weren't going to hang around waiting for them.

The column turned left onto a five-lane road, keeping to the sidewalk and one lane on the left side. The road was lined with lush trees, like overgrown Bonsais, which shifted from black to dark green in the first morning light. The road was also bordered by parking lots, and high-rises that looked like either resorts or residential buildings, a few with lights still burning behind their windows. The road itself stretched to the horizon, farther than Yaz could see. Along with the others, he just got busy eating up the distance.

Every minute or so there'd be a little shooting, mostly from the front. Shortly after, those in back would step over or past twisted bodies in pools of viscous black liquid, lying on the road or sidewalk, or in adjacent parking lots or lawns. An occasional glance to the rear showed they weren't being followed – yet. And Yaz still didn't have to engage.

More than once, he detected flashes of dark movement off in the shadows to his left, and thought he heard hissing or wheezing. But the patrol moved past before they resolved. And Yaz knew, as the mission brief dictated, that moving was better than shooting.

Still, it was a lot of moving, and Yaz felt his limbs burning from the strain and exertion. The other reason a mile was longer than it sounded was they were once again loaded down with combat gear – but not the same as in San Francisco. Having had to swim their asses out of there, all had shed, and most discarded, their tactical vests and plate carriers. The Marines put to sea with a lot of spare gear, so they'd been able to replace most of what had been lost. But no one had anticipated an open-water swim, so they only had a few spare vests and plates, not enough for everyone.

Now, for this mission, guys had stuffed their pockets full of magazines, and shoved more into assault packs. Fick, unsurprisingly, had jungle-taped one upside down in his M16. They were going to have to get replacement vests and plates at some point.

But today they had to make it work.

# ENJOY THE POSSIBILITIES

*Honolulu – Ala Moana Center*

Not long after turning onto the five-lane road, they turned off it again, into a mixed commercial/residential development, with a big three-level parking deck, all of it anchored by a high-rise.

They had to cover a stretch through a narrow tunnel, parking deck on one side and overhead, high-rise on the other, claustrophobic and tense, with Marines putting down stumbling dead on the road ahead, as well as coming out of the parking structure right beside them to the left. Soon they passed out of this again, breaking contact, and turned onto a wider road.

The order went out not to engage unless necessary, but just keep moving, fast. Everyone knew taking on the entire former population of Honolulu was a fight they couldn't win.

They reached the base of a vehicle ramp, wide and a quarter mile long, rising up along the outside of the parking deck before turning 90 degrees out of sight to the right. This was the point where they really had to break contact. The LT led the Marines into a run as he fielded his last update from their top cover.

*"Reamer, your target site still shows dead and cold."*

The LT didn't spend the wind to respond as he rounded the bend, pounded up the last stretch, and emerged out onto the top level of the three-story parking deck – which itself was a sprawling, open, stadium-sized parking lot, with only a handful of vehicles still parked in it.

When the rest of the Marines stepped out onto it, they got

hit by a blast of wind, the same offshore breeze, but a mile inland now, blowing free through the exposed and elevated area. To the right of the ramp, on the south edge of the lot, sat an equally gargantuan building.

Their target site. Sam's Club.

This was the ground they had to hold, and the fight they had to win. But they needed to keep it from kicking off as long as possible. The fire team assigned to hold the top of the ramp, namely 1/2, spun to the rear – and found nothing following them up. They'd broken contact. But the first group to approach the store found something waiting for them.

In a big, wiggling pile.

* * *

*Well, so much for a secure target structure,* Yaz thought.

Their planning had included a number of assumptions, among them that the warehouse would be sealed up. It was possible some of the rear loading entrances would be propped open, though they tended to swing shut and auto-lock for security reasons. And the front entrances were automatic sliding doors, which would shut by default.

Unless they had bodies wedging them open.

It looked like someone had shot these ones to pieces as they tried to enter the store, and they now lay in a pile, most unmoving, a few wiggling, and one or two trying to crawl toward the Marines. The sliding glass door kept banging into them as it kept trying to close itself. Not only were they going to have to destroy the still active ones in the pile. But someone was going to have to clear them the hell out of there.

Yaz started distributing surgical gloves.

Then he pitched in and got to work.

* * *

Yaz had a bad feeling this wouldn't be their last bad surprise. And it turned out it wasn't even their last bad surprise in the next minute. Just inside the entrance they found another crowd of tottering dead, all on their feet – and all reaching up and moaning at something overhead.

Pivoting around the briefed mission plan, the Marines self-organized, each fire team grabbing a job that needed doing. First 2/2 dispersed into the parking lot to secure the stairwell doors at the four corners. With these chained or nailed shut, the only way up there would be the ramp – a single point of entry and exit. At the same time, 1/1 got to work on the body pile in the entrance. Finally, 2/1 pushed inside the building to deal with the crowd in the lobby.

Some of those had already sensed the Marines moving bodies, and stumbled over to investigate. Others remained fixated where they were. All got put down with clean headshots. When it was over, Fick lowered his weapon, put his left hand on his hip, looked up, and muttered:

"Jesus Couch-Surfing Christ. That's not just gay, that's fucking Navy gay." He glanced at Yaz. "No offense."

The other Marines gathered around and looked up at what had been riveting the attention of the dead guys. It was a TV hanging from the ceiling, playing a 30-second ad on a loop.

This showed a schlubby-looking guy picking out a necklace at the jewelry counter... then, behind him, in ghostly outline, an imagined version of him giving it to a woman over a dinner table. Then there was a dude standing in front of a half-dozen large-screen TVs… while a ghost version of him and his friends leapt up, shouting at a football game on TV. Then a seriously fat dude, watching his ghost self sleeping on different reclining chairs. Finally, a Sam's Club logo appeared, while voiceover and text said:

"Sam's Club. Enjoy the possibilities."

Reyes shook his head. "Damn, some Raiders we are, man. Raiding a fucking warehouse store."

"Hey, could have been worse," Brady said, glancing at 1/1 dragging bodies outside. "Could have been Walmart. Imagine the whale-sized dead guys we'd have to drag around there."

Yaz tried to look away from the body pile under the TV, but didn't succeed. He could see the racial mix was about half Asian, minority white, a few Pacific Islanders. They wore a lot of flip-flops and sandals, tank tops and cut-off jean shorts, through which tattoos and fat rolls peeked through. It wasn't People of Walmart, but it wasn't appetizing.

Yaz's stomach was already uneasy from the smell of rotting flesh. But then the warehouse took a lurch around him, and he reached out for something to steady himself. There wasn't anything – until Brady suddenly appeared, holding him up.

"Hey, you okay, Doc?"

"Fine." Yaz didn't elaborate. The dizziness passed.

Fick turned, scowled, and stabbed his thumb over his shoulder at the TV. "Somebody get that shit turned off."

The quickest way turned out to be just shooting it.

* * *

The next phase, to clear and secure the structure, was the most exhausting. The rear loading doors were secure, and only another fifty or so living dead populated the place.

But the warehouse was just absurdly huge.

Most of those in the clearing op ended up covering more ground than the original mile of the insertion march. Finally, Fick jogged back to the front, where the LT had the handset from Chesney's backpack radio up against his head. Yaz stood nearby, puling security for the HQ element. Fick was soaked in sweat and breathing hard.

"Target structure secure," he said. "Swept and cleared. All three fucking acres of it." Their mission workup had told them the warehouse was 134,000 square feet. But, as usual, you didn't know the terrain until you walked it.

"Forklift trucks?"

"A-ffirm," Fick said. "More than we can use, a whole fleet of 'em. We tested out three, and they started up just fine. There's also a shitload of hand carts in, uh, the hand cart aisle."

"Nice," the LT said, and turned away to provide updates to CIC on the long-range radio. When he finished, he turned back to see Fick dropping his rifle mag to check the contents. He then looked at the body pile under the destroyed TV. "I wonder if we should be stabbing, instead of shooting."

"Hey, sir," Fick said, "you want to kick it *Walking Dead*-style, be my guest. I don't personally like getting that close to the dead diseased bastards." He reseated the mag, then nodded outside. "Where are we out there?"

"The lot's clear and secure. Ramp's still quiet."

Fick practically smiled. "So now we can go back and hand-hold the swabbies up the aisle."

"Uh, no, actually. Small delay on their end."

Fick ground his jaw. "So the Fuck-up Fairy is paying us another visit already." He turned to leave.

"Where you going?"

"Back to check on our security positions. With a quick swing by the lube aisle…"

Not even the LT had to ask what that was for.

* * *

"Rob, how could you lose your flak jacket *and* your life vest?"

"I work in Stores, down in the bilge of the damned ship. There'll never be any shooting down there, and I couldn't fall overboard if I tried. They won't even let me up top."

Rob Callum's supervisor for the work party was twenty years his junior, and she was not amused. "You're a Storekeeper First Class. You're supposed to know where your shit is."

"I'm three weeks away from retirement. They can bill me."

"Okay, just come on, we're out of time."

Wearing only his dark blue coveralls, Callum followed the young ensign down the last stretch of passageway, emerging out onto the fantail deck. Spread out below was a flotilla of small craft, floating in the warm morning light. It included the *Kennedy*'s launch, as well as half the utility craft and runabouts from the other ships in the strike group. All were already loaded up with sailors.

And all wearing their flak jackets and life vests.

Awed by the sight, Dooley muttered, "It's like the Little Ships of Dunkirk." Then he climbed down to take his place.

"Don't fall in," the ensign said, following behind.

* * *

"Don't shoot anyone in the ass," Fick said to Kemp, slapping his backside as he ran by, trying to keep up with Graybeard, Brady, and Reyes, all hauling ass out the front doors. Kemp was unaccustomed to the weight of the Mk 48 machine gun, which he'd inherited from Flynn, who fell in San Francisco.

So 2/1 was under-strength, but four guys was deemed enough to escort the sailors in, particularly since the arriving group would include additional shooters. Or, at any rate, persons with guns, namely Naval Security Forces.

Fick followed them outside, as did the LT, his RTO, and Yaz. In the full light of morning, they watched 2/1 head down the ramp toward the 1/2 guys strongpointing it. They were going to have to perform a military maneuver known as a passage of lines. When lines are quiet, this was low-risk.

But as Graybeard led his team toward the backs of 1/2, he heard shots. When he reached them, he could see a handful of sprawled-out bodies down at the ninety-degree bend in the ramp. And even as he watched, another curious dead guy stumbled around the corner, looking up and reaching out.

And then another. The defense of Sam's Club was on.

And the clock was seriously ticking.

# THE RAPE OF SAM'S CLUB

*Honolulu – Sam's Club, Parking Deck Ramp*
*{One Hour Later}*

"Dude – why didn't we just barricade this thing with a couple of overturned eighteen-wheelers or some shit? Then people could just climb over."

"Too obvious. Plus not retarded enough."

This griping was between Lawton and Raible, junior guys in 1/2, the defenders of the ramp. Now, an hour after taking up this position, they had to raise their voices over the firing and moaning. They were also having to traverse their weapons up and down as they built a body pile at the bend, and dead kept climbing over it, causing it to tumble over in little meat avalanches.

"Fire discipline!" barked Sergeant Vorster, 1/2's Element Leader. "Plus shut the fuck up."

The wall they'd built was both good and bad news.

The pure bad news was their ammo situation. There'd been delays at every stage of the op, and now the five defenders of the ramp were burning through ammo at an unsupportable rate. Already, two other fire teams had come down to do an intravenous ammo resupply, depleting their own stores of rifle mags. And if anyone was organizing an ammo drop from the *Kennedy*, no one had told 1/2 about it.

There was also no talk yet of them getting relieved. But standing there and firing nearly nonstop was starting to wear them down. Though the whipping gusts of wind, in the bright Hawaiian sunlight, were at least keeping them cool.

The reason they were still standing there and shooting was the rest of the personnel for this escapade had only just reached shore, got organized, and started moving thirty minutes ago – nearly two hours late. The plan for them coming into friendly lines involved coming up the ramp, which the Marines were supposed to hold open for them.

But now it was completely closed out.

No one could safely scale an infected meat wall. So they were probably going to have to shoot their way back in. Or something.

"Fucking POGs, man," Lawton said.

Raible just shook his head in agreement. It was Persons Other than Grunts who had slowed up progress so disastrously. Every aspect of the mission that was the responsibility of the Marines had gone like clockwork. But now they were all going to die because the swabbies couldn't light a fire. Raible looked over his shoulder when he saw Vorster go off the line to confer with Gunny Blaylock and Gunny Blane, the two ops sergeants.

"Negative!" Vorster said, nodding at the meat wall. "Coming in this way is a no-go!"

"Roger that," Blane shouted back. "Okay, we gamed this out. We'll bring 'em in via the first alternate infil." He stepped away, twiddling his radio channel selector and pressing his earpiece.

"You guys okay for now?" Blaylock said.

"Absolutely," Vorster said. "Until the ammo runs out."

* * *

*"Reamer Two One, this is Reamer Two, how copy?"*

"Solid copy, send it," Graybeard said, still moving, but not shooting. He was leaving the gunplay to the friskier pups, and keeping his focus on navigation, comms – and riding herd on their flock of 55 unskilled, untactical, and scared shitless sailors. They were all military personnel, and all had been through Navy Basic Training. At the very least they'd been taught how to shut up and march. But this was like herding cats.

*Check that,* Graybeard thought. *Cats have dignity.*

Among them were two NSF guys, who'd been sent along for security at the dockside. So now the Marines were also having to keep those guys from shooting – a prospect they honestly considered the most dangerous part of their day.

But that was why they got the assignment. Not only was 2/1 regarded as unkillable. But their Element Leader, Graybeard, whose operational history stretched back to the first Gulf War, had survived so much horrendous shit without a scratch he'd surprise everyone if he reported to sick bay to get so much as a boil on his ass lanced.

Blane's voice came back in his ear. *"Be advised, Two-One, primary infil route closed out. Repeat, the ramp is a no-go. You need to come in via alternate Alpha, northwest stairwell, over."*

"Roger that, no worries. New ETA fifteen mikes."

Graybeard squinted ahead as his parade of circus clowns moved down the last enclosed stretch of road before the ramp. They were already competing for this space with scores of stumbling dead, which were being put down by Brady, Reyes, and also Kemp with his chattering Mk 48. All these dead Hawaiians were heading in the same direction, following either the shooting, or just the moaning of the others.

The planners of this caper had believed the dead would only turn up in force with the noise of the first helicopters.

*That's what we get for thinking,* Graybeard thought.

The change in plan had them covering more ground, and out on it longer. But Graybeard was happy to cut a loop around that shit up ahead, and bring his patrol in from the rear.

He switched radio channels to brief his guys.

\* \* \*

"Hey," Blane said, trotting up to Fick and the LT, who'd moved their CP to outside the front entrance of the warehouse. "Since Two-One's coming in the back door, is there any reason we're waiting to shut the front one?"

"Good point," the LT said, getting on his radio. "Seven Nine Combat from Reamer… We report Doris, repeat, Doris."

Blane smiled. "Doris" was the pro-word to indicate they were tucked up at the target site and the next phase of the air op could commence. Then he realized they weren't actually all tucked up. He grabbed Fick and ran toward the ramp.

They needed to get 1/2 off it.

\* \* \*

Drake stepped from the Bridge out onto the observation deck, wanting to see this in person. There was little in life so thrilling as the carrier launch of a combat jet aircraft. Granted, it was happening a little too close to the four helicopters already out on deck – their two Seahawks, the Marines' Defiant, and the huge King Stallion that had dropped down to them from heaven. Three of the helos sat in the parking spots just forward of the island, with the last on one of the aircraft elevators.

Two already had their rotors turning.

The F-35 was hooked in at the start of the bow-deck run-way, worryingly close to them. And when it fired up its after-burning turbofan engine, only the blast shield behind kept it from immolating the four helos. Then again, if it had launched on the angle deck instead, it would have screamed by them close enough for its right wing tip to caress their rotor discs.

Either way, this seemed to Drake like a truly dangerous dance, and a lot of rotors spinning at 400 RPMs in close proximity to a 29,000-horsepower engine. Then again, no one ever said a carrier flight deck was a safe place to work. But today was getting not just crazy, but redneck crazy.

"Hold my beer," Drake muttered to no one.

And they hadn't even gotten to the dangerous part yet.

Finally, the EMALS towbar dropped and the F-35 tore off down the deck like a bat out of some tropical hell, shrieking into the pale blue sky and banking left, accelerating and climbing, leaving sonic booms trailing behind.

Drake checked his watch.

*Well,* he thought. *At least that went better than last time.*

\* \* \*

"Hey," Lawton said to Raible, the two of them eyeing the ramp they'd just left undefended, or rather defended only by a meat rampart. "What's minimum safe distance on GBU-39s?"

This was of some interest, as the lower section of ramp was about to get served with a GBU-39/B Small Diameter Bomb. With guidance by GPS and inertial navigation, plus radar, IR homing, and semi-active laser guidance, they were said to be incapable of missing. Nonetheless, everyone in 1/2 was backing away from the ramp toward the building, seeking hard cover.

They'd been around the block enough times to know air strikes never got put in the wrong place.

Until they did.

"Eh," Raible said. "This is probably far enough." He nodded at the five-foot concrete wall ringing the deck, obscuring the ramp from view. "If you can't see the explosion, the explosion can't see you, right? I heard that once."

"So a paper bag over the head should do the trick."

"Again, please shut the fuck up." This was Vorster, who with the others now crouched down against the front wall of the building. Fick, who'd pulled them off the line, had ducked inside, which didn't make anyone feel more relaxed. And they could also see Gunny Blane hauling ass diagonally across the deck toward the northwest stairwell, at the same time the Marine guarding it opened the door, and a whole gaggle of spooked-looking sailors spilled out of it.

And started running across the deck toward them.

The sound of screaming crossed the sky, followed by a streaking gray dart, and a smaller black one from beneath…

Falling straight down on them.

* * *

*Ah shit*, Graybeard thought, as he spotted Blane running at them, and heard what he was shouting. He also remembered Number 13 from Murphy's Laws of Combat:

*If at first you don't succeed, call in an air strike.*

Then he got really busy trying to herd his colony of Navy cats over toward the north edge of the parking deck, away from the impact point, his own guys and Blane assisting.

But it was too late.

The southwest corner of the deck exploded, with noise, light, fire, debris, and super-heated air all rolling across the deck toward them. Everyone freaked the fuck out, scattering and diving.

Graybeard just sighed out loud.

* * *

It turned out no one was injured, at least nothing worse than scrapes and bruises from sliding on concrete.

And at least not this time.

And, twenty minutes later, the mission was finally proceeding along something like intended lines. The 55 naval personnel, most but not all Stores ratings, and used to working in a nice safe warehouse environment, went tear-assing into the Sam's Club, happy to get away from bombs falling on their heads, however small their diameter, not to mention the surging herds of undead down on the street.

And eight minutes later they started coming back out, riding on a fleet of rumbling forklift trucks, or else rolling hand carts in front of them, all piled high with boxes, bags, plastic crates, and giant aluminum tins. These got dropped off and organized into a supplies dump and marshaling area, 25 meters in front of the store entrance.

The stuff that wasn't already on pallets got palletized by guys buzzing around like crazed bees with huge roles of plastic pallet wrap, cargo nets, and wooden pallets liberated from the warehouse. Inside, others ran around with tablets and colored marking tape, identifying items for transport back to the carrier.

The Rape of Sam's Club was in full swing.

# GOAT RODEO

*Honolulu, Sam's Club – Parking Deck*

Fick, Blane, and the LT just hung out near the entrance surveying the progress.

"I love this shit," Fick said, rocking on his heels.

"What?" Blane asked. "Watching other people work?"

"Exactly. Hey, isn't that the Suppo?"

He gestured at an officer holding a tablet and a clipboard in either hand, running alongside a hand cart piled high with dry goods.

"Yeah, I think so," Blane said. "You've got to like a senior officer who hangs his ass out in a combat zone."

"Eh," Fick said. "Maybe he's just a goddamned control freak. Speaking of which…" He hit his radio.

"One-Two, sitrep on your sector, over."

\* \* \*

Sergeant Vorster stole a look over his shoulder before hitting his radio to respond. There was nothing to see behind them except the bend in the ramp, which he and his team were down below now. This left them out of sight of the others, hence the radio check-in. And 2/1 was still tasked with holding the ramp.

The difference was, there was no ramp anymore. Not past the point where they stood, at any rate.

"One-Two," Vorster answered Fick. "Position secure."

*"Copy that. You guys okay?"*

Vorster faced forward again and surveyed the ragged cliff edge just past the toes of his boots. Beyond and below the eight-foot drop was a riot of scorched concrete and metal debris, mixed with body parts, some still wiggling, or even moaning.

The fruits of the F-35's bombing run.

This eight-foot gap between them and the street below was their margin of safety. They'd put in the air strike so close to the base of the ramp, and around the bend, to ensure the safety of those working up top. One downside they hadn't considered was they'd had to jack one of the forklift trucks to push the body pile at the bend down the ramp and over the edge.

But the bigger downside was they now enjoyed only a modest vertical gap between them and the rest of undead Honolulu. Not least because they'd just bulldozed about a hundred bodies down into it.

Dead still stumbled in from the street, moved to the foot of the destroyed ramp, and reached up with mottled fingers, staring with burning and occluded eyes. The ones up front were starting to get squashed down by those pushing in from behind, like people crushed in a soccer riot, the body pile slowly rising toward the ramp edge, a few inches at a time.

"Yeah, we're fine," Vorster said, looking down into those evil eyes and ravening mouths. "Until the dead start climbing their asses on up here."

*"How long we looking at?"*

"Hard to say."

*"Oh, hard to say is it? Hard to say? Hard to say? I'll tell you what's fucking hard to say. It's hard to say, 'Oh my God, someone please help me, there's a man in my office with a FLAMETHROWER', that's what's hard to say! Over."*

"Roger that, Master Guns. Two hours. Three max."

*"Copy that. Keep me posted. Out."*

Looking around, Vorster suddenly realized there were five of them there, basically not doing shit. He didn't like Marines standing around not doing shit. He also didn't like being out of visual communications. It felt too close to being cut off.

"Raible, Lawton," he said. "Go strongpoint the bend."

As he watched those two trot back up the ramp, he heard and then saw the first Seahawk flying in from the coast, cruising in over the top of the deck and going into a hover.

*Thank Christ for that,* he thought.

He looked down into the face of the dead 300-pound Samoan dude reaching up at him with green grasping fingers.

He shot him in the face and took a step back.

\* \* \*

As Raible reached the bend along with Lawton, he could see for the first time the mountain of provisions growing in the marshaling area, not to mention the first Seahawk hovering over it. The idea had been to get everything packed up and staged there first, before the noise of the helos drew the dead.

*News flash,* Raible thought. *The dead are already here.*

He and Lawton just watched as one of the cargo-handling dudes climbed up on one of the big-ass stacks of pallets and started stabbing up at the bottom of the Seahawk with a load beam. This was a metal pole with a locking keeper on one end and an attach point on the other, to connect the sling-load to the aircraft. But first this guy was going to have to catch it on the belly hook of the hovering helo – in a stiff wind.

Raible shook his head. *What could possibly go wrong?*

He sighed and turned to face the dead again.

\* \* \*

Fick and Blane listened to the LT radioing back to CIC, sending updates on their progress, namely that they were finally moving some goddamned supplies out of there.

He was having to shout over the engine and rotor noise of the two Seahawks, one of which had just gotten hooked up to its first load, then lumbered back into the sky and turned south, toward the water and the carrier. It moved like an old man, careful and slow, shuddering in the gusting wind, due to having five tons of palletized dry goods hanging beneath it.

The second Seahawk came in over the manmade mountain of supplies and started getting hooked in as well.

"Man," Blane said. "I wouldn't want that job."

"Yeah," Fick said, turning his face up to the warm sun, higher in the sky now. "Luckily it's them fucking this chicken. All we have to do is stand back and watch the feathers fly."

Blane laughed. "I'm just glad this mission is finally progressing. Moving the ball down the field."

Fick squinted. "I wonder – hey!" he said, yelling at the Suppo as he scurried by, coming back out of the warehouse through rumbling forklift trucks and skidding hand carts.

"Yeah, what?" the Suppo said, looking disinclined to stop.

"How do you know the weight of those pallets doesn't exceed the cargo capacity of the helos?" If there was some kind of a giant-ass scale out there, Fick had missed it.

The Suppo smiled and tapped his temple. "All right here, Master Guns. All up here." With that he dashed off again.

And even as the second Seahawk lumbered off into the sky,

the sound of louder and heavier whumping and engine noise descended toward them. The Marines looked up in awe as the sky-whale shape of the King Stallion started to drop into a hover over the marshaling point. It looked like someone was levitating a submarine. And it was time for this behemoth to pick up its first load – four times as big and heavy as the ones the two Seahawks had just lifted out.

"Jesus," Fick shouted over the rotor storm, watching the operation with squinted eyes. "If it was me responsible for that, I'd be sweating like a blind lesbian in a fish market."

Blane just shook his head.

* * *

"Goddammit," Drake said, coming back inside the Bridge. He no longer wanted to look at the goats currently being rodeo'd out on the flight deck. Or maybe he just didn't want to be too close to it. "Get me PriFly," he said, then realized it was quicker just to do it himself. He snatched the handset from his station and punched it up. "PriFly, Bridge."

*"Bridge, go for PriFly."*

Drake recognized the voice of the Air Boss himself. "Yeah, what's it going to take to get those helos moving again?"

*"Probably you ringing the Deck Department and giving them shit about it. It's their cargo-handling guys who are sodomizing the proverbial canine on this one. Nothing to do with me."*

Drake ground his teeth. "Roger that."

He looked back out the front screens, where he could still see the first Seahawk to return holding an unsteady hover over the cargo-loading point amidships, while the second came in and lined up behind it. Below, green-shirted cargo-handling guys were trying, and failing, to get the load beam unhooked, and release the sling-load of pallets. That the aircraft above it kept swaying from side to side in the stiff wind, plus rising and falling, was not helping the process one bit.

Nor were all the guys in green who kept arriving to help.

Worst of all was the proximity of all this to the Defiant, the Marines' extraction helo, still sitting out on the elevator, its pilots on cockpit standby. The first Seahawk's load was at least down on the deck – though a bad enough gust of wind might make the helo drift enough to drag the load across it, after which all bets were off. Even more worrisome was the second Seahawk that was lined up, its five-ton load still literally twisting in the breeze.

And then Drake spotted what was at first a gray speck, then a huge speck – the King Stallion, also heading their way, and also needing to drop off its load of shit and go out again.

This was turning into one snarled-ass traffic jam.

"PriFly, Bridge – I do not want that King Stallion overflying this vessel. Not until the Seahawks have cleared out. That much is still your job, right?"

*"Bridge, PriFly. Roger and wilco. Now if you'll excuse me, I need to get our F-35 back on the deck safely. Out."*

Drake put the handset down as he heard the shriek of an incoming jet from the stern, followed by the screech of tires burning down the angle deck, causing the whole island to vibrate.

And he closed his eyes and just tried to breathe.

* * *

"Safety first, kids."

"Copy that."

This was USMC Captain McBrien, speaking to USMC Lieutenant Soper, pilot and co-pilot, respectively, of Batcopter One – the helo currently sitting with its face hanging out on the *JFK*'s aircraft elevator, in the middle of what was turning into Cirque du Soleil with Seahawks and sling-loads. Both just stared blank-faced out their front cockpit glass at the amateur-hour production taking place not far enough out in front of them.

But then both looked to the left, equally blank-faced, as an F-35 shrieked down the angle deck barely ten meters away, decelerating from 200mph to a stop in less than 300 feet, due to the arresting wire caught in its tail hook.

Neither pilot commented. They'd seen it all before.

Their sleek and nearly black helo used to be the lead aircraft in a flight of two SB-1 Defiant advanced joint multirole helicopters. But now Batcopter One flew alone. This was because her sister aircraft, Batcopter Two, had gone down trying to get Team 2 of the Marines the hell out of the collapsing and self-immolating vortex of San Francisco.

These guys still had their aircraft, but the way things were shaping up, they didn't much like their odds of it surviving into the third week of the post-Apocalypse. It would be ironic if the whole world went down to zombies, but they bought it in a run-of-the-mill aviation disaster on this wind-buffeted flight deck.

But that's why they got paid the big bucks.

Both were Marine Corps aviators, which meant both had qualified as Naval aviators only after attending the Basic School, like every other Marine officer. Being able to fly advanced rotary-wing aircraft in demanding and dangerous combat conditions was just layered in on top of all that.

Now, the two pilots just cooled their heels, hanging out while suicidal idiots played grab-ass with 10,000-pound sling-loads, twirling and swinging underneath 18,000-pound aircraft – which weren't designed for the purpose, and were piloted by naval aviators who definitely weren't trained for it.

Their radio went: *"Hey, assholes, scoot over."*

They instantly recognized the voice of their Defiant pilot counterpart, Captain Reusser, flying with his co-pilot Lieutenant Wiegand. Today, those two had been shanghaied into piloting the King Stallion, and heaving around even bigger sling-loads. They weren't really trained for that job either, or even that aircraft. But you didn't get assigned to fly advanced demonstrator helicopters by not being adaptable.

McBrien hit his radio. "You two having fun in that rotary-wing 747 you're joyriding in?"

*"Hey, don't piss us off, or we'll land on top of your asses, and crush that little sportster of yours. Now make way."*

"Love to, man. Just as soon as these jittery Seahawk-jock sons of bitches get themselves unfucked and clear out."

*"Fine,"* Ruesser came back. *"We get paid by the hour."*

McBrien checked his watch.

"Sure hope the ground-pounders on target do, as well…"

# PAY THE PIZZA GUY

"Well, isn't this just turning into the shopping trip from hell."

"Roger that."

This was Fick, along with the LT, who'd just returned from checking out the state of the destroyed and besieged ramp in person. The LT was young, and didn't mind running his skinny ass around. Not least since he was battling to feel in control of this mission he was nominally in charge of.

"How's it looking down there?" Blane asked.

"It's a ticking clock. Bomb, rather. The tide's rising fast."

Blane said, "Hell is empty. And all the devils are here."

"Come again, Gunny?" the LT said.

Fick laughed. "You're just like your mother, sir."

The LT just let that one go. He looked back toward the ramp. "I never thought we'd be on target this long."

"No one did," Blane said.

They'd now spent over three hours holding this position, watching the helos go out with tons of supplies then come back in for more. Luckily, flight time back to the carrier was less than two minutes, and the pick-ups and drop-offs had started to become routine and regular, though they'd never really be safe.

Fick said, "We also didn't expect all of undead Honolulu to decide to come shopping today." He turned to eye one of the forklift trucks rumbling out the front doors, which had been wedged open again. "Hope they don't want pasta."

The Stores guys were bringing out the most calorie-dense stuff first. They'd already built several gigantic piles of bagged rice and beans, plus nuts and seeds, which got carried off through the air, then rebuilt almost instantly.

"Or toilet paper," Blane said, seeing a cart full of that go by.

"Seriously?" Fick said. "What the fuck. They're swabbies – they can wash their asses with salt water. I don't want to fucking die out here for quilted softness."

With this, they heard firing resume from down the ramp.

The LT said, "Brady and Reyes were right – once the dead start coming, they never stop. What we didn't anticipate was that they'd literally pile up."

Blane looked at the younger man, his expression kindly. "We're Marines, sir. We learn – but always the hard way. Usually, we bite off more than we can chew, and learn painful lessons, sometimes by filling body bags. Then we apply them to the next war, once they've become useless. It's the same every time. You're right on schedule."

"Wish the damned mission was," Fick said.

* * *

"Hey, Sarge, you need us back on the line?"

This was Raible, radioing Sergeant Vorster. Positioned back at the bend, he and Lawton could see both ends of the action – the forklifts and helos coming in and out up top, and their three teammates once more engaging down below.

*"Nah, you're fine for now. We're just mowing the grass."*

From their more elevated position, Raible could see the other three taking aimed single shots at dead trying to walk up the rising body pile, and putting them down farther out, before they could become part of the pile themselves.

"Howdy boys, anything I should know about?"

Raible and Lawton spun to find Fick behind them, rocking on his heels, smiling like it was payday. They straightened up, and Raible said, "All good, Master Gunnery Sergeant."

Fick nodded. "Just remember, you guys have got two jobs – secure your sector, and pay the pizza guy."

Raible and Lawton looked in at each other, baffled.

"Yeah, there's no pizza guy. So now you realize you have one fucking job."

The two junior Marines grinned and nodded.

Lawton pointed at the Seahawk over the marshaling area, with another guy standing up on the stacked pallets attaching a sling-load. "How many trips are they gonna make?"

"Where does an 800-pound gorilla shit?"

"Wherever he wants?"

"Exactly. They're gonna make as many trips as they can, to keep the strike group alive as long as possible. Basically, as long as we can hold this position. So no pressure."

Fick turned when he heard noises behind him, even above the rotor and engine racket – a thundering crash, followed by a high-pitched scream of pain.

"Ah, shit," he said, taking off.

* * *

"Doc, c'mon!"

Yaz followed Corporal Meyer at a run, both following a random sailor in blue coveralls, still wearing his flak jacket and life vest. Racing out the front door of the store, dodging carts and forklift trucks, Yaz quickly saw what had happened.

A big stack of goods had been carelessly loaded onto a fork-lift truck, then knocked off – possibly by a hanging sling-load blown around by the wind – which then tumbled onto a Stores guy working down in the city of foodstuffs. His buddies, plus the two NSF guys, their rifles flapping and banging around on their slings, were pulling giant and stupidly heavy tins of canned vegetables off him, while he continued to holler in pain.

By the time Yaz got there, kneeling down, med ruck off and on the ground, the victim had been excavated. Yaz pulled on gloves and zoned out the ambient shouting, firing, moaning, and chaos as he was trained to do. And as he leaned in and started a visual examination of the casualty…

The hollering sailor went gray and fuzzy.

His screams faded away, along with background noise.

And then the whole world went black.

# BORN AGAIN

*Honolulu – Sam's Club, Lobby*

When his senses dialed back up, it was like being born again.

Except Yaz was alone.

He slapped at his chest and found his vest was off him for some reason. Turning his head to the left, he could see his med ruck lying on the tile floor beside him. Extending his focus, he finally worked out he was lying inside the warehouse, in front of the checkout aisles, off to the left of the entrance.

The only human figures he could see were the destroyed dead ones, previously piled up under the TV, but which had been dragged off to the side and out of the way. That was it.

And for one second, Yaz panicked.

*Where the hell was everyone?*

They couldn't have left him. Could they?

And then everyone appeared all at once. It must have been some weird lull in the forklift and hand-cart traffic, because now they started blasting by, just fifteen meters to his right, moving in both directions – loaded ones bouncing in from the back of the store and going out, empty ones returning for more. And standing over and behind him…

Was Corporal Meyer.

He smiled at Yaz, then squatted down.

"Oh, good," Meyer said. "You're alive. I'll get Doc Milam."

"No," Yaz said, sitting up, and patting himself down. "I'm fine. What the hell happened?"

"No idea. You just passed out. We carried you in here to get you out of the way, and keep you safe."

"Why'd you take my vest off?"

"Dunno, maybe to help you breathe?"

Yaz nodded, climbed to his feet, found his vest, got it strapped on, then grabbed his weapon and his med ruck.

"Where you going?"

"Back to work."

As Yaz exited, dodging traffic, Meyer stayed on his elbow, as if to catch him in case he keeled over again. When they hit open air, Yaz could hear heavy small-arms fire, plus grenades whumping off, all of it out of sight down and to the left. He also saw Marines running across the lot toward the ramp. Whatever was going on down there, it didn't sound good.

When he faced ahead toward the marshaling point, he couldn't see his patient, the seaman who'd gotten half-crushed by giant cans of tomatoes. Turning again, he saw he'd been moved up onto the curb in front of the store, where Doc Milam was palpating his abdomen.

Meanwhile, the op was continuing – empty helos buzzing in, heavily laden ones powering out, Stores guys replenishing the pile every time it got knocked down. The difference now was the louder sounds of battle – and the general vibe that things were coming to a head.

Everything felt frantic now – and under threat.

Yaz threw his ruck down and squatted beside Milam.

Milam didn't even look over. "I got this." He nodded behind him. "Ensign back there rolled an ankle getting this guy dug out. Go get a compression sleeve on it." This was vaguely disappointing, but Yaz had no choice but to comply.

When he moved out of the shadow of the warehouse, he

saw one of the Seahawks was actually touching down – not at the marshaling point, but in an open area of the parking lot 50 meters to the north. The instant it did so, Marines started pulling out heavy rucks and a couple of crates from its cabin, down onto the pavement. When they reloaded their own weapons and vest pouches from it, piled them onto a hand cart and started speed-rolling it toward the ramp, Yaz knew what that was.

An ammo resupply.

\* \* \*

"Thank God," the LT said, getting out of the way as the cart went tear-assing by, picking up speed down the ramp, the two Marines on either side not battling all that much to control it. He had moved their mobile CP to the bend in the ramp, where they could monitor the fight they were actually in. It had turned back into one, after the bombing of the ramp, shockingly quickly.

"Nah," Fick said. "Not God. Your ops sergeant here."

Blane shrugged. They always prepared an ammo resupply as a contingency, even when they had no intention of using it. Especially then. You never knew when you were going to find yourself in some *Black Hawk Down* shit, unexpectedly having to fight balls-out all night. And if you got into that pickle, the last thing you wanted was a bunch of sailors digging around in your armory going, maybe a few boxes of these?

You wanted that shit staged and ready to go.

The good news was they were back in ammo. The bad news was they couldn't get any more shooters on the line. They already had two fire teams, ten Marines, standing shoulder to shoulder, firing into the rising tide of dead – knocking it back down, and trying to keep it at bay by shooting and lobbing grenades farther out. They also had the two squad machine-gunners lying on top of the concrete walls to either side, firing controlled but increasingly long bursts down into the undead lynch mob. That looked dodgy to the LT, but Vorster took responsibility.

And the machine-gunners looked like they were having fun. It wasn't every day you got to fire belt after belt into a crowd, with no moral concern or disciplinary ramifications. And as the dead were slow, stupid, and had no regard for their personal safety, they were like rotten fish in a Honolulu-sized barrel. Guys were occasionally whooping out loud, as more ammo got passed around.

It was kind of looking like an enjoyable day out – until the ammo ran out again. Or the dead overwhelmed them.

It was all fun and games until somebody got eaten.

"Be right back," Blane said.

\* \* \*

"Ah," Blane said. "Back from the dead, I see."

He'd gone up top and found Yaz squatted down in front of his new patient, such as she was, waiting for her to get her boot laced back up, holding a torn-open packet of Tylenol.

"I think Meyer brought me back," Yaz said, looking over his shoulder at the young Marine, still standing nearby, protectively. "Some kind of lovely voodoo."

Blane nodded. "Magical Negro, eh?"

"Ah, shit, I am definitely not going there."

Blane smiled. "Anyway, glad to see you on your feet. We were all a little worried."

The female ensign, whose nametape read *Hayden*, finished

lacing her boot and stood up unsteadily, Yaz rising with her and assisting. "How's it feel?"

She winced as she put her weight on it. "I can walk, but probably not run. God, that's how everybody gets killed in *The Walking Dead*, isn't it? Shit."

"Don't worry, ma'am," Blane said, nodding at the marshaling area. "We've got helicopters in this show."

Yaz handed over the Tylenol, crumpled up the packet, and looked around for a trashcan.

Then he remembered the world had ended, and tossed it.

* * *

Trotting back to the CP with Yaz, Blane saw the battle below had grown even more furious during his brief absence. He looked back up top at one of the Seahawks lumbering off with another twirling load, then said to the LT and Fick, "We're kind of pushing this down to the wire, don't you think?"

"Hey, what could possibly go wrong?" Fick said, smiling up into the brilliant sunshine. "Especially here in paradise."

The LT sighed. "Last time I talked to the Suppo, he didn't seem real keen on leaving – not until this place had been completely sucked dry."

"The Suppo can suck me dry," Fick said. "Anyway, we were supposed to have learned this lesson last time. The more we shoot, the faster they come." He nodded down at the front line below. "We can't win this fight. We can only get away."

The LT looked to Blane, who said, "You're ground commander. It's always been your call."

The LT hit his radio. "God Six, Reamer, how copy?"

*"Solid copy, Reamer, send it."* That female voice again. Serious. Emotionless.

"Yeah, interrogative: can we get an update on how surrounded we are, and how riled up the city is, over?"

*"Roger that, Reamer. You are completely surrounded – with dead moving toward your AO from every sector, all the surrounding streets, in every direction we can see."*

"Copy that. Estimate of enemy strength?"

*"I'm gonna say between brigade and division strength…"*

The Marine leaders eyed each other. They couldn't fight 15,000 dead, if it was a full-strength division coming for them.

*"…but hang out long enough and it will be a corps."*

Fick said, "I think I liked it better when we could only see what was right in front of us."

The LT eyed the length of ramp that was left. "Can we put in another air strike? Higher up? Buy some more time?"

Blane eyed the Marines down on the ramp, then looked back up at all the sailors, forklifts, and helos still swarming the top of the deck. "Maybe if we'd thought of that in the first place, or earlier on. But at this point? It would be begging for blue-on-blue. I think that ship has sailed."

The LT peered over the top of their skirmish line, at the sea of dead bodies stretching out of view beyond it. "How about calling in CAS? Try to destroy them *en masse?*"

Fick shook his head this time, and made a circle with his thumb and fingers. "This is how much cross-training we've done with the carrier air wing on close air support." He nodded back up top. "Never mind with those fucking guys."

"Okay," the LT said, knowing his Team Chief was right.

When he looked forward again, he saw Sergeant Vorster turn, come off the line, and trot back up toward them.

"We're out of time, aren't we?" the LT said.

"Affirmative. But that's not the bad news."

"What is, then?"

Vorster pulled the LT over to the concrete barrier, Blane and Fick following. When they looked out over the edge, they saw what the bad news was. Not only were the dead up to the level of the destroyed ramp.

They were piling up on all sides of the structure.

The shore team was now floating in a sea of infected dead people. And the closing ring felt like the grip of cold fear.

It was seriously time to go.

# MACH JESUS

*Sam's Club – Parking Deck, Ramp*

"Well, that explains the smell," Blane said, wrinkling his nose. It had truly gotten horrendous, and not only down on the line.

"This is just the luau version of San Francisco," Fick said, stepping back. "Déjà vu all over again."

"I'm calling it," the LT said, turning and looking around. "Anyone know where the Suppo is?"

"Is my face red?" Fick asked.

"Pardon me?" the LT said.

"I said, is my face red?"

"No, Master Guns. It is not."

"Well then the Suppo's not up my ass, is he?"

The LT shook his head. "Fick, come with me. I think I can actually use you." He nodded at Chesney, his RTO. "You, too."

The three turned and started running up the ramp.

* * *

Raible took time to slot another empty mag into his pants cargo pocket. They'd been instructed to hang on to empties. No one knew for sure when or if they'd find more.

As he slid a new mag in, slapped at the bolt release, and resumed firing, he also found himself stepping backward, to stay even with the others in the line. They were edging away from what was no longer a ragged ramp edge, but just a transition from concrete to meat. The tide had reached shore.

And it was about to spill over them.

As dead guys reached up and clawed at the ramp, trying to pull themselves over, then got shot in the head and went limp, Raible glanced over his shoulder to try to see what the hell was going on with the rest of the mission – and if there was any sign they'd be getting the hell out of there any time soon. But all he saw was the LT and Fick disappearing, and Vorster trotting back, not looking in any particular hurry.

"Hey, Sergeant," Raible shouted. "What's up?"

"What's up is your weapon, putting steel on target."

Raible turned, raised his rifle, and continued doing so.

* * *

"You see that?" The Suppo jabbed his thumb over his shoulder at the gigantic mountain of food piled up behind him. "Does that look moved over to the carrier to you?"

Neither the LT nor Fick could deny that what they'd come to think of as Mount Pasta looked undiminished. But this was because it was being constantly replenished by the Suppo's army of worker ants. And the size of the pile spoke to the bounty of Sam's Club, not their failure to move it. They'd already transported several metric fuck-tons out of there.

The LT opened his mouth, but the Suppo cut him off: "Because my orders are to top the carrier's galleys – seventy days' worth of food, not a meal less."

"Sir," the LT said, "It's my responsibility to advise you—"

But he got cut off again. "No, you be advised, Lieutenant."

The Suppo touched the gold oak-leaf cluster on his collar, the insignia of a Lieutenant Commander – O-4 to the LT's O-2. "Your job is to protect my people while we get this shit done. And we're not fucking done yet."

The LT exhaled, looked over to Fick, who for some reason was keeping his mouth shut. So the LT drew his shoulders back and pulled himself up to his full height. And the insecurity fell away from him. "Yeah, sir, actually, you are fucking done. Because my job is to get us all back alive so we can do it again next time. And this time is fucking over."

The Suppo touched his rank insignia again, and opened his mouth – but this time the LT cut him off. "This is my operation, Commander, and my operational authority supersedes your rank. We walk. So kindly get your guys ready to extract – now." He spun Chesney around and got on the radio. "Seven-Nine Combat from Reamer... Lucille. I repeat, Lucille... Roger. Out."

As fate had it, the Sea King was just that moment flaring in to pick up another load. Almost before the LT got off the horn, it diverted, banking and sliding over to the right, then simply set down outside the marshaling area.

"This is bullshit," the Suppo said.

The LT was already jogging off with his RTO.

But Fick stayed a little longer. "It may well be bullshit," he said. "But if you don't like it, you can continue not liking it, and if you still don't like it you can like it anyway. Also, if you and your crew of glorified Uber Eats drivers here have any interest in getting the fuck out of Dodge, I strongly suggest you move at the speed of Mach Jesus and get your asses on that majestic Marine Corps aircraft. Have a nice fucking day..."

He was halfway back to the battle on the ramp before muttering over his shoulder:

122

"…sir."

* * *

*"Lucille,"* LT Campbell said across the air mission net. *"Batcopter Two, you are go for extraction of your Marines. Be advised, LZ is reported hot, ground team in close contact."*

"That's us," McBrien said, acknowledging CIC before changing radio channels, while his co-pilot, Soper, started cranking the engines and rotors. Sitting there on the *Kennedy*'s flight deck, they already had the APU running and switches set, so they could be in the air in 90 seconds.

With only one Defiant now, they were also going to have to make two trips to extract the two teams of Marines. As Soper flipped the battery switch, tested auto re-ignition, then hit the starter button and waited for correct rotational speed, he scanned the deck and airspace ahead, thanking God the death-defying cargo-unloading festival wasn't happening above the flight deck right that second. He also listened to tower traffic as McBrien radioed for clearance.

"PriFly, Batcopter One at Elevator Two, request air taxi for VFR flight, destination Sierra Charlie One."

*"Batcopter One, PriFly – exit via heliroute Whiskey, squawk 7040, air taxi holding point Helipad Two."*

"Roger, PriFly."

By this point, flight deck crew had already unchocked their wheels, and both sets of rotors were winding up to insane RPMs. The pusher propeller in the tail allowed them to maneuver across the deck themselves, without a tow from one of the tractors. In seconds, McBrien rolled them forward from the elevator onto the marked HLZ, closer to the island.

"PriFly, Batcopter One is ready for departure."

*"Batcopter One, PriFly, stand by for take-off clearance."*

McBrien drummed his fingers on the cyclic. This was the nerviest part of any mission, waiting to launch. He did as instructed and stood by – for five seconds. Then he got on the radio again. "PriFly, we have priority tasking from CIC mission commander to extract troops in contact, how copy?"

*"PriFly copies all. Batcopter One, Helipad Two, cleared for take-off, wind eighty degrees twenty knots – but gusting to forty. Seriously – watch those crosswinds. And fly safe."*

Ten seconds later, the Defiant powered off the deck, then put its nose down and accelerated hard, blasting out over the front edge of the flight deck. As they roared away, they passed a Seahawk bringing in what was to be the second-to-last load of cargo, their rotors practically brushing.

"You jackasses have fun on your trapeze," Soper said.

\* \* \*

"Fire in the hole, motherfuckers!" Fick bellowed, loud enough that most of the Marines on the line, backing up the ramp while firing nonstop, turned to look. And what they saw was Master Gunnery Sergeant Fick, standing like a colossus…

With another LAW rocket on his shoulder.

Everyone between him and the enemy shoved their way to the sides, then around behind him. While Fick waited for his fire lane to clear, Yaz shook his head and said, "Again?"

Fick smiled his scary-looking smile. "You think I'd leave these behind after last time? Hell, I'm not even going for a shit without rockets anymore."

Running by, Vorster said, "That'll solve the problem of you stuffing up the goddamned toilets."

"Hey, can I help it if I crap like an elephant?"

Eyeing the rocket, Yaz said, "Where'd you hide it this time?"

"Is my face red?"

"Don't answer that," Vorster said. "It was in the ammo resupply."

With everyone behind him, and the King Stallion rising up over his right shoulder like a phoenix, Fick popped the last safety, took aim, and let the rocket go. It shrieked into the front edge of the sea of dead crawling over the edge of the ramp, vaporizing some, dismembering others, and knocking more back into the crowd. It also destroyed a big chunk of the remaining concrete underneath, which had a similar effect.

That of buying them time.

"Listen up!"

The Marines turned to see the LT trotting back down to them, at the head of every Marine not already down there. "Team Two on the line! Team One, get your asses on the helo." Not even looking, he jabbed his thumb over his shoulder as the Defiant swooped in and dropped down onto the deck behind him.

The two teams conducted another passage of lines.

And while Team One deserved the relief, nobody had to ask why Team Two was staying back and holding the line while the others extracted. It was so the LT would be last man out.

Yaz hefted his weapon, and got ready to use it.

And hoped those Defiant pilots flew fast.

* * *

They flew so fast, and Team 1 loaded up so efficiently, that they overtook the King Stallion, returning its 55 sailors to the *Kennedy*.

At the last second before departure, the Marine pilots of the King Stallion, Wiegand and Reusser, had to have a heated argument with the Suppo about taking one last sling-load out with them. Wiegand tried to explain the aircraft couldn't lift with a full load of passengers, and also 36,000 pounds of shit hanging underneath. This didn't seem to land, so finally Reusser said, "Hey, man, get the fuck on or get the fuck off."

He decided to get on.

Two minutes later, the King Stallion touched down on the carrier's flight deck like a building flaring in – but by then the Team 1 Marines were already racing off the Defiant, which had beaten them there and parked in the spot adjacent to the island. The bigger bird landed on HLZ3, which left some margin for error. What left less margin for error was both Seahawks hovering overhead again – and, as before, the cargo handlers on deck struggling to get the first sling-load unhooked.

The winds were now kicking up even worse than before, and the Seahawk pilots, who'd never trained for this mission, were struggling to hold hover as the gusts knocked them around. The second helo wasn't doing much better than the first, holding position just off the port side, waiting its turn.

Down in HLZ1, McBrien, the lead Defiant pilot, turned as a gloved hand banged on his cockpit glass. It was Master Sergeant Saunders, acting commander of Team 1, who gave him a thumbs up, and shouted:

"Everyone out! Door secure! You can lift!"

McBrien nodded, turned to his instruments, then looked up at the crowded skies overhead, as well as the unloading operation of the King Stallion. There were three times as many guys unassing that helo, but they were doing it six times slower.

McBrien got on the radio: "PriFly, Batcopter One at Helipad One, request clearance for immediate dust-off, over."

*"Batcopter One, PriFly, negative, repeat negative. Airspace too conflicted. We need to clear some of these other aircraft before you can lift. Hold position and stand by for clearance."*

McBrien ground his jaw as he looked at the open cargo door of the King Stallion, where a female ensign was limping out, assisted by two sailors, her arms around their shoulders. But then four guys started trying to unload a sailor on a gurney, the one who'd been injured in the mishap at the marshaling point.

Even as this was going on, the wind gusted again, knocking the gurney around – but, much worse, pushing the Seahawk overhead toward the island and the HLZs, far enough that its 10,000-pound sling-load started to drag across the deck... directly toward the King Stallion.

"Ah, shit," McBrien muttered to Soper.

# SHOW OF FORCE

"Ah, shit," Ruesser said to Wiegand, in the cockpit of the King Stallion. They looked at each other and then out the front glass again, at the five-ton sucker punch coming straight at their faces, both knowing there was absolutely nothing they could do about it. Even aside from the fact that the cabin was still being unloaded, they had no ability to maneuver on deck, dependent on tractors for that. And there was no time. They were just going to have to sit there and take it.

And taking it might mean getting pushed over the edge of the flight deck.

But the blow never came.

Instead, the line connecting the load to the Seahawk passed inside the 80-foot rotor disc of the King Stallion – which severed it instantly. In the same instant, the Seahawk above unexpectedly got 10,000 pounds lighter and took off toward the heavens, wobbling madly as the pilot fought to maintain positive control.

The second Seahawk pilot reacted to this, backing farther off the port side – but was only able to do so slowly, with its own hazardous load twirling underneath. Suddenly, the sky overhead wasn't Cirque du Soleil – it was like a barnstorming stunt show crossed with *America's Worst Aviation Disasters, Caught on Home Video.*

With Team 2's extraction helo parked in the middle of it.

* * *

"LT, we need to displace!"

The LT tried to think, to make his mind function – which was hard to do while firing his own weapon on the line. Standing up to an arrogant superior officer was one thing, but combat leadership skills could only be earned. And while it wasn't unheard of for a platoon commander to engage the enemy with his men, it was still something you tried to avoid.

Now the LT's understrength Team 2 had gotten backed all the way up the ramp, finally spilling out onto the parking deck. The good news was they could spread out into a wide arc, and get every gun on the line. The bad news was they were running out of ammo again, with no resupply inbound. The worse news was there was nowhere left to retreat. They'd sealed off and controlled access to this target site too well. Now they were looking at dying in place – if that Defiant didn't get back pretty damned soon to extract them.

And then, with everything else the LT was trying to process, the voice of God, Rain the Growler EWO, jumped back in his ear. *"Reamer, how you doing? Doesn't look good down there."*

The LT didn't bother answering, not least since he didn't have the bandwidth for it.

*"We got authorization for a show of force flyover."*

That made the LT laugh out loud. What the hell was that going to do? It didn't even work on dollar-a-day Taliban AK-humpers, and it sure as hell wasn't going to scare off the dead. Nonetheless, a few seconds later, the sky turned to screaming and a series of sonic booms exploded in a line overhead as the sleek jet flew over, put itself on its tail, and shot up into the sky again, belching exhaust onto the swarming dead on the ramp.

This actually did get their attention, causing hundreds of them to look up, reach for the sky, and cease pressing forward... for five seconds. Then it was game back on.

The stench of cordite burned the Marines' nostrils and the clacking and snapping of suppressed rifles was drowned out by the moaning of hundreds of dead in full frenzy. It was as if they smelled blood – or sensed their opponents up against the ropes, their flesh inches from the grill.

And now were coming in for the kill.

Nonetheless, Yaz felt bizarrely safe, tucked in between Blane and the HQ element on his right, 2/1 out past them on the right flank, Meyer and 2/2 on his left. Also with 2/2 was their Assistant Element Leader, SSG Coulson, who'd insisted on going out despite having a major artery surgically reconnected days earlier. Until now, he'd been in a static post at one of the stairwells, to save him running his patched-up ass around.

But now he had to move and shoot with the others.

Yaz fired carefully and selectively, and was definitely slotting his empty mags back into his vest pouches. These were special-snowflake Beretta polymer mags, and it was unclear when he might find more of those again.

*Probably not even in Sam's Club,* he thought.

But then he had to get his head back in the fight, and shoot and move at once. The Marines were still walking backward, which expanded the gaps in their line, and let the dead spread farther out across the deck. Animated dead bodies stumbled forward, got shot, fell forward, splashed black gore and brain matter on the concrete, then got climbed over by ones behind, who did the same thing. It was like the front edge of a lava flow, churning forward, the tide spilling out and growing endlessly.

The Marines could keep destroying the front edge.

But that scarcely even slowed it, never mind stopped it.

Yaz was close enough to hear when the LT did what he was trained to do and radioed for support. "Seven-Nine Combat, Reamer Actual, requesting urgent sitrep on air extraction, over!"

*"Reamer, Combat, be advised we have a slow-motion air-traffic disaster going on here. We're jumping through our asses to get it cleared up, so we can get your air back in the air, how copy?"*

"Seven-Nine, Reamer, solid copy. But be advised if our extraction flight doesn't get here in the next ten minutes, you can save them the trip and the fuel, over."

*"Roger that, Reamer."* Campbell's voice sounded sympathetic, but not flustered. *"Listen, Lieutenant, can you do me a favor – and hot-mic your radio for me?"*

The LT didn't have the time, space, or luxury of asking what the hell that was for. He just did it.

"LT," Fick repeated. "We need to displace. We gotta go!"

"Fine, but where to?"

Fick nodded to their left – at the only possible place left for them. Suddenly it was obvious.

One last chance to enjoy the possibilities.

* * *

McBrien considered radioing PriFly again. But it was pretty obvious they already had their hands full, doing emergency air-traffic control duty for a floating airport circus.

The severed cable from the first Seahawk, still attached to the ball of cargo, was whipping around the flight deck in the wind like a cat o' nine tails, while sailors who'd exited the Sea Stallion took cover underneath it, its seven 40-foot-long blades still whumping overhead. The second Seahawk had been directed to land on the bow runway, setting its load down first, then just sliding over to set down beside it. After that, they could unhook the line at leisure, if anyone was still alive. Trouble was, they'd only just started maneuvering to do this, creating an even more hazardous situation ahead.

Mainly, and worst of all, the first Seahawk was still trying to regain positive flight control somewhere up over their heads, after being sling-shotted toward the sun. Now it was also being kicked around the skies by outrageous crosswinds.

And there was still a chance it might crash.

Knowing the futility of this, McBrien reached for his radio to request permission to depart again. But then the radio went on its own – relaying traffic neither pilot had expected to hear. And which did nothing to soothe their sense of urgency.

*"—keep moving, keep moving! We'll hold here!"*

*"How do we get these fucking doors closed?"*

*"Too late, they're right on us, just get inside! Move, move!"*

*"Where's the roof access?"*

*"Fuck it, we'll figure it out – go, go!"*

All of this was punctuated, and half drowned out, by non-stop gunfire, explosions, shouting… and moaning.

"Okay, fuck all this noise," McBrien said.

"Foxtrot Alpha," Soper said.

LT Campbell, who was responsible for patching through the Marines' team-net traffic, came back on the air mission net.

*"Hey,"* she said. *"You guys do what you gotta do…"*

# DEFIANCE

*Honolulu – Sam's Club*

"Note to fucking selves! Learn how to close and lock auto-opening fucking store doors!"

"Roger that. Will do, if we live."

"Yee-hah, motherfuckers! Marine and dead guy rodeo!"

Due to the multiple patched-through radio connections, what had failed to come through to the pilots in the Defiant was the Marines' hooting and laughter. What had sounded like sheer terror and heavy breathing was actually most of them laughing their asses off. It was the standard combat adrenaline, plus good old schoolyard fucking around and giddiness.

Admittedly, they were being pursued by thousands of walking dead monstrosities, but the dead could only walk, while they could run – even Coulson, in a pinch – and now they had a city-sized warehouse with hundreds of thousands of consumer items to put between them and the dead.

It had really only been the LT freaking out, because he was ultimately responsible for getting them out of there alive.

After a brief struggle trying to get the front doors shut, never mind locked, the rear element, namely leadership, decided to pack it in and just follow the others toward the office areas in back, which they assumed would have stairs leading to the roof. Yaz, who'd been covering the guys working on the door, only realized Fick had disappeared when he appeared again, with a

16-pack of Charmin Ultra under one arm, and a 12-pack of Sam Adams under the other.

"You hypocritical son of a bitch," Yaz said, falling in behind him, realizing now he really had to cover the Team Chief, since it wasn't clear he could fire his weapon.

Looking defensive, Fick said, "Hey, I said salt water's good enough for swabbies. My old leatherneck ass is tender."

"And what about the beer?"

"Sam Adams needs no defense. Anyway, I tucked these away when I thought I could just grab 'em and hop on the helo at leisure. Didn't count on this escape-and-evade bullshit…"

As the team moved past the endless aisles, 2/2, who'd never been inside, marveled at the massive arrays of crap.

"Look at the size of those wide-screens!"

"A hearing aid center? Seriously?"

"Disco pants and haircuts."

"This place has got everything."

"What the fuck does that mean?"

"You never seen *The Blues Brothers*?"

"Shut the fuck up," Graybeard finally said, again.

Now everyone on Team 2 was together in a tight column. HQ – the LT, Fick, Blane, SSG Gifford, and Chesney the RTO; 2/1 – Graybeard, Brady, Reyes, and Kemp; 2/2 – SSG Cartwright, Coulson, Meyer, Dunham, and Graves; and finally Yaz. They had to transit the entire back edge of the warehouse, two football fields in length, ducking in and out of offices. At the end of it, Fick delivered the inescapable verdict.

"There's no fucking rooftop access," he said.

"How'd we not contingency plan for this?" the LT asked.

"Not enough time," Blane said.

Marines had now started taking shots down the long aisles toward the front of the store at the closest dead guys, who had nearly reached them again.

"Look," Graybeard said, "there's got to be at least a ladder up the back of the building."

"How do you know that?"

"Because I saw a dozen air conditioning units and an acre of solar panels on the roof, in the aerial imagery at the briefing. They've got to be able to service them somehow."

"Good point," the LT said. "Come on!"

The dead had not only caught up with them, they'd largely filled up the building, so it was probably good the Marines were looking for a rear exit.

Whether they'd ever get off the roof was another question.

\* \* \*

*"Batcopter One from PriFly, come in."*

Drake looked up. Someone had piped the air-control traffic into the Bridge, because that seemed to be the most immediate set of crises they had to face. Drake figured it beat listening to the Battle of Sam's Club, which sounded like everyone was about to die any second.

*"Batcopter One, this is PriFly. Be advised, you are NOT cleared for take-off OR taxi. Conditions too hazardous. Hold position, repeat, hold position. Batcopter One, acknowledge."*

Drake stole a look at the back of the Bridge, and the Captain's Ready Room – and decided if one more goddamned thing went wrong, he was going to quit. Or at least go bodily drag the Captain out there, and make him pitch in on managing this exploding goat rodeo.

But then the radio traffic drew his attention back – and got him up out of his chair and over to the screens to spectate.

*"Hey, you hotshot sons of bitches in Batcopter One. This is the fucking Air Boss. And in case there's some part of that you don't understand, Air is what I control. And Boss means I get to decide you don't get to fucking use it right now."*

Drake stepped out onto the observation deck, which he knew might get him killed, considering everything going wrong out there. The out-of-control Seahawk with the lost sling-load was still overhead, doing some kind of lethal acrobatics. The other one was trying to land without catastrophe, due to being on a string attached to a ten-ton anchor on the deck, and being blown around by a gale. At the same time, people cowered around the King Stallion, and flight deck tractors and personnel rolled and scrambled in all directions, with most people covering up their heads.

*This,* Drake thought, *is why we have sea trials.*

And then, right at the center of this tempest, the Defiant, blades whizzing, started to maneuver through, around, and under it all, powered by its pusher propeller. It rolled right on out of the HLZ, hung a sharp left, juked around the F-35 – which was in motion again, towed by one of the deck tractors – and finally emerged out onto a clear section of deck almost at the stern.

*"PriFly, Batcopter One departing, squawk 7040."*

*"You arrogant motherfuckers."*

*"Sorry, Air Boss. But you've got six-plus acres of flight deck here. And we just needed a little clear spot."*

*"You assholes are defying a direct order. Which means it's the 'Boss' part of 'Air Boss' you don't understand."*

*"Yeah, I guess we are. But which part of 'Defiant' did YOU not understand? Alpha Mike Foxtrot. Batcopter out."*

Drake had to think about that one for two seconds.

*Oh yeah. Adios, motherfuckers.*

He watched in something like awe as the sleek black helo rolled straight off the back edge of the boat, achieving positive lift in the same instant, then roared up and away, tear-assing into the sky and banking away toward land.

"Well," Drake said, seeing it was away safely, and everything else out there starting to resolve and calm down.

"I guess that could have gone worse."

\* \* \*

"Jesus," Coulson said, looking down the ladder. "How many can there possibly be? And when do they stop coming?"

Brady and Reyes both shook their heads. They thought they'd covered that one. Right now, they were also having to wait for Coulson, his gimpy leg slowing everyone down. All four-teen operators were hauling their loaded asses up a ladder bolted onto the rear wall of the warehouse, after exiting out a cargo door below. The dead filling the area beneath them weren't even the ones that had followed them into the store.

They had spilled around the whole building.

The parking deck out front was now completely submerged in a rising sea of the dead. You couldn't even see any concrete.

Fick was last up the ladder, and last out, not much of a Tailgunner Charlie with the draw-string handle of his Charmin hooked over the buttstock of his rifle, and the Sam Adams tucked under his left arm. This left him climbing with one hand, his weight threatening to pull him off the ladder with every step. As he finally hauled himself up over the edge of the rooftop, he could see the Defiant buzzing in from the coast to extract them, and heard someone say:

"Any reason to think the roof will hold that thing?"

"Only one way to find out, brother."

But they didn't have to find out, as the Defiant went into a hover five feet above the deck, and the co-pilot hauled open the cabin door and kicked a rope ladder out.

"Great, one more goddamned climb," Fick grumbled.

The fourteen of them lined up, waiting their turn.

Blane said, "Why do I have a feeling hanging out on rooftops waiting for extraction is going to be a major feature of our new existence?"

"Yeah," Reyes said. "While the dead swarm on all sides."

"Hey," Brady said. "Who cares as long as the Team Chief can wipe his ass in quilted comfort."

"Hey," Fick said, "You stay in your fucking pay grade. Which is now officially one that doesn't get a Sam Adams."

They were giving each other shit. But also having fun. Not only because they were Mike Charlie, mission complete. But because they were all getting out alive.

Together.

Yaz smiled into the sinking sun, feeling happy, but also ill at ease. He stood close to an air conditioning unit…

In case the world started to go black on him again.

# L'ENFER

*Pop! Spooooshhh…!*

A bath of bubbles sprayed and spilled down the champagne bottle, as Jenkins held it over the heads of hooting and cheering Marines. Fick wasn't the only one who'd engaged in a little personal pillaging of Sam's Club. More than a few, especially those holding the interior of the warehouse, had shoved bottles of anything expensive or French-looking in the packs of guys in front of them, underneath body armor, into pants cargo pockets…

And now they'd gone through too many bottles for anyone to be all that careful about not shaking them up first.

Also, everyone had just spent a week stuck in quarantine. The good news was Drake had agreed to Doc Walker's recommendation that they bring their isolation period down from two weeks to one. All the intel they had said the infected turned at most two or three days after exposure. The bad news was this time the Marines had been stuck in there with 55 increasingly smelly sailors and eight helo pilots.

The real good news was they'd taken no casualties on the mission. And that was worth celebrating.

Now the celebration was too big and boisterous to fit in the Team Room, and had spilled into the passageway outside, as well as a couple of adjacent compartments. Inside, Fick was DJ'ing from the laptop at the desk, the tinny little desktop speakers blaring Disturbed.

"Shit," Lawton said, "next time let's grab a Sonos home audio system, and get that bitch installed in here!"

"We've got bigger problems," Fick said.

"What?"

"I think the Internet's packed it in. Spotify has, anyway. Saw that one coming."

"No problem," Yaz said, smiling and weaving. "I've got music. I've got fucking awesome music. Hang on."

He stumbled through the throng of revelers, out the hatch, and down the passageway toward his cabin. Finding and holding onto his keycard required some focus, and then locating his MP3 player took ten minutes. But he was in the zone of the drunk and singleminded. When he stumbled back out into the hall and refocused, there she was.

Rain. Just walking by his cabin.

"Hey!" Yaz said. "Hey."

She turned, but didn't look all that keen to stop.

Yaz tried to compose himself, and tried on a smile, as he caught up to her. He said, "How you doing?"

"Just fine." She had little choice but to stop now.

"Nice to see you overhead on the mission. Vroom!" He made a swooping motion with his hand.

She just blinked slowly and exhaled. "Yeah, I saw you, too."

"How'd we look?"

"Busy. But you survived. So I guess that's good."

Yaz squinted at this, then shifted gears. "So, listen, we're all celebrating the success of the mission, not to mention escaping quarantine alive, down in our Team Room. It's right there. You should totally come by. Have a drink. We've got bubbles. Least you deserve after watching over us."

"No, thanks," Rain said. "Maybe next time."

"Hey." Yaz turned to see Chesney, who lived in his cabin, walking up along with Blane, who didn't.

Blane smiled. "Hey. Was just worried about you."

"What was it you said last time? I'd been gone too long. I'm fine! You remember Rain, EWO on our overwatch flight."

"Whoah-ho," Chesney said. "So it was you guys who took an hour to get your asses in the air. Thanks for leaving us sitting in a hostile city with our faces hanging out."

Rain's expression went dark. "Wasn't us. Talk to the deck crew, particularly those assclowns in the shooter's capsule."

Blane tried to smooth this over. "There were hiccups at every stage. But we all pulled together and got it done."

"I don't know," Chesney said. "A fuck-up here, a fuck-up there, pretty soon you're talking real money."

Yaz used a line he'd picked up from Tier-1 guys. "It's all the little turds that add up into one big pile of shit."

Rain didn't smile. "We did our job."

Yaz said, "Hey, one team, one fight."

"I don't know," Rain said. "It wasn't our team that caused the delay. It was those other guys."

"L'enfer," Blane said, "c'est les autres."

"What the hell does that mean?" Chesney said.

"'Hell is other people.' From a play by Jean-Paul Sartre."

Chesney looked like he was trying to focus. "I think I've wandered into the sober intellectual bastard party. I'm gonna head back to the drunk asshole mosh-pit party. Just need to lie down for a minute…" He disappeared into the cabin.

As the hatch closed, Yaz said, "Do you believe that?"

"What," Blane said. "That hell is other people? Nah. And reading Sartre isn't good for you."

"That doesn't mean he was wrong," Rain said.

Yaz tried to smile again. Their festive celebration had suddenly gotten dark and heavy. Squinting at Rain, he realized this was a person he didn't understand yet. "Is that why you're not coming to the party?"

In answer, she just turned to leave. "See you around."

Yaz watched her go, equally intrigued and repelled. This woman seemed to be operating under very different principles from the ones driving him.

Or maybe even antithetical to them.

* * *

"I gotta go for a shit," Fick announced to the increasingly drunken dance mob in the Team Room.

"Great, another one of your elephant craps," Vorster said. "Don't forget your rocket launcher. Also, let me know which toilet stall to stay away from."

Fick stopped and turned unsteadily, still holding a bottle of Sam Adams in one hand, dripping condensation. He cleared his throat. "I eat like a tiger! I crap like an elephant! I can drink three hundred cups of wine at a sitting!" He paused to glug from the beer. "I have married three wives, made love to a thousand women! I outplay anyone on the lute and the flute! I write immortal poems by the thousands!"

The nearby Marines looked at him like they had no idea who the hell had replaced their normal grizzled Team Chief with dark sparkling Folgers crystals.

"WTF, Master Guns?" Lawton asked, drink in hand.

Fick's shoulders sagged again. "It's from a book I read in seventh grade."

"What kind of fucked-up Whiskey Tango school did they send you to?"

"I loved that book." Looking sad, Fick just turned and wandered blearily out the hatch.

"Man, you think you know a guy," someone said.

"Didn't really buy the crap about the flute. Or lute. Whatever."

Jenkins said, "I fell asleep on fire watch once. I guess my head must have tilted back and my mouth opened up – because when I woke up, Fick's face was six inches from mine, and he had his index finger stuck all the way in my mouth, but not touching anything. He said, 'You're lucky it was my finger.'"

"Holy shit, dude."

"Yeah, I definitely learned my lesson on that one…"

* * *

Blane eyed Yaz as the two walked back to the Team Room, Marines and sailors stumbling past them in the dim passageway. He was trying to figure out how worried to be about what ideas Rain might be putting into Yaz's head.

Speaking of which, what Blane was really worried about was Yaz blacking out at the target site. But he decided now wasn't the time to discuss it. Tomorrow would be another day, and one on which they'd all be sober.

*Or maybe we won't be*, Blane thought, as they fought their way back inside, and saw the general merriment had grown even merrier. As a senior NCO, he was probably going to have to put the hammer down on this. A little drinking and celebration was fine, but Marines needed to save the truly crazy shit for shore leave.

But he never got the chance.

The lights flashed twice, and when everyone turned to face the hatch, the LT was standing in it. And he didn't look happy. You could almost hear the needle scratch as the music cut out. Not having to raise his voice, he said, "Hey, did someone rescind General Order Number Ninety-Nine while I wasn't looking?"

Most sailors and Marines knew it was Navy Secretary Josephus Daniels – infamous buzzkill and supporter of the Temperance Movement – who'd implemented that rule in 1914: "The use or introduction for drinking purposes of alcoholic liquors on board any naval vessel, or within any navy yard or station, is strictly prohibited, and commanding officers will be held directly responsible for the enforcement of this order."

Then again, despite the LT's sharp words, he really just looked worried – like he was going to get in trouble for this.

"Sorry, sir," Blane said. "We were just winding down." He picked up an empty champagne bottle upside down in a helmet full of ice. "I think we've run dry anyway."

A knock sounded on the outside of the hatch.

It was Commander Drake, ship's XO. He was in his usual unpretentious khaki uniform, and also looked humble – the opposite of a senior officer who wants everyone to come to attention when he enters the room. Like he knew he was on their ground. He gestured behind him, where an enlisted sailor had two rough wooden crates tilted back on a hand cart.

Drake said, "The Suppo thought he'd get in the Captain's good graces by bringing these to the Officers' Mess." He looked around. "But the men who deserve them inhabit a lower deck."

He stepped aside as the sailor tilted the cart forward and shoved the two crates off it. One was labeled *Moët & Chandon* in fancy script, and the other, *Veuve Clicquot*.

The entire compartment erupted in wild cheers — followed immediately by chants of, "*X-O, X-O, X-O, X-O…!*"

Drake put his hand up, waving off all the praise as unnecessary and embarrassing. He made way as Fick came back in, and addressed his final comment to him and the LT: "Just do me a favor and try not to destroy 02 Deck."

"Aye aye," Fick said saluting. "Hey, sir, you know how it is — give a Marine a rubber mallet and he'll flatten an anvil."

"Yeah, I know. And lock a Marine in a room with only an anvil, and it will end up broken, missing, or pregnant…"

More cheers erupted from the room.

Drake turned to go, but paused and stuck his hand in the top crate. "Think I'll just grab one of these for later…"

He nodded and left.

Fick cut off the noise just by holding up his beer, and casting his laser gaze across the men, who all piped down. "To Captain Day," he said. "A hard pipe-hitting Recon Marine."

Everyone raised their glasses.

"And Corporal Flynn," Blane said. Someone shoved a cup into his hand. "Who died on his gun, defending his brothers."

They all drank in silence, and remembered that while this mission had incurred no casualties…

The ZA had already taken its first harvest from them.

# DEATH IS CHASING US

*Honolulu – Sam's Club*

*When Yaz's senses dialed up, it was like being born again.*

*And, once again, he was totally alone.*

*He didn't have to slap his chest to know his vest was off him. He'd lived through this scene before. He reached out to verify by touch that his med ruck lay on the cold tile floor beside him. Ahead was the expected pile of twice-dead bodies – destroyed while watching a 30-second Sam's Club ad on eternal repeat.*

*God knew what their experience of eternity was now.*

*This time Yaz didn't panic. He knew he hadn't been left behind. He knew Corporal Meyer was watching over him. And that his other team-mates were just outside the warehouse. He got to his feet, strapped on his vest, grabbed his weapon and med ruck, and glided back out the propped-open doors.*

*He needed to get back to work.*

*The badly injured sailor was still being dug out from giant cans of tomatoes, and still howling in pain. Yaz took a knee beside him, got his med ruck slung open, gloved up…*

*And the howling man's face went gray and fuzzy.*

*Oh, God, Yaz thought. Not again…*

*His patient's screams faded away, as did the sounds of helicopters, firing, shouting, and moaning.*

*And once again the whole world went black.*

\* \* \*

This time when Yaz awoke, he was truly alone.

The infinite embrace of the empty black cosmos stretched out on every side except one – the cold hard surface of the deck beneath him. Overhead, he could see a canopy of stars – but also lights burning in the top three levels of the island, rising out of the giant warship behind him.

He was out on the goddamned flight deck.

At night. And completely alone. A steady wind whistled over the top of the ship, and over his supine body. The ship must be underway. Using his elbows and hands, he sat up. He was both confused and scared, but looking around, he had to admit this was a majestic sight – being out on the flight deck of a supercarrier underway in the middle of the ocean.

As to how the hell he got here…

And then his face sagged. His head obviously wasn't working right. Something had to be seriously wrong if he was having nightmares about the mission – while sleepwalking. This was not good. He started to climb to his feet, but then startled and spun around, going into a defensive crouch.

Somebody was standing behind him.

"Oh, good. You're alive."

For one second Yaz, honestly had no idea if he was awake, or still dreaming. But then he started breathing again. It was Corporal Meyer.

*Thank God.*

Yaz had to prevent himself from performing the script from last time, saying "What the hell happened?" The last thing he wanted was to appear confused and incapable. But somehow, despite him not asking the question, Meyer answered it: "You just passed out."

Yaz shook his head and blinked. "What?"

"Knock, knock," Meyer said.

"What?"

Meyer made a fist and knocked at the air in front of him.

Horrifyingly, the air made a knocking sound.

It, and Meyer, kept on knocking.

Yaz shook his head and tried to focus…

\* \* \*

And he woke up in his rack, covered in sweat.

But not alone this time. This was obvious from the rumble of snoring coming from the rack below him, as well as from the two on the other side of the cabin.

And the hatch actually was knocking.

For some reason, Yaz was the only one who woke up. He pulled on his pants, padded over, and opened it up.

Behind it stood Gunny Blane.

"Buy you a coffee?" he said.

"Yeah," Yaz said. "Sure."

Five minutes later they were back in the 02 Deck Mess, sparsely patronized at this hour. Once they both had mugs of coffee, Blane cupped his, looked across the table, and said:

"May as well get to it. I'm worried about you deploying."

"What?"

"You got medical sign-off for operational status."

"I did."

"Yeah, I know. Because I've got the paperwork." He looked down and blew on his mug, then looked up again. "My question is: how much lying did you do to Doc Walker to achieve that?"

Now Yaz looked down at his own mug. Finally, he said, "I might have been slightly selective in what I told her."

"What did you leave out?"

Yaz hesitated. "Headaches. Some dizziness."

Blane exhaled. "Okay. That's not the end of the world. A lot of guys have lingering issues with TBI, from IEDs and whatnot. And we've all had to play through injuries, both for training cycles and operationally. That's baked into special ops. So is fudging a little on medical, probably."

Yaz nodded, relieved – temporarily.

"But it's also my job to consider the operational status of the whole team, and their safety. What if one of my Marines gets injured – and you black out while treating him?"

Yaz took a breath, sobered. "I feel fine. It's not going to happen again."

"How can you know that?"

Yaz had no good answer to this. Finally, he just said: "I can't screw this up. I need to be part of this team."

Blane nodded. "I hear you. I really do. But you're seriously going to screw it up if you let someone get killed on your watch. You hear what I'm saying?"

Yaz nodded. "I do. But you can't keep me back from missions. I have to go out. I need to do this job."

"I need you to do it, too, believe me. Why do you think I had you flown out here when I did, even as the world was ending? Two MSOTs and one SARC is bad juju."

They both sat and just sipped coffee for a while.

Finally, Blane said, "Okay, here's how this is going to go. I'm not going to rat you out to Doc Walker."

Yaz nodded, so grateful he felt himself tearing up.

"But you have to tell me if you have any more episodes. Any dizziness, headaches, blacking out. You got me?"

"Yes."

"Promise me that, and I won't take this further."

Yaz just nodded again.

Blane smiled, shifting gears to lighten the mood. "Maybe you got addicted to the action, too." He nodded down at his coffee. "It probably wasn't the food."

Yaz laughed, then shrugged. He looked up, trying to decide how honest he could be with this man. The question answered itself. He said, "It's what you were talking about last time we were here. About us getting back to being a tribe."

Blane nodded. "Kicking it old school."

"But also now chased down the street by dead people."

Blane laughed. "I'm not sure how much has changed there, either. Death has always been chasing us. This just makes it a little more literal. And, you know, more urgent." He checked his watch. "Speaking of which. Got a command debrief at 0800."

Yaz said, "And our team hot wash at 1200."

Blane rose. "See you there, brother."

Yaz sat alone and stared at his coffee. And then he realized... he had already lied to Gunny Blane – by not telling him about having blacked out in the shower.

He had already betrayed his brother's trust.

# MEMBRANES

*JFK – Flag Bridge, Briefing Room*

Drake took a beat to survey the faces around the table, and the others standing around it, holding up bulkheads. He kept tweaking who he wanted in these meetings, and if he kept this up he was going to have to find a bigger room.

Finally, he nodded across the table. "Suppo. Go."

"Everyone already knows our goals for the Honolulu mission. We're still cataloging and stowing what we brought in, as well as updating the Stores manife—"

The hatch banged open. "Begging your pardon." It was the Captain. Everyone shuffled and stood up, but no one had thought to save him a seat, so somebody had to make space, which resulted in four people trying to do so at once.

The Suppo resumed. "We're still updating manifests. But I can tell you now we achieved less than our target of filling every galley and getting us back to seventy days endurance." He paused to look over at the three Marines.

The LT looked down at the table. He figured this was where shit rolled downhill, and onto his head. The Suppo was going to get payback for the LT ending the mission early, and pin the blame on him. And he was fine with that. His major worry was Fick, and that he'd make things worse with his famous mouth.

But then the Suppo said, "The failure to hit our target was down to the situation on the ground, and the pressure on the shore team and on our security. The Marines fought like hell to keep us there as long as they could."

The LT exhaled.

"Bottom line?" Drake said.

"Pending a final number, best estimate is sixty-five days. That's how long the carrier's got. Before we've got to do it all again."

The LT smiled – 65 was pretty damned close to 70.

"And the strike group as a whole?"

"That calculation is just dividing by 1.5 – 7,500 souls in the strike group, versus our 5,000. So forty-three days."

Drake exhaled, as did some of the others. That wasn't nothing. Another 43 days of life, he'd take. "Last time we talked, you were developing a plan for cutting down rations."

"Yes, sir."

"Because people are going to have to get used to a lower standard of fare, what with the world having ended and all."

"Aye, sir. I think they'll figure it out pretty fast, when every meal starts getting built around rice, beans, and pasta. I've got my guys building new meal plans. We won't know for sure until we start feeding everyone. But current estimate is you can multiply by 1.5 again on the new ration plan."

"Nice," Drake said. "So back up to sixty-five days."

The Suppo nodded. "The other development is since we're shifting to dry goods from fresh food, we can store much more. There's a lot of storage space on this boat, and if we get the chance to raid the General-Mills factory, we can pile up boxes of pasta in the Stores warehouse down below, the hangar deck, even out on the flight deck. Not to mention on the *Rainier*."

"That's a lot of pasta."

"And the bakery is still running. There will always be fresh bread, as long as we keep bringing in flour and yeast."

"Sounds like Italian every night."

"Some jarred tomato sauce and garlic granules and it's a party. I'll keep those on the list. We can also look for hard cheeses. Most of them were developed before refrigeration, so some can keep for years."

Drake just blinked. That was probably more about cheese storage than anyone in this meeting needed to know. But it was nice to think the post-Apocalypse wouldn't be as grim as everyone thought.

"Reactor Officer, go."

She nodded and said, "You have our full readiness report and updated maintenance history, as ordered."

Drake had seen the email go by, but didn't want to admit he hadn't read it yet. He'd been kind of occupied with the shore mission, and keeping the flight deck from turning into a helicopter demolition derby. "Top line?"

"We're all squared away, sir. As I said before, these reactors barely have the plastic off them. And they had exhaustive testing – containment, reactivity control, safety margins – before being lowered into our hull. Everything's quadruple-redundant. And my guys are all top guys. Everyone wanted this assignment, so we got our pick of the most experienced, from officers down to MMs, EMs, and ETs."

Those were the nuclear-trained Machinist's Mates, Electrician's Mates, and Electronics Technicians, enlisted petty officers trained at the Navy's Nuclear Power School, and all of whom already had experience working on one of the Navy's 93 other nuclear power plants – 71 on subs, 18 on aircraft carriers, and 4 training and research plants.

Drake said, "Okay, but what are the sustainment issues you're going to face – things you'll no longer be able to get, without putting into port or dry dock, and without support?"

"Nothing. The whole point of them is to be self-sustaining."

Drake didn't buy it. "What's the weak spot? Our vulnerability? What could go wrong?"

She seemed to give this some thought. "I guess those same personnel. If we lost people in critical roles – or, God forbid, the whole section."

"And then? If you can't get replacements from Fleet?"

"Then everyone left on board is pretty much screwed, sir. Don't take this the wrong way, but nuclear reactors are kind of complex to run. Never mind get started once shut down."

"This isn't funny," Drake said. "What happens if there's an outbreak in your section? And you do lose everyone? Because if those reactors go down, we're not only dead in the water, propulsion-wise – we're also *dead, in the water*. Not only do we lose propulsion, we lose the 750 megawatts of power those things produce. Nothing runs without it, including the desal plants. Without which we're dead in a week."

He paused and squinted in thought. "Okay. I want you to relocate your team's billets – as far from the reactor frames as possible. So if something does happen in the control room or reactor compartment, your guys off duty aren't endangered. Let 'em camp out on the Sparrow-and-CWIS decks, I don't care." He indicated the heads of the Admin and Safety Departments. "Get together and figure it out."

"Aye aye, sir."

Drake shifted gears. "Life support, go."

The officer in charge of the desalination plants passed down two printed and bound documents, each nearly an inch thick. Drake flipped through the first couple of pages of each, one for readiness and the other a full maintenance history. There was no summary page for either.

"Again, top line," he said.

"For both plants, I'm able to report we're at full readiness, and maintenance is fully up to date."

"Great. But, again, sustainment issues? Risk points? Like I said, none of us stays alive without them. What do we need to do to keep them working long-term, without support?"

"You'll find that in the first annex in back, sir, but the biggest issue is the membranes." He paused to look around the table, evidently trying to judge how much of a background lecture people were up for. "Sir, desalination by seawater reverse osmosis, or SWRO, is a membrane process, with four stages – pretreatment, pressurization, membrane separation, and post-treatment stabilization. It's in the third phase, the separation process, when water is passed through permeable membranes that stop dissolved salts while letting the water pass through. Over time, those membranes clog up, and have to be replaced."

Drake had a one-word question: "When?"

"Totally depends, sir."

Drake sighed, failing to mask his annoyance. "*When*."

"Most manufacturers claim a three-year replacement period. But it really depends on several things: the plant's pretreatment system, how well we maintain the feed-water quality by filtration, and chemical cleaning of the membranes themselves. Also, how closely we monitor the feed-water pH. All of that we control. What's harder to control is the SDI."

"SDI?"

"The Silt Density Index. It's a measure of the fouling potential of suspended solids in the source water."

"So you're saying it depends on the quality of water we start with? That is, whatever we're sailing through."

"Yes, sir. Sewage, pollution, floating oil and waste from other vessels, or even our own waste, all increase SDI. Out here on the open ocean, the replacement period is pretty predictable."

"But otherwise?"

"SDI starts to climb closer to shore, near the mouths of rivers which have agricultural run-off and pollution, and near oil platforms or shipping ports, which spill a lot of fuel and other crap. Eventually, the membrane pores start to become scaly or blocked. This reduces the flow rate, and our fresh-water production capacity. Eventually it falls to zero."

"And then?"

"Then they have to be replaced. Ideally, sooner."

"Tell me we keep replacements on board."

"No, sir."

Drake ground his jaw. "Why the fuck not?"

"For one thing, they're expensive. The desal plants we run are the biggest in the world for offshore use."

"What's offshore use?"

"Anything not land-based – ships and oil rigs, offshore platforms. Anyway, ours are the biggest they make, and there aren't many, so the membranes are pricey. Also, ONR has been doing research into third-gen desal technologies and experimental prototypes – nanoparticle membranes, ceramic and polymer ultrafiltration, biomimetic membranes… As you know, sir, strategic projections have us operating in littoral and coastal waters more and more."

Drake sighed. "Meaning dirtier water with more particles."

"Exactly. Even out in open water, there are now big algae blooms in ocean dead zones. So better desal tech has become an urgent operational requirement. The expectation is they'd roll out to the newest and most advanced ships first."

"Namely us," Drake said. "And let me guess, no one wanted to spend money on last-generation tech, like these membranes, only to throw them away when the new stuff comes in."

"Exactly. But the main reason we don't have replacement membranes is we just expected to put into port a lot more often than they need replacing."

"All right," Drake said. "I need you to get to work and find me replacements. And I need you to get on it now."

"But, sir, as I said, we've got years in these things. Why now? It's not urgent."

"No," Drake said, obviously battling to tamp down his ire. "But it's critically fucking important. Which makes it one of those quadrant-two tasks – high importance, low urgency – that always gets kicked down the road while we're doing all the urgent but unimportant crap. Until one day it's too late. And if these things are expensive and only go in the biggest desal plants, I'm guessing they don't grow on trees."

"No, sir. I don't suppose they do."

"Right. And I don't want to sit around watching our water production decline until one day suddenly we're rationing water, and, oh, shit, the only replacements are in Utah."

"No, sir. I don't suppose we do."

"The other reason I want you to get on it now is the Internet's going down on us. With our normal supply chain and support networks out of action, I expect you're going to figure this out the way everyone else does. By Googling it."

"Yes, sir. I'll get it done."

"Please excuse me." This was the Captain, standing up, re-sulting in everyone else around the table also doing so. There was a pregnant pause while he looked around, his gaze settling on Drake. "Um, there was that other thing, XO. The radio transmission. Were you going to cover that now?"

Drake's face remained a mask. "Sir, you'll recall we agreed to keep that need-to-know for the moment."

"Ah, right. Of course. Excuse me, then."

He shuffled out and everyone sat again, Drake last. He thought, *Wow, last to arrive and first to leave.* But maybe they were better off that way. He looked around and said:

"Okay. Next up. Raiders, go." But then he squinted and said, "That is your official unit name now, right? No longer MARSOC, Marine Special Operations Command?"

The LT nodded. "That's correct, sir. The Marine Special Operations Battalions are now formally the Marine Raider Battalions. The commandant made it official at our last change of command ceremony."

Drake almost smiled. "Named for the legendary World War Two unit, the first elite Marine operators, right? Long-term ops, behind enemy lines, no logistical support."

"Yes, sir. We hope to honor their legacy."

Fick opened his mouth. The LT kicked him under the table.

Drake nodded. "I'd say you earned the name this week."

"Thank you, sir." The LT nodded. "You already have my written after-action report."

Drake sighed, his smile fading. If he had time to read all these reports, he wouldn't call meetings. He was also afraid this *Groundhog Day* feeling was going to be another major feature of post-Apocalyptic life. "Again, top line."

"No casualties in our teams, as you know. Two injuries among the rest of the shore team, one serious. Our operational plan was decent, and achieved the commander's intent – well, sixty-five out of seventy. We also learned some significant lessons, mainly about the enemy, which we're going to drill down in our team hot wash today."

"I sense the bad news coming," Drake said.

"Yes, sir. Small-arms ammo. We burned through an atrocious amount. Today is also ammo manifest day. But I can tell you it's in the ballpark of fifty percent of our stores."

Drake sighed. "Which means you can do one more mission."

"Yes. But only if nothing goes wrong or kicks off between now and then. And which also means, respectfully…"

"That we're going to have to hit a military installation."

"Yes, sir. We've got to top up on NATO five-five-six and seven-six-two for the rifles, nine-mil and forty-five ACP for pistols, belted seven-six-two for the machine guns, grenades, both hand-thrown and self-propelled forty-mil—"

"Okay, okay," Drake said, waving this off, along with the barrage of metric measurements. "I trust you know what you need, and will tell me where to go to get it." He paused to scan the room. "Anything else?"

The Admin Department head raised a hand. "Sir, I've got the updated personnel roster you requested – including the matrix of suspected versus confirmed desertions or su—"

Drake cut him off. "We'll take that offline. Dismissed."

# A DUCK'S DICK

## JFK – Bridge, Observation Deck

"LT, are your Marines doing what I think they are down there?"

"Yes, sir. Building a CQB village."

"Close-quarters battle training. Out on my flight deck."

"Just temporary, sir. And three of the four runways are clear."

"You get any kind of authorization for that?"

The LT looked away from Drake and eyed Fick. The four of them were once again out "getting some air" on the observation deck, in what seemed to be a post-briefing ritual. Really, this was Drake coming to rely on the advice of his Marine leaders. Ultimately, whatever the org chart or chain of command said, you tended to work with the people you liked and trusted.

This time, no gale blew, but only a fresh morning breeze, through slanting sunshine and a light scattering of cumulus. But there were also a bunch of jarheads down below, busying themselves with paper targets, scrap lumber, and hand tools.

The LT said, "The Captain authorized it, sir."

Drake said, "Did he? Well, good to know he's still capable of making a command decision. Was this a good one?"

"Oh, absolutely, sir," Fick said. "The Marine Corps is like America's pit bull. They beat us, mistreat us, and every once in a while, let us out to attack someone."

Both the LT and Blane rolled their eyes, recognizing the quote, but didn't say anything. Fick went on.

"And since it kind of looks like we all might be out here a while, we need to give 'em a padded sleeve to tear into and thrash around on. Because, believe me, the last thing you want is your pit bulls getting fat and happy."

"What he means," the LT said, "is you don't want your Critical Skills Operators letting their perishable skills—"

"Perish?" Drake said.

"Yes, sir," the LT said. "Exactly."

"Because they're critical." They knew Drake was being a smart-ass, but no one answered, though Fick looked tempted. Drake nodded downward. "And you think that will help?"

Fick smiled. "Does a duck's dick drag through the weeds?"

Drake blinked, trying to maintain his stern expression. "I trust there won't be live fire on my flight deck?"

"Negative," the LT said. "Simunitions only. And blanks."

"Try not to scare anyone to death with the noise."

Blane spoke for the first time. "Speaking of which, Commander, may I ask what that was about, with the personnel roster? The desertions and… suicides?"

Drake's amused expression melted away. He looked around, but there was no one else within earshot. "This doesn't leave this group. But we've been losing people. In ones and twos at first. But then more. Personnel not reporting to their duty stations at start of shift. Obviously, we've all had a lot on our minds, but best we can piece together, it started outside San Francisco Bay. A handful of life rafts disappeared. But also we think some people just swam for it."

Fick boggled. "What, back into that shit storm on shore?"

Drake shrugged. "Back to their families."

Blane said, "They had to know they'd never make it?"

"Maybe. But evidently they still had to try. Hell, the admiral's whole staff cleared out, flying off in the C-2 they flew in on. That thing's not going to make it back to DC without refueling."

"Any idea what happened to them?"

"You mean, do we know what happened to them? No. But, yeah, I've got some idea of what happened to them."

"Christ," Fick said.

Drake shrugged. "Worrying about ourselves is worry enough. More of our crew went missing off the coast of Hawaii. Worst of all, there were some during the passage across the Pacific."

Blane shook his head. "And those people…"

"Yeah. Definitely not going back to their families. They were just going. Those were the suspected suicides. But there have also been a few, four to be exact, that we didn't have to wonder about."

Blane said, "Because you found the bodies."

"I wish I could say those were going to be the last. But I doubt it. Listen, we're scrambling to set up more frequent morale and welfare checks. I don't know how this is going to play out. The world's never ended before, except in a million movies, books, and TV shows. But we can presume it's going to be tough on people's mental health. So I suggest you keep a close eye on your own men, starting now."

"Roger that," the LT said.

"So," Drake said, as if he'd been getting around to this. "The ammo situation. I'm guessing with your initiative, and mad planning skills, we're not starting from scratch."

"No, sir. We're looking at Changi Naval Base, Singapore."

"Why there?"

The LT nodded. "As you'll know, it's a Republic of Singapore naval facility – but as a result of the local Five Power Defense

Arrangements and a 1990 agreement, U.S. naval and air forces have been allowed to make use of the facilities. Including…"

"Storing ammo, ordnance, and stores. Genius."

"Yep," Fick said. "Several metric shit-tons of fuck-shit-up."

Drake said, "But without U.S. military personnel based there. Or not many, anyway."

"Yes, sir. Few or none. Much less risk of blue-on-blue."

"And, mainly, no need to—" Blane said.

"Yeah, got it," Drake said. There would also be no dead people walking around in U.S. military uniform, possibly former friends and colleagues of the Marines and sailors. And who they would then have to shoot in the face.

The post-Apocalypse was horrible enough without that.

The LT said, "It should also allow my Marines to replace everything we had to leave behind in San Francisco – vests, mags, helmets, ESAPI plates, a few belts and boots."

"I love it," Drake said. "Where are you at with planning?"

"Concept stage. Aided by both Wikipedia and Google Maps still being up."

"Use 'em as long as you can. We're seeing web sites and services going down fast. Our engineering and telecoms guys tell me it's the power grids. When a coal- or oil-fired electricity plant stops getting fuel trucked in, the local grid fails – instantly, because there's no storage capacity. They all just keep the juice flowing in real time."

"Until they don't," Fick said.

"Until they don't. And then any data center wired to that grid only stays up as long as the power in its USP batteries lasts, usually just a few hours. Or, if it has backup diesel generators, when the fuel for those runs out, in a few days. This is all going to get worse. And it's probably not ever going to get any better."

Blane said, "What about communications satellites – which among other things connect us to the Internet at sea?"

"I wouldn't worry about that. The Comms Department assures me the geostationary ones will stay up for years without maintenance, and their solar arrays will work for fifteen or twenty years. Though…" and Drake glanced up "…the low-earth-orbit ones will start falling out of the sky when they run out of fuel to boost their orbits."

The others looked up to the mostly clear skies, then just breathed the clean salt air for a minute. Like suddenly this moment was worth savoring.

Because it was going to end.

"Okay," Drake finally said. "Thank you, gentlemen. Based on what you've told me, I'm going to have the Nav Department start putting together a voyage and passage plan – for Singapore." Then he looked at Fick and the LT. "But right now I need a word alone with your Operations Sergeant."

Fick looked vaguely relieved, and the LT vaguely confused. But, as always in the military, you didn't have to understand orders – you just had to obey them. The commander and senior NCO saluted and headed down the outside ladder, to swing by the construction of their urban combat training site.

And make sure no one was nailing anything to an F-35.

# FIGHT YOUR WAY
# TO YOUR RIFLE

*JFK – Raider Team Room*

When Yaz stepped inside, after finishing his coffee, shower-ing, and waking up properly, he found himself arriving at the same time as his favorite Assistant Ops Sergeant, namely Staff Sergeant Gifford. Gifford had Corporal Kemp in tow – the most junior guy in 2/1, and their new machine-gunner, since Flynn got killed getting out of San Francisco. Gifford carried a tablet, and both wore cammies with side arms.

All of them reaching the hatch at the same time, Gifford ignored Yaz and just went in, but Kemp smiled and said, "Hey, Doc," making way for him to go in first.

"Thanks," Yaz said. "You guys doing an ammo count?"

"You guys playin' cards?" Gifford said. Yaz got the refer-ence. It was Flounder in *Animal House* – the new guy who was never going to fit in, asking a dumb-ass question.

"Yeah," Kemp said, ignoring Gifford and just answering, as he followed Yaz inside. "Counting and re-counting every round, even the crates that are unopened, for some stupid rea-son." Kemp was pretty clearly hungover, but seemed intent on doing his job well anyway. That was one of the things about young guys, Yaz remembered – they could function on an hour of sleep, after two bottles of champagne.

Inside, Yaz saw a handful of Marines lounging around,

including Gifford's counterpart, Staff Sergeant O'Bannon, Assistant Ops Sergeant for Team 1, sitting at the desk in front of the laptop. "About time," O'Bannon said. "Got the numbers for the ammo room?"

"Yeah," Gifford said. "Assuming everyone complied and checked everything back in, rather than keeping a couple mags under the mattress. Just gotta go through the overflow stuff in here, then we're done."

"Beam me what you've got, will you?"

"Wilco."

Yaz moved to the lounge area on the right, where Meyer was on the Xbox again, this time with Dunham, the pair playing *Resident Evil 6* in local cooperative mode, each fighting side-by-side on a split screen on the huge wall-mounted flatscreen, Dunham on the couch, Meyer perched on a crate, both with wireless controllers in hand. Yaz sat down to spectate and kill time until their hot wash.

"*Resident Evil*, huh?" Yaz said. "That's a little close to home. Fighting off infected from a bio-terror attack."

"Who said we had a bio-terror attack?" Meyer said, not taking his eye off the screen. "You know something we don't?"

Eyes also glued to the screen, Dunham said, "It's perfect tactical training. This is like, totally a training evolution."

Meyer snorted. "It would be if you didn't suck."

Making his way around the room to Meyer on his crate, Kemp said, "Kindly move your ass. Gotta check inside."

"Why?" Meyer said, engrossed in the balls-out zombie battle onscreen. "It hasn't been opened since last time."

"If you think that answer will be satisfactory to this United States Marine Corps, you've been spending too much time on Phobos."

166

Meyer smiled and stayed where he was, not pausing his strafing barrage of shotgun blasts. "As long as you promise to jump back in when you're done. I need my battle buddy back. Dunham here's killing me. Literally."

Yaz picked up his feet as Kemp stuck his head under the couch, presumably to make sure there were no hidden crates of missiles down there. As he did, Yaz saw the young man's side arm closer up now – a chunky autoloader, desert-tan with textured grips, like most of the Marines carried. Yaz said, "I didn't know enlisted under E-5 got side arms."

Kemp stood up. "In MARSOC we do. Also, machine-gunners always do, for personal protection."

Yaz nodded. "Ironic. The most junior guys."

Gifford stepped over, scratching his chin stubble. "It's not fucking ironic. If you're carrying a Mk 48 as your primary weapon, you're not gonna be able to snap-fire it."

Kemp smiled. "Or even bring it around in tight corners." He unsnapped the thumb break of his belt holster, pulled out the pistol, reversed it, and handed it over to Yaz. "M45 CQBP, Close Quarter Battle Pistol."

"Beautiful weapon," Yaz said, feeling the weight.

"Yeah," Kemp said. "But I'd give it back in a second, along with the Mk 48. For one more day with Flynn around."

The mood in the room fell, but for no one more than Yaz. Flynn was the Marine he'd failed to save. He handed the pistol back. Kemp holstered it and moved to the crate Meyer was sitting on. "I said move your ass."

Not looking away from the game, Meyer said, "I will when you get a haircut, you hippy bastard."

Kemp's hair was definitely pushing up against the grooming standard, more than some of the others, including the senior

Marines, who would be given more latitude. He almost had a flop in front, making him look more like a frat boy than a hippy. Yaz guessed he was 21, maybe 22.

Gifford rubbed Kemp's scalp with his knuckles, equally vigorous and affectionate. Then he shoved Meyer off the crate, causing him to get killed in the game.

"Goddammit," Meyer said. He looked back to Kemp, who was opening the crate. "As much linked seven-six-two as you burned through on that mission, I'm surprised there's anything left to count."

"Hey," Gifford said. "This trigger-happy hippy saved our asses. If he hadn't unloaded when he did, we would have been pushed back sooner, and that parking deck gotten overrun a hell of a lot faster, us with it."

"Okay," Meyer said. "We love our full-auto serial killer."

Yaz said, "It's true. Otherwise, we might not have had the chance to get into the warehouse, or up to the top of it."

"What?" Gifford said, squinting into the tablet. "The one you were napping in? While Marines were fighting?"

Yaz fought to hold his tongue.

But Kemp rushed to his defense. "Don't listen to him, Doc. You may not be a leatherneck, but you're still the most important guy here, because you keep the rest of us alive. When the shit comes down, we'll have your back."

Yaz smiled, grateful. Then he looked back to Gifford. Maybe this guy was never going to like him. But he couldn't resign himself to permanent hostilities with anyone on this team, especially as it was such a small one. "Hey, Staff Sergeant, the flight deck's open for exercise later. How about a run?"

Gifford snorted. "No, thanks. I lift. Cardio's for people who can't shoot."

"Yeah," Meyer said, respawning onscreen, and glancing over at Kemp's side arm. "And a pistol is the perfect tool for fighting your way back to your rifle. Speaking of which, who's getting in on this CQB training up top…?"

Soon the others were chattering about that.

And Yaz's various humiliations, large and small, faded.

For now.

# THE ARK

Silence reigned with only Drake and Blane left out there, as the former cast his eye upon the Marines' construction project, then over to the dozen F-35s still parked at the edges of the flight deck. "I wonder what the odds are we're going to be in another fight that requires those aircraft."

Blane said, "Well, one sure helped secure our target site."

"We could have taken that ramp out with a single shell from a destroyer's deck gun. Would have been cheaper."

"I'm not sure money matters much anymore."

"No. You're probably right."

Drake turned and looked at Blane, like he was trying to take his measure. Finally, he said, "Britain still stands."

"Beg your pardon, sir?"

"Pretty sure you heard me. Great Britain's still standing. The UK. It didn't fall. Everyone there's still alive. Well, almost everyone. But a hell of a lot more than anywhere else."

Blane just squinted in wonder. "How?"

"The 11/11 attacks. Those two British Airways triple-sevens that went down, a few days before everything went to shit. Stupid-ass jihadis accidentally timed it perfectly – Britain grounded all international flights, and pretty much stopped train and ferry traffic, while they tried to work out what the other targets were, based on the intel they had. What they didn't realize was this would save the country."

170

Blane shook his head. "My old platoon sergeant used to say he'd rather be lucky than good any day."

"Well, the Brits sure were. The lockdown, their whole counter-terrorism response, gave them a few days to hunker down against the waves of refugees, and the army of dead following behind, rolling across Europe. It was too fast, and too much, for anyone else to react to or deal with."

"How many?"

"How many what?"

"How many still alive?"

"They don't have a final number yet, at least not for us. But they think at least fifty-five million. That's England, Scotland, and Wales. Northern Ireland didn't make it. Or Ireland, for that matter. They also had a few big outbreaks in the cities, which they managed to put down. And they've still got packs of dead roaming the countryside, with the military hunting them down. They're not out of the woods. But they're in the fight."

"You've got to love the Brits. Like World War Two all over again – all of Europe falls, and they still stand."

"That's a more apt metaphor than you know. They had to fight a second Battle of Britain – or, I guess, a reverse Dunkirk – to keep from being swamped by the refugees, many of them infected, trying to cross the Channel."

"Defending their island home."

"Yeah. But it was the advance warning that gave them the chance to do so. Everywhere else, it happened so fast, most people went down before they knew what to be afraid of."

Blane shook his head. "Okay, Commander, forgive me, but I have got to ask – why are you telling this to me?"

"I'll tell you why. But first you need to understand why I'm not telling anyone else. Almost no one else."

Blane squinted into memory, from the meeting. "This was what the Captain was talking about. The transmission."

"Yeah. The old man nearly spilled the beans."

"Okay. So why don't you want others to know?"

Drake sighed. "Because if people knew there was someplace left to go, they're gonna want to go there. Best case is we come under enormous pressure to take everyone to Britain. More desertions in the meantime. Worst case, maybe outright mutiny. Hijacking the *JFK*, or the whole strike group, steaming across the world to the one decent place left."

Blane cocked his head. "Would that be so bad?"

"Yeah," Drake said. "It would be. Because we're the only eggs not already in that one basket. And Britain could still fall. Like I said, they're not out of the woods yet. And every other nation in the world has gone down, so it's not clear how you stay alive and run the last country going, surrounded by an army of seven billion flesh-eating bastards. If Britain does go down, tomorrow or next year, then that makes us…"

"The ark," Blane said. "For humanity."

"Exactly. We've now talked this through with their Ministry of Defence, who have a direct line to the PM and Cabinet. And everyone's in agreement. The *Kennedy* strike group has to stay away. And we have to survive on our own. At least for now."

Blane shook his head. "There's no one else out there?"

Drake shrugged. "Small pockets of survivors, scattered here and there. The Brits have started putting together a registry to keep track of them, the ones they've made radio contact with. But these are all small groups, and all cut off. To the best of everyone's knowledge, no other nation-state, or government, has survived. Britain is it."

"Britain – and us."

"Yeah. And us."

Blane shook his head again, trying to reconcile their dark and surreal reality with the beautiful day out on that windy and sun-splashed deck. "So if we're the ark, what do we do? Just stay at sea, and stay alive, until the dead rot to pieces? And we get the planet back? Then start over?"

Drake shrugged. "I don't know. It's above my pay grade. And too much, and too far off, to think about. Hell, I don't even know if we'd be enough breeding stock to start over."

"Actually, yeah," Blane said. "I'm pretty sure we would."

"Go on."

Blane squinted into memory. "They think humanity went through at least one genetic bottleneck, when the Toba super-volcano eruption, seventy thousand years ago, blocked the sun and caused a thousand-year winter. After that, Homo sapiens dropped down to just a few thousand people."

"Well, that'd do it."

"Maybe. Some think a pandemic around the same time may have been a factor."

Drake snorted. "So everything old is new again."

"Also, the native population of the Americas may be descended from as few as seventy people who crossed the Bering land bridge. I think I remember the magic number, to restart the race, without risk of inbreeding, is ninety-eight."

"They teach you that at Parris Island?"

"I read a lot," Blane said. "Again, why are you telling me this? And not our commander, or senior NCO?"

Drake exhaled and scanned the horizon. "I'm not sure, honestly. The LT is capable and gung-ho, but he's wet behind the ears. Fick is exactly the blunt object he needs to be for that job, but he's a little all over the place. You're next in the chain of command. And steadiest. But it's not even that."

"What, then?"

"You've got a good face?"

Blane laughed, but didn't buy it.

"I don't know," Drake said, turning to look out over the railing again, face to the wind. "It was something you said. The day we met, when your team came aboard. I was going down the row, shaking hands, just sort of ritually welcoming everyone. When I came to you, I said thanks for being here. And you said something different to the others, which I couldn't forget. You said, 'It's a privilege.' I said something like, 'What, getting stuck down in a smelly compartment belowdecks in the surface fleet?' And you said: 'It's a privilege every time out.'"

Blane faced into the breeze. He'd forgotten about that.

Drake scanned the horizon. "My experience of Marines on board is they tend to keep to themselves."

"Yeah, well. I was never into that us-and-them stuff." Blane also looked around, at the empty ocean surrounding them. "And definitely not now."

"Copy that," Drake said. "Also, I know Gunnery Sergeants always look out for their Marines. But I got the sense you'd also make sure your Marines looked out for us."

Blane just nodded.

"Listen, there's one other thing. When I said it was just Britain, us, and small pockets of survivors, that wasn't all of it. There are also American military personnel in Britain."

Blane arched his eyebrows.

"Aside from the ones already stationed in the UK, some from other units based in Europe, or even farther away, managed to fight their way there. They're still trickling in. Also

174

remnants of some European military forces. Almost all of them SOF guys."

"No surprise there."

"No. Anyway, point being, if things go south for us, and the strike group falls, your Marines might be able to escape. Maybe you'll already be on shore. And now you know…"

"There's somewhere else left to go."

"Exactly. And that's why I need someone on your team to know about Britain. Now try to forget it all. I need for this to not get out." He looked back inside, at an enlisted information specialist standing by his station.

"I've got to go. Got a Genius Bar appointment."

Blane laughed and watched him leave.

# NO BAD IDEAS

*JFK – 02 Deck Briefing Room*
*{Ten Days Later}*

This time the briefing room was less than half full – only the two teams of Marines, a dozen Weapons and Stores personnel assigned to help carry ammo out, and a handful of CIC, air-wing, and small-boat personnel for mission support.

This time the LT ran the briefing – and the show.

"Welcome to Op Dakka," he said.

One of the younger Marines in the second row, and one of the gamers, said, "As in – 'more dakka'?"

"Exactly." The LT grinned. "One of the privileges of special operations is getting to name our operations whatever the hell we want. And our mission objective on this one is more dakka, for us gunfighters to dakka-dakka with. The good news is this time we're not going to have to defend a target site while dozens of sailors extract mega-shit-tons of food. This time it's only a couple of tons of ammo and ordnance. And a handful of non-Marines to help us with it."

He paused to scan the room. "But be advised, this objective is as critical as the last one. Because without ammo, there's not going to be a whole lot more food in our future."

He hit a button to lower the lights, then another to fire up the video display, then leaned into his laptop and called up an overhead view of an enclosed port facility. The surrounding harbor, nearly square, was obviously manmade.

"Changi Naval Base – Singaporean, but with docking, fueling, and resupply rights for U.S. and allied navies." He paused to look at all the glinting eyes shining back at him. "And not only will we not have to hold a perimeter while helicopters haul dozens of sling-loads out… there won't be any helicopters on this one. And the perimeter should hold itself."

He saw skepticism on the faces in the front row.

"This is a military base, ladies and gentlemen. It's got its own secure fence-line. And we won't be flying there, or flying out. Instead, it's going to be nice smooth sailing…"

He flipped sides.

"…just as soon as we secure this bad boy."

\* \* \*

"Good morning. I'm Ensign Hayden." A female officer in her mid-twenties, she had a round freckled face and pale blue-green eyes. Like most junior officers, she looked and sounded earnest – and young. She didn't smile.

Yaz recognized her from treating her rolled ankle in Hawaii. Evidently she'd recovered enough to go out again. Plus gotten promoted to being in charge on this one.

She said, "It's my job to lead the combined team from the Weapons and Stores Departments, and to help you get all the cans of whoop-ass you need back here to the flat-top."

She called up her own Powerpoint slide deck.

"Right now I'm going to give you an overview of cargo handling and ground transport." She flipped from the intro slide to another overhead photo of the port. "How far will ground transport have to stretch?" She pointed at a spot on the photo. "That's the dockside, at water's edge." Then she moved the pointer a half inch. "And that's the ammunition and magazine stores warehouse. The whole point of this place is to supply the fleet. So very easy loading and unloading."

She paused to flip slides.

"As to how we'll get the ammo out of the warehouse and across the dock…" The display now showed a stock photo of some kind of low, flat, white vehicle, like a huge steel pallet on wheels, with an enclosure for the driver in the front left. "Inside the warehouse should be a small fleet of seven-ton pallet and container transporters."

"Bumper cars!" Brady shouted from the front row, where he sat along with most of the senior Marines. "Much more fun than forklift trucks."

"Which you also didn't get to drive," Reyes said.

"Which sucked," Brady said.

Fick leaned across Reyes and stuck his face two inches from Brady's. "Come here, devil dog. Look into my deep brown eyes. When it looks like I give a fuck, let me know."

Hayden still didn't smile.

She just flipped slides.

* * *

"Nice to see some of the same smiling faces from last time."

LT Campbell was again briefing for CIC, and mission support. The Marines got the sense she liked to be hands-on.

"Let me tell you about our intel, and why we're confident about this target site. We know with a high degree of certainty there are still several cubic ass-tons of ammo cached here. We know it because COMLOG WESTPAC, the virtual command based at Changi, was the principal USN replenishment facility for fifty-one million square miles of Indian and Pacific Ocean. So this place is almost nothing but munitions and ordnance."

Brady was slumped down in his chair, his long legs sticking straight out ahead and touching the foot of the podium. He smiled his beautiful smile and said, "So it's basically like the ammunition store at Ragnar Anchorage?"

From his right, Graybeard said, "This isn't the *Galactica*, man, and we're not on the run from the Cylons."

"Oh, no?" Reyes said. "It's kinda perfect, actually. The dead did wipe out all our colonies."

"Yeah," Brady said. "But the question is, does the radiation field at this place adversely affect Zulu technology?"

"Shut the fuck up," Graybeard said, tiredly.

Fick leaned over again and added, "Before I adversely affect your technology. Or start revoking birth certificates."

Campbell waited for them to finish.

Saunders raised his hand.

"Master Sergeant," Campbell said.

"Yeah, any reason to think any of it'll still be there? Now that we're all in the post-Apocalypse, ammo is kind of going to be worth its weight in, well, ammo."

Campbell nodded. "Two reasons. One, there's so much ammunition, ordnance, and heavy weapons cached there that even if the Singapore Navy threw the doors open when civilization fell, it's hard to imagine who'd be able to carry it all out in the time they've had."

She flipped to what appeared to be live drone video. "Two, not only was the facility heavily guarded, fortified, and locked down. But current ISR shows the base and port facility secure and intact."

"That's what Sam's Club looked like," Reyes said.

This time Fick just hit him.

Campbell said, "Your total TOT on this one is going to be a lot shorter. You'll be making less noise with no helos. But mainly, any noise you do make inside, including shooting, is guaranteed not to bring the whole city down on you."

"I am assured of this," Fick muttered. Now Graybeard hit *him*. He was surely the only one who could get away with it.

Campbell just grimaced. "Any dead from outside the base will be stopped by the perimeter fence. It's twenty feet high, solid stone, and topped with razor wire."

Brady said, "Which the fucking dead—"

"Yeah," Campbell said. "We know. Which they'll eventually pile up over. We get it. But, like I said, if things go remotely to plan, you'll be out of there long before that."

"And when the hell has anything ever not gone to plan?" It was also Fick who said this. The others just looked at him. He shrugged and hit himself.

Campbell just shook her head. "Any other questions?"

Graybeard raised his hand.

"Master Sergeant," Campbell said.

"Yeah, one question and a follow-up."

Campbell smiled. "Go on."

"If it's so secure and locked down, how do we get in?"

"It's our warehouse, and we've got full basing rights." She held up a white keycard. "Just badge yourselves in. This is basically an all-access pass, to most secure areas of the base."

"Nice," Graybeard said.

"And your follow-up?"

"What about dead inside the walls?"

"Unsurprisingly, we do see a few wandering around, mostly just standing around at this point. And you'll probably encounter more inside the target structure. But nothing you gentlemen can't handle."

She paused and scanned the faces of the Marines.

"Get past them, and Smaug's treasure is all yours."

* * *

Yaz, in his old seat in the fourth row on the right, mostly zoned out of the briefing about insertion and extraction, given by the small-boat guys from the Deck Department. Instead he was looking around the audience for her.

For Rain.

He did spot the male pilot, Angel. But when the LT took the stage to wrap up, Yaz figured the Growler crew didn't rate a speaking slot this time. They'd already been introduced, and would be doing the same job on this mission.

And Rain evidently hadn't even bothered to turn up.

* * *

"Okay," the LT said, Fick standing with him up front now. "Anyone else have input, feedback, or pushback at this time?"

Fick scanned the Marines, his face serious. "Come on, don't be shy. Questions, comments, moans, groans, bitches, or complaints – now's the time. There are no bad ideas."

"Ha," Brady said. "How about taking down Sam's Club?"

"Yeah," Reyes said. "That was definitely a bad idea."

Fick leaned toward Brady. "Stab yourself in the neck."

Reyes drew his K-Bar, reversed it, and handed it haft-first to Brady, who just ignored it.

The LT gritted his teeth, patience straining. "How about possible threats? Anything we've missed in our assessment?"

Reyes raised his hand. "What about gangs, sir?"

Sergeant Lovell snorted from behind him. "You are aware we're not deploying to South Central?"

Reyes turned around and stuck his finger an inch from Lovell's eyeball, then faced forward again. "Seriously. Singapore had a pretty big gang problem. They'd go around slashing people with those curved machetes."

"How do you even know that?" Brady asked.

"Lotta immigrants from Singapore in LA. 'Nuff said."

The LT nodded, looking like he was trying to take this on board. "I'll do some research on it tonight. But, honestly, in terms of survivors, we're more concerned about the Singapore military – both because their odds of surviving would be higher, and because they'll be a lot better armed."

"Fine," Reyes said, slumping in his chair. "It's all fun and games until someone slashes your Achilles tendon."

"All right," the LT said. "Anything else? If not, let's all try to get some rest. We roll out at oh-dawn-hundred."

He brought up the lights.

"Dismissed."

# RAGNAR

*South China Sea, Two Miles West of Singapore*

As soon as the Marines hit the rear dock of the *Kennedy* to load the launch, Yaz realized what had been missing from the mission briefing – and maybe from the planning documents themselves, although he didn't get to see them.

An annex on the weather.

Like the enemy, the weather usually got a vote, especially in special operations. It had been a huge factor in the mountains of Afghanistan, where an overnight fall of snow could make the passes and mountain trails impassable, and violent thunderstorms rolling up the valleys could make close-air support ineffective, and helo extraction impossible.

There would be no mountains or helos today.

But it was summertime south of the equator, and as the Marines and sailors stepped out into the boat, just before dawn, it was already 80° and climbing – and the humidity made them gasp for breath, and their uniforms stick to their bodies underneath their body armor and assault packs.

It was also the start of the monsoon season.

And they'd only covered a mile of ocean before the low and heavy skies opened up and unleashed a downpour on their helmeted heads. The rain fell not in buckets, but in tubs, and Yaz watched the level of water in the open-top boat rising, wondering if they were going to have to bail – literally or figuratively – before they made it to their insertion point.

But, up ahead, through the thick mists of heavy rain banging the surface of the sea, the manmade sea-wall that ringed the harbor finally came into view, its entrance big enough to admit even the largest warships. As it did, the rain stopped again, like somebody turning off a tap.

The Marines sat hunched in the boat, soaked to the skin, hot steam rising off them, determined not to be miserable, and not to rent the weather space in their heads – to stay mission focused. But with weather this mercurial, Yaz thought...

It was probably going to turn on them again.

\* \* \*

The launch entered the opening in the sea break, then turned right, then left, then right to enter the harbor. Ahead, to the north, two huge piers appeared, jutting straight at them out of the dockside, the hulking buildings of the base rising up behind. Alongside those piers, and also moored along the perimeter sea-wall, surrounding them on all sides, and rising up out of the mists...

Sat the hulking gray shapes of still and silent warships.

The Marines could see these included destroyers and a couple of frigates, variously flagged as Singaporean, Australian, and Malaysian. Then they passed an aircraft carrier, a British one, with its distinctive upward-curved flight deck. And finally a littoral combat ship, a landing helicopter assault ship, and a dock landing ship...

All three of them U.S. Navy vessels.

But, under whatever flag, they were all ghost ships.

Gray, motionless, and silent, they rose up out of the steaming water, menacing the Marines in their little launch.

Nonetheless, the boat turned left, toward the surrounding pier on the west side, engines settling to a smooth idle as it coasted in to the dockside. This was built for huge oceangoing vessels, so fully ten feet high, but a ladder descended to the water, and the launch bumped up against it.

Right between two of the U.S.-flagged vessels.

Pre-positioned in front, the Team 1 Marines started climbing up, those behind covering them and edging forward to keep the boat balanced. But the first Marine hadn't even reached the top of the ladder when the first Zulu arrived to investigate. It stuck its head over the edge and reached down toward the leader, Master Sergeant Saunders.

Two Marines in the boat fired simultaneously, both nailing the dead guy's head. Two things they should have thought about first but didn't failed to happen – the body didn't drop into the boat, where it would risk infecting the others, and its brains didn't splash all over Saunders on the ladder. Instead, both body and brains flew backward and out of sight. Saunders slipped up onto the pier, others following. A few more suppressed shots sounded as silent Marines disappeared up top.

Last up was Jeschke, Team 1's RTO, and as he went by, Fick slapped him on the ass and said, "Today's Friday. Try not to fuck it up." Jeschke grinned and kept climbing.

The launch burbled off again.

Team 2 was now on their own.

* * *

The same scene played out at the bigger main dock on the north side of the harbor, which abutted the hulking warehouse and port buildings. This time Yaz was last out, and decided pulling himself up the ladder in a soaking uniform, trying to breathe what felt like the air of a steam room, was just no fun at all.

Then again, he wasn't there to have fun.

As he pulled himself over the lip of the dock, he thought about how this job really never stopped being difficult, scary, and painful, and wondered again why he did it. He knew ultimately it wasn't the adventure, the physical challenge, or the adrenaline rush when the bullets started flying. It wasn't even the satisfaction of living a life of service.

No, it was the group that preceded him up that ladder.

And believing he could have a place within it.

There'd been some bumps so far. But Yaz knew he just had to keep doing his job, keep getting along with the others, and give himself more time to settle in – and them more time to accept him and get used to him.

And mainly he had to not fuck it up for himself. Again.

Because now there were no other options if he did.

But then his mind snapped back to the present, and he remembered his job right now was covering his sector – which, as usual, was their six. Probably not much was going to come at them from the direction they'd just come, but it didn't pay to assume. Aiming his rifle out over the water, he listened to the footsteps and suppressed shots behind him, and watched the launch moving off again. When the shooting finally died down, he stole a look over his shoulder.

Scattered on the dock were six bodies, in Singaporean or maybe Malaysian uniform – Yaz couldn't tell the difference between the two flags if the fate of what was left of the free world depended on it. Four Marines were already dragging them out of the way, wearing the blue nitrile gloves Yaz had distributed after raiding the hospital to top up his own supply. Hauling on arms or legs, they dragged them fifteen meters down from a steel door in the warehouse, and piled them up against the wall.

Yaz brought his rifle back up, turned, and tried to stay switched on. Then he decided to make himself more useful, and stepped out to the edge of the dock to take a look around below, in the soggy but brightening morning light.

Sure enough, there were two threats no one had seen when they rolled in. Both were bodies floating around the pier pilings. One wore a lifejacket and floated free, head tilted back – and mostly gone. Someone had shot off most of this dude's face, suggesting he'd been undead before becoming actually dead. The second one floated face down, one arm draped over a section of piling, head mostly submerged.

It occurred to Yaz to put a security shot into the second one. But the firing behind him had stopped, and he didn't want to bust into the silence. They were all quickly learning that noise was seriously not their friend. They were fortunate to have encountered so few dead here so far, and even luckier not to have met any survivors. Yaz considered how Zulu fighting probably had some advantages over fighting the living. Not least because the dead couldn't use weapons.

Looking to his left, he could see the outside wall of the base on the east side, adjacent to the water. He just hoped the advance intel and ISR were accurate.

And this place of ghosts really was secure.

* * *

As the Marines set security on the dock, the LT moved to that nearby entrance, a heavy steel security door, just down from a much bigger steel slatted roll-up door. It had an electronic card reader beside it, and when he waved his white keycard in front, it blinked from red to green.

And then he simply pulled the door open.

Two Marines from 2/2, Coulson and Dunham, one senior and one junior, stayed to strongpoint the entrance, while the rest of Team 2 pushed inside to clear the structure. Yaz moved from the dockside to stack up and follow the others. Coulson and Dunham had the rear sectors now, and when the Marines were moving, it was Yaz's job to stay close, so he was seconds away if someone got hit. Seconds often meant the difference between survival and death.

After they all slithered inside, Coulson watched the door close and the light change to red, before turning out again to cover his sector – half the water and the dock to the east, with Dunham doing the same to the west. Coulson had pulled this duty because he was dead-reliable and unflappable, but also because his leg wound meant he still wasn't going to be the 100-meter dash champion for Team 2. Or any team.

As Assistant Element Leader, he was also wired into the command net, and heard the LT report to CIC and the other leaders on the ground: *"Seven-Nine Combat – Reamer Two has inserted. Clearing target structure now, over."*

*"Solid copy, Reamer. We no longer have eyes on. Keep us posted – regular updates."*

*"Combat, Reamer, wilco."*

* * *

Ensign Hayden stood at the prow of the ship's launch on its second trip, feeling like General Washington crossing the Delaware. One difference was Washington didn't have to stand tippy-toe to see over the back of the gunner. Though it was a lot of fun to think what the Continental Army would have done to the Hessians with a six-barreled minigun.

Hayden was tempted to smile, but didn't, due to the seriousness of her responsibilities on this mission. The flash of humor was also squashed by the humidity, the stifling heat and moisture already causing her to sweat through her clothes. Her blue-and-gray pixelated camo working uniform, beneath the flak jacket and life vest, was also stiff and starchy due to her having only worn it once before. Before the Hawaii mission, she'd never had an assignment off the boat, and until now it had been service khakis at her duty station.

She'd also never been in charge of a shore working party.

Looking down, she twisted her foot around, feeling the last pain and swelling in her ankle, after the mishap outside Sam's Club. She had it taped up, and she'd be fine today. That's what she'd told command, anyway. Then she touched the holstered M9 pistol on her duty belt. While she had qualified on the weapon at Basic, she hadn't fired it since, and presumed she wouldn't have to. Still, it underscored the seriousness of what they were doing today.

Going out on hostile ground.

She took a look back, at the towering gray mass of the *Kennedy*, shrinking in the gray heat haze behind them – and then down again at the two dozen enlisted sailors and petty officers she had the privilege of commanding today. More than a few of them were older than her, some a lot older, which was a source of awkwardness she knew she had to overcome if she was going to hack it as a junior officer.

Within a few minutes, the boat had retraced its journey, and the support crew had covered the same route as the Marines before them. They finally pulled up alongside the main dock, engine idling. As Ensign Hayden assisted the others up the ladder, she heard someone behind her say:

"Holy shit, dude. Floater."

She turned and saw two of her sailors ogling a body in a life vest, floating on the surface of the water a few feet away, its mostly missing head turned to the sky. This was a horrible sight, particularly close up, and Hayden had to tear her attention away from it, in order to keep the others focused.

"Hey, Rob," one of the junior storekeepers said. "There's your replacement life vest right there, dude."

Hayden had no idea how serious the suggestion was, but several sailors – including old Rob Callum, who had to be at least twice her age – leaned over the side to check it out.

"You men keep moving," Hayden said.

And then they did move – shouting and scrambling back toward the other side of the boat, threatening to capsize it. A soggy and rotted hand had just landed on the gunwale – followed by a waterlogged but mostly intact head.

With jaws gnashing.

And Rob went flailing into the water on the other side.

# KEYCARD

*Singapore – Changi Naval Base, Dockside*

With only two of them on security outside, Coulson decided the swabbies could get themselves up the ladder and onto the dock on their own. But he soon realized how wrong he'd been. Only about half had climbed up when the silence was torn by terrified shouting, and punctuated by the resounding splash of something big going into the water.

Coulson only needed one guess what that was.

His senses were also jacked enough to hear wheezing underneath all that. He headed for the ladder at dock's edge, seeing Dunham moving to cover him. It was a good reaction, supporting his teammate, but Coulson needed him to stay on the door, and started to wave him back—

When his right leg went out, his knee slamming the deck.

*Dammit*, he thought. *Trick artery.*

As he steeled himself against the pain and climbed back to his feet, he saw Dunham had already reached the dock edge and started engaging something below. By the time Coulson arrived, it was slipping from the gunwale back into the water. He pivoted right, where some young sailors were pulling an old one back into the boat. Just like that, it was over.

Threat suppressed, man overboard recovered.

"Everyone okay?" This was the LT, racing up with Fick, Gifford, and Chesney, all of them emerging from the same door they went in a few minutes before. The other Team 2 leader, Blane, was still inside, presumably running that show.

"Fine," Coulson said. "You come back just for this?"

"No." The LT nodded behind him. "Structure's clear."

"That fast?"

"It was clear to start with. No one home."

"Nice," Coulson said. "I approve this mission."

The LT stepped to the edge of the dock and looked down, where he could see the headshot dead guy floating face down in the swells – and the soaked sailor who had caused those waves, shaking himself off like a dog in the back in the boat.

As the sailors resumed climbing up, Fick stepped to the dock edge beside the ladder, hands resting lightly on his weapon, rocking on his heels. As the half-drowned sailor and the others filed by, Fick just shook his head and said, "If you live a Jerry Springer life, Jerry Springer shit will happen to you."

Gifford evidently thought this incident wasn't as funny as annoying, and said, "Hey, can one of you shit me a few more Marines – so we can do everything ourselves next time?"

Ensign Hayden was last out, her new uniform all but creaking as she climbed the ladder. Unexpectedly, Fick came to attention and snapped a salute.

"Welcome aboard, ma'am," he said. For Marines, any place you went – ships, naval bases, FOBs in the mountains or desert – you were coming aboard.

She stopped and saluted back. "Thank you, Sergeant."

But evidently no one had told her you never addressed Gunnery Sergeants or Master Sergeants – never mind Master Gunnery Sergeants – merely as "Sergeant."

Fick just smiled frighteningly in response, and said, "Looking sharp, ma'am. Love the aquaflage." The blue-and-white digital camo uniforms had been the subject of ridicule ever since they rolled out, with awkward questions asked about why shipboard crew needed camouflage at all. Fick added, "Battle Dress Oceanic, I believe?" That was the other term of abuse.

Hayden managed a tight smile. "They're phasing them out."

"Too late for you, ma'am." He saluted again and waited for Hayden to move off, though it was more slinking off.

Nearby, Coulson nodded at Dunham, both battling to stifle their laughter, then headed back toward the secure door. But the LT stopped them.

"Not there," he said. "Push out. This area's secure."

And it looked like it was. They had perfect visibility 200 meters in both directions down the dock. And, aside from the pile of bodies near the door, there was absolutely nothing on the dock itself. No place anyone, living or dead, could hide.

But out beyond that section of dock was a different story.

They'd known from the start the base was too big to clear, never mind hold, with only 28 shooters. The alternative was to maintain a smaller perimeter and deal with any dead that trickled in when they got there. They were also betting intel was correct, and the outer wire secure, so dead from the city couldn't inundate them, as they'd done in Honolulu.

The LT walked Coulson and Dunham thirty meters out on their left flank to set security. Before leaving he said, "Keep me updated on what you've got coming in from this side. And radio for support if it gets too much to deal with."

But even then Coulson was raising his rifle to take aim at a tottering figure 200 meters out, down at the far end of the dock. He took up a textbook standing shooting posture, cheek welded to his stock, right elbow chicken-winged out, rifle barrel laid in the thumb web of his support hand, just in front of the maga-zine well, other four fingers pointing at the sky.

He fired once.

The tiny figure in the distance dropped to the deck.

"Shouldn't get too crunchy," he said, lowering his weapon.

The LT smiled and patted him on the back. Their left flank was in safe hands. He turned away, trotted back to the oth-ers, and got two more 2/2 guys – their Element Leader, SSG Cartwright, as well as CPL Graves, another senior/junior pair – into a mirror-image position on the right flank, facing east. The last of the 2/2 Marines, Meyer, took Yaz's old position at the dock edge, watching over the tied-up launch and the harbor.

This would be their security bubble. Now they just needed to get their nervous support crew to work inside of it.

So they could all get out again with Smaug's treasure.

As he trotted back, the LT switched channels and said, "Reamer One, from Two, sitrep."

*"Stand by, Two."* That was the voice of Master Sergeant Saunders. And he was speaking in a barely audible whisper.

That was probably a good sign. Probably.

\* \* \*

Inside the warehouse, Yaz stuck by Blane, where he instinctively felt comfortable. When they'd first entered via the secure door, it opened onto a long corridor – one in total darkness, as soon as the door shut behind them.

The twelve operators pulled their NVGs down and fired up IR illuminators on their barrel rails. In the spectral cones of green, surrounded by menacing black, they cleared a suite of bare offices, which let off either side of the corridor. Despite PCs on desks, and files and papers scattered around…

No one was home, either living or dead.

It was only when they emerged from the corridor at its end that they entered the warehouse proper, with supplies stacked to the 36-foot ceilings in thick rows stretching to the back wall. As 2/1 pushed ahead to clear that maze, the leaders hooked around to the right, back toward the front wall, and into an open area ending with the roll-up cargo doors. And parked there were six big pallet transporters, all in a row.

This was also where Fick and the LT found Blane and Yaz, after badging themselves back in and passing through the corridor. The difference this time was they'd got the lights on.

"Nice," the LT said. "So there's still power."

"Yeah," Fick said. "Otherwise—"

"Yeah, otherwise the card reader wouldn't have worked." The LT shook his head. It was amazing how much you took for granted before civilization cratered. He'd heard Singapore was some kind of advanced economic superpower, so maybe their power grids were staying up longer. He just hoped they stayed up for the next couple of hours.

In the stark overhead lighting, they could now see the six big-ass, low, flat pallet transporters – as well as, in the other direction, what they'd come for: towering stacks of crated and palletized ammunition, explosives, and other supplies, all of it rising to the ceiling and stretching out of sight to the back, like the warehouse at the end of *Raiders of the Lost Ark*.

Fick whistled. "Piss in my mouth and call me R. Kelly."

The LT looked around, and spotted a junction box on the wall with two buttons on it, one black and one red, which controlled the front cargo doors. He made a balled fist, but paused at the sound of suppressed rifle shots from outside. That would be their perimeter security, dropping the odd Zulu wandering in from the rest of the base. This gave him pause and he looked to his senior enlisted.

Blane said, "Sir, why don't we get everything loaded up first, then roll it all out in one go. There's only twenty meters of dock to cover out there, and also—"

"Also we keep the mission objective under positive control. And maintain a single secure point of entry."

"Exactly," Blane said.

"Man," Yaz said, regarding the colossal stacks of supplies. "That's gonna take some loading."

Fick grunted and said, "With enough lube and patience, the elephant can fuck the ant."

"I don't even know what that means," the LT said.

"One day you'll understand, young Jedi," Fick said, then moved back to the office area and down the corridor to the outside door. He stuck his head out and raised his voice for the sailors mustered there. "Okay, who here wants to pick up a whole bunch of really heavy shit? Bear in mind if I don't get volunteers, you will be voluntold."

The bemused Stores and Weapons crew filed inside.

Then they got to work, overseen by Ensign Hayden and directed by the 2/1 guys – Graybeard, Brady, Reyes, and Kemp. The Marines ran around like kids in a candy store, one for highly destructive kids, pointing out and marking pallets, boxes, crates, steel cans, and Tuff-Boxes full of small-arms ammo, explosives, grenades, rockets, belted rounds… All of it getting stacked into piles on the pallet transporters.

They even found U.S.-issue Rhodesian tactical vests, plate carriers, and ESAPI plates, which quickly got distributed to the

Team-2 Marines who had lost theirs swimming out of America. It was like a Tupperware party for pipe-hitting operators.

Yaz just hung out, cradling his weapon, keeping an eye on the proceedings. There was a lot of heavy stuff moving around, some high off the ground. But it was more a matter of occupational health and safety than combat medicine.

Everything was going like clockwork this time.

* * *

An hour later, the half-dozen Stores and Weapons augments were covered in sweat and panting – but the six transporters were full, piled with the best and most useful ammo and ordnance in the warehouse, as decreed by the Marines.

Ensign Hayden wiped sweat from her forehead before it fell on her tablet, which she was using to create a manifest of everything selected for transport back. They'd gotten a surprisingly large portion of the contents of the warehouse loaded up. Now they were getting into decreasing marginal returns – the Marines pointing out stuff that might be fun, but wasn't exactly critical.

As the supervisor, Hayden didn't have to pick up anything, but she was still feeling gross and sweaty – only the office areas had air-con, and the main warehouse was heating up fast – so she decided she could really use some air. She reported this to Yaz, probably because he was nearby. "I'm going to go out and just check on the status of transport."

"I'll escort you," Yaz said, turning to do so.

"No need," she said, holding up the white keycard. "I can come and go. Also, it's like fifty feet away, with a squad of Marines guarding each end."

Yaz thought about insisting, but she was already off.

Also, he remembered the LT declared the area secure.

* * *

Thirty minutes later, when they decided they couldn't safely pile another loose round on the transporters, the LT punched the button to roll up the cargo doors. It was only then…

Yaz realized Hayden hadn't come back.

He presumed she'd stayed outside, and when he stepped out, he took a look around for her, but got distracted by firing from Coulson and Dunham to the right. Out past them he could see a dozen bodies littering the dock, out to 200 meters. But then when he turned to scan for her in the opposite direction, he had to clear out as the engines of one, then two, then all six pallet transporters turned over and started rumbling out onto the concrete dock.

They were so far ahead of schedule the next mode of transport hadn't arrived yet. The six loaded vehicles lined up in two rows, and the sailors driving them shut the engines down again. Yaz looked to his right at the backs of Coulson and Dunham, who'd stopped firing, then at Cartwright and Graves in the opposite direction, who'd never started.

A lonely gull called from over the water in the still and silent morning.

And then a clattering, rolling burst of full-auto gunfire exploded from the east.

Yaz hit the deck and got his rifle pointed in that direction, where he could see Cartwright and Graves doing the same thing. But after that they reacted to contact perfectly – Cartwright returning fire, a rapid flurry of nonstop single shots, draining his 30-round mag, while Graves low-dashed to the cover of the transporters behind them. Then he turned around and opened up to cover Cartwright, as he got up and sprinted to cover.

Whoever was engaging them from down on that side of the dock was putting out blistering fire. Yaz scrambled forward into the lee of one of the transporters, then moved forward to get his gun in the fight. And then he realized...

They were all taking cover behind explosives and ammo.

# PARANG

*Singapore – Changi Naval Base*
*{Four Hours Earlier}*

Dòujī sat upon the wall. And he let the warm sun dry him.

The rains of the monsoon didn't bother him. Nor the stickiness of the humid and rain-sodden air. Nor the passage of time. He was happy here, sitting just as he was. Perhaps because he had a role, a job to do.

And a group to do it for.

His name was Mandarin for "fighting cock." Dòujī had literally been named for a bloodsport. He fingered the razor-sharp edge of the parang in his lap – technically just a very large knife, it was more like a machete, but optimized for the heavy jungle vegetation of the Malay peninsula. It had a heavier blade than a normal machete, plus wider beveling on the blade, to prevent it from binding to wood during the cut.

This also kept it from getting stuck in bone.

Dòujī knew this from first-hand experience.

He looked up again, scanning the wide expanse of the naval base laid out before and below him. Climbing up the outside of the perimeter wall, now that the cameras and active defenses were down, was easy. Wire cutters cleared away the razor wire on top. And the few zombies doddering around below, the sailors from Singapore and elsewhere who hadn't escaped the fall of the base, paid him no mind. As long as he stayed silent, and still, they went about their business.

Whatever the business of the dead was.

When the time came, Dòujī knew he could dispatch them with his parang. He looked down again and fingered the nine notches on the wooden handle, one for each man he had killed in single combat – knife fighting. But the notches weren't the real badges of his victories. Those were the knots of scar tissue on his arms, hands, shoulders, thighs, and torso. An old adage said, "If you fight with a knife, expect to cut" – and Dòujī did, and had. He'd spilled liters of his own blood on the streets, and spent many weeks in bed healing up.

But he had never lost a fight.

"You should see the other guy," he would say to his brothers in Salakau when they came to visit him. And, so far at least, the other guy had always spilled more blood. And none of them walked away, to bed or any other place.

They had been carried away.

Dòujī was wicked fast, he knew the location of all the most vulnerable parts of the body – where the largest veins and arteries rose closest to the surface of the skin – and he knew how to protect his own.

Mainly, he knew how to handle his weapon.

Many of his brothers in Salakau also carried parangs, but they preferred guns – handguns, submachine guns, street sweepers, whatever they could get their hands on. Salakau meant "369" in Hokkien, a dialect of Chinese – the numbers 3, 6, and 9 added up to 18, signifying the 18 saints of the Shaolin Temple. Salakau, a long-time fixture of the streets of Singapore, was half street gang and half secret society.

But its members, especially Dòujī, were all in.

\* \* \*

Now Dòujī sat on the wall, and breathed the air, and waited.

He volunteered for these shifts because he liked the solitude. And because he relished the prospect of getting in some action with his parang – with either living or dead, he didn't care which. But mainly because it allowed him to serve. To be of use to the group. They all knew there were weapons and ammunition stored in the naval base – much better and deadlier than the cheap crap they were able to buy on the black market, before the dead came back to life.

Since the fall of the city, they had managed to break into a couple of Singapore Police Force stations, and take the weapons in there, including one mounted on a special tactics vehicle. Trouble was, by the end, most of the weapons were in the hands of police out trying to quell the unrest – and then trying to defend themselves from the dead.

But now, if Salakau could get their hands on the military-grade weapons in the naval base, they would be the most deadly and dominant group of survivors in the post-Apocalypse. They would take what they liked, kill who they wanted, and own the streets of Singapore – forever.

But the trick was getting in.

And if it was Dòujī who got them in, his star would be ascendent – and he would be in a position to take over leadership of the group. That would mean killing their current leader. But Dòujī was fine with that. This was how things worked on the streets.

But, for now, there were the peaceful shifts on the wall.

It was simply a matter of waiting for someone to come out of one of the secure warehouses. Which would allow them to go in, either by catching the door or just killing the person who left and taking their security keycard.

Dòujī slid his parang back into its scabbard, pulled his phone out and checked for a signal, then checked Bluetooth was on – and finally looked at the last object sitting on the wall beside him. Looking like a sleek black remote control, it had only two big buttons, and white text on the front, which read:

*Durascan D600.*

Some in the gang had suggested they start killing zombies and search their pockets until they found a keycard. But it was only the American warehouse, the big one in the middle, that they knew for sure had weapons and ammo. So far, no one had seen a zombie in American uniform.

So today Dòujī watched, and waited, for someone to leave. What he hadn't expected was…

For someone to arrive.

When he heard the roar of a jet flying overhead, he dropped off the wall on the inside and covered up beneath the bushes and trees at its base. But as he monitored the sky, the clouds blew clear just long enough for him to spot a glint in the sky, even higher up.

The dumbass on duty yesterday had sworn he spotted a drone, overhead at high altitude. No one had believed him, but Dòujī had been intrigued enough to take the next watch himself. Now he knew that the dumbass had been right.

And he knew he needed to act fast.

\* \* \*

The newcomers were American – and had brought a security keycard with them. This was the jackpot.

By staying low to the ground, and sticking the top of his head around the building edge, Dòujī could see them get the door of the warehouse open. He was in the alley between it and the next one, where he hid himself as soon as he spotted the boat cutting across the harbor. Peeking out was a risk – there was a chance the Americans on the dock would see him.

But he needed to see them.

What he hadn't counted on, and didn't know how to deal with, was how many they were, and how well armed. It looked like the prize inside the warehouse would belong to them and not Salakau. Dòujī had already called the brothers, and got them moving. But without a keycard to open the front gates, they could only climb the walls and drop down inside, just as he had, armed with only what they could carry.

But maybe it would be enough.

# SPRAY AND PRAY MAFIA

*Changi Naval Base, Main Dock*

Despite the fury and surprise of the attack, it went nowhere and stalled out fast – for more reasons than Yaz had time to count. Still under cover, he peered through his optic and assessed the tactical situation.

The most obvious aspect was the Marines were highly trained and switched-on, and knew exactly how to react to contact. They also had the cover of the pallet loaders – albeit potentially explosive cover – while the attackers were fully exposed, racing across the bare expanse of concrete dock from the east. Even the ones still dropping off the wall only had the bushes and a few trees there, more concealment than cover.

Most importantly, every Marine was a rifleman first, and all of them could shoot. The Singaporean and Chinese gang-bangers in shitbird post-Apocalyptic streetwear could not. They were rocking cheap Tec-9 machine-pistols, even cheaper Hi-Point handguns and .38 revolvers, and at least one bolt-action hunting rifle. Even if the weapons had been reversed, the Marines would have lit up the attacking gang members all day, and cut them to pieces.

But these guys couldn't hit shit.

They were the Spray'n'Pray Mafia.

Rounds came in all over the place, cutting the air, skittering across concrete, thunking into the warehouse, a few pinging off the pallet loaders or thwacking into the ammo crates on them.

Ignoring the incoming, Marines put out disciplined and effective fire, taking down one, two, eight of the running attackers, sending them sprawling out face down on the dock, or running wounded for cover. But the only cover was between the warehouses that fronted the harbor to their right.

Yaz didn't even get a shot off before the enemy was routed and scattered from the dock, cowering in those alleys. In the next few seconds, they started leaning out and letting off badly aimed or totally unaimed shots and rolling bursts. They were still a threat, but mainly because they were hitting, when they hit anything, the piles of crated ammo and ordnance.

And Yaz wasn't the only one aware of this.

Staff Sergeant Gifford, Yaz's best buddy in Team 2, was up on the front line, in front of it actually, out beyond the transporters and down on one knee, leaning forward and putting out heavy and accurate fire. As he went empty and dropped out his mag, he twisted at the waist and shouted, "We need to push out and roll them up! Two-One up, on me!"

The LT, who had just reached the corner of the loader behind him, shouted, "Hey, Sergeant, we've got numbers and cover! Let's be conservative, and not get anybody shot today."

Gifford snarled, ignoring the incoming fire, and said, "We've got them on their back feet. Let me finish it."

Even as he said that a round thwacked into a crate beside the LT's head – one marked *30 GRENADE HAND FRAGS / DELAY M67 W/FUZE M213* along with a lot number.

Gifford laughed at this, or maybe he was laughing at danger in general. "We need to suppress the threat before something goes boom – or everything all at once."

The LT looked inclined to see the wisdom in this, but then put his hand to his ear and shouted into his chin mic over the gunfire. "Combat, Reamer, I do not copy your last, repeat all after 'multiple victors'…" But even as he hunched over trying to hear, his mind now inhabiting a different space, two more rounds whacked into the grenade crate.

Fick moved up behind him and said, "Hey, sir, you need to let your pit bull off the chain."

A loud chattering started up behind them, and when Yaz turned, he saw Kemp down on his belly in front of the door. His MK 48 was emplaced on solid concrete on its bipod and putting out disciplined 5- to 7-round bursts at short and regular intervals. As trained to do, he was providing a base of fire, both to suppress the enemy…

And for assaulting Marines to advance under.

Looking forward again, sensing a chance to make himself useful, and maybe even impress Gifford, Yaz pushed up and said, "Hey, I'll join the attack."

Gifford looked over his shoulder at Yaz, then farther back at Kemp, and shook his head. "Negative. Go back and pull security for Kemp." When Yaz hesitated, he yelled, "Do it!"

Yaz nodded and complied, turning and leapfrogging pallet loaders as he moved to the rear. He ducked his head under the snap of rounds cutting the air, while staying out of Kemp's fire lane, until he reached the young Marine's position. And it was true that a machine-gunner at work was vulnerable – he'd neither see nor hear any threats coming from his sides or rear.

So Yaz took cover nearby, inside the front of the warehouse, under the rolled-up cargo doors where the pallet loaders once sat. From here, he could face the rear, keep his eye on Kemp, cover the area, and monitor radio traffic.

What he couldn't do was watch the fight – but only listen.

First he heard a long and violent chain of ground-shaking

explosions from way out to the east – this would be an opening grenade volley launched down-range. Then the nearby volume of fire ramped up, as the 2/2 guys added to Kemp's base of fire. After that, Yaz just had to imagine 2/1 racing forward with Gifford in the lead. And he had to admit their Assistant Ops Sergeant – however much of an asshole he might be, however much he personally disliked Yaz – was a brave son of a bitch.

Despite all that, and despite having an important job to do, Yaz still felt like Corporal Upham in *Saving Private Ryan* – banished to stay in the rear with the backpacks, while the real soldiers assaulted the German machine-gun position. But then, almost as soon as he thought that…

The next part of the movie happened.

Somebody got stitched up by the enemy machine gun.

Hearing frightening updates on the team net, Yaz turned and peered out around the corner, eyes narrowed, heart racing, looking toward the front – where, way down the dock, but flush with the buildings, he could just make out two Marines dragging a third one back around the corner from the adjacent alley, hauling him by his vest.

That third man was not moving.

Somehow Yaz knew it was Gifford. And he figured the man was either dead, or soon would be. He looked back in the other direction, then down at Kemp. He was belly-down in the rear behind his Mk 48, with a dozen Marines between him and the enemy – as well as two others, Coulson and Dunham, still providing security on the opposite side, facing away to the west. He was as safe as anyone could be in a firefight.

Yaz touched his med ruck, broke cover – and took off.

* * *

When Gifford led the charge around the corner into that first alley, barely slowing his balls-out run or high rate of fire, he quickly discovered the limits of aggression – specifically, when the enemy's numbers, disposition, and capabilities turn out not to be what you'd thought they were.

The instant he rounded that corner, he found himself face to face with a whole approaching column of vehicles, mostly pick-up trucks, racing directly at his face from the front gates of the base. And at least one of them had a mounted machine gun. It opened up, and due more to bad luck than anything else, caught Gifford with a long burst, which felt like a piano landing on his chest, also wrenching his right arm and stinging his cheek.

He'd barely hit the deck, slamming into it with his back and hammering the air from his lungs, before Brady and Reyes grabbed the arm-holes of his vest and hauled him out of the line of fire, while Graybeard shot to cover them, and put it out on the radio.

"Contact north, multiple victors with crew-served weapons, one man down…"

Still flat on his back, Gifford tried to refocus his eyes, and tried to resist as Brady started to unstrap his vest. But his ceramic plate had stopped most of the rounds, while one creased his right cheek – and the last went cleanly through his right arm, just above the bicep. Even as Gifford sat up, he hazily saw a fifth man squatting down beside them.

It was Yaz, unslinging his med ruck and gloving up.

"The fuck you doing here?" Gifford barked.

Yaz took Gifford's arm, and said, "Let me see that."

"I'm fine, you asshole," Gifford said, shrugging him off.

"I've heard guys with six holes in them say exactly that."

Gifford shoved him in the chest. "Well I've got exactly one

hole in me. These fucking guys are spraying and praying, they can't hit shit." He squinted off behind Yaz toward their rear. "And I told you to pull security for Kemp."

Yaz deflated, but said, "You've got at least one GSW…."

"I'm fine," Gifford said, climbing to his feet. "Fuck off!"

There was nothing else to be said, so Yaz fucked off, shrugging back into his med ruck, hunching against the incoming and outgoing fire, and jogged back toward the rear. He was nearly back to their lines when he looked up and saw a figure emerge from the secure door of the warehouse and fall on Kemp with what looked like a machete.

No one heard Kemp screaming over the gunfire.

Once again, Yaz took off at a dead run.

# TAILGATER

Dòujī maintained his stealthy position in the alley, watching the Americans and waiting for his backup – his brothers in Salakau. He was still worried they were biting off more than they could chew by attacking American soldiers. They looked professional, well-armed, well-organized, and alert.

And even more were arriving in another boatload.

Dòujī reached for his phone to wave the brothers off… when God smiled on them. He heard shouting and a loud splash from underneath the dock, and then the two soldiers guarding the front door, one after the other, ran over to the dock edge. Dòujī knew this was his only chance – it might get him killed, but if it worked, his status in the group would be assured forever.

He broke cover and dashed along the front of the warehouse toward the door, right behind the backs of the two soldiers. He hauled on the handle.

*Fuck.* Still locked.

He heard gunshots and turned to see one of the soldiers firing down into the water, but then lower his weapon as the other reached him. One or both would surely turn around any second, and another rifle shot would end him. In desperation, he looked around. There was nowhere to hide. Except…

A pile of bodies by the wall of the warehouse.

Dòujī ran to it and lay down facing the wall. The smell was

horrid, and the bodies leaked black gunk on the concrete, but he could stay out of the worst of it if he pressed up against the wall. Now he had no choice but to lie there…

And will himself not to move.

\* \* \*

Two hours was a long time to lie motionless in a pile of dead and diseased bodies. On the other hand, Dòujī was able to open his eyes and look around a little, and as he did so he realized the only Americans outside were facing away – two toward the east end of the dock, two west. He could hear bustling activity inside the warehouse, through the wall.

But nobody else came or went… until someone did.

The door opened and a woman in blue camouflage fatigues emerged. Dòujī slammed his eyes shut and stopped breathing. He heard footsteps as the woman approached one pair of the soldiers, those to the east. They exchanged words, but quiet and distant, and in English anyway, so Dòujī had no idea what they were talking about.

And then the woman turned around, came back – and badged open the door. Like a wraith, Dòujī rose to his feet, staying in a low hunch, and padded at high speed toward it…

Catching it just before it closed.

When he followed the woman inside, he was startled to find her turned, looking straight at him – evidently waiting for the door to close before she went on. Someone had trained her well enough to not get followed into a secure area by a tailgater. But what she hadn't expected was that she actually would be. Still, she reacted quickly – opening her mouth to shout, grabbing at a holstered pistol with her right hand, and tightening the grip of her left to protect the keycard…

But she succeeded in none of those things.

Because, fast as she was, Dòují was much faster.

In two seconds, and five quick cuts, he had her bleeding out mutely on the ground, and then proceeded to drag her dying form into one of the offices just off the corridor. He shoved her trembling body under the desk, dug out the keycard from her clutching fingers, got out his Durascan NFC & RFID Reader/ Writer, and then read the security token data from the card. He transferred it to his phone by Bluetooth, and sent it as a message to the others.

Somewhere on the other end, they would use the string of hex data in the token to clone a new but identical security card – one that would let them in the front gate of the base, along with their vehicles, and with much heavier weapons.

Finally, Dòují hid himself behind the desk.

And he waited for his moment to strike.

# UNLEASH HELL

*Changi Naval Base – Main Dock*

Yaz was now running flat out, but also somehow frozen, unable to act – transfixed by what he could see being done to the young Marine ahead of him. Basically, Kemp was being hacked to death in front of his eyes. The fact that none of the other Marines could see this, all facing away as they were, made the situation even more sickening and surreal.

Yaz felt as if he had no mouth, and he had to scream.

Later, he would obsessively recount the reasons he hadn't shot sooner – his hurtling run, the manic motion of his target, the Marines in his sight picture ahead, including Kemp himself, the roar and snap of incoming and outgoing fire – and, mainly, just how lethally fast it all happened.

Finally, too late, he raised his weapon and engaged.

* * *

Kemp felt like he was having another great day out – and should have volunteered to hump the Mk 48 ages ago. Granted, it was a fair bit of weight, but it was pretty hard to beat as a section support weapon. In spec-ops, the idea was usually to use stealth and cunning to defeat a larger force, so the big gun generally only came into the fight when things went to shit.

But, so far, Kemp had gotten to rock out with it on each of their first two missions in the post-Apocalypse. Yeah, firing long bursts into a crowd of already dead people was good fun. But it was even more gratifying to support his teammates and their assault – to be a role player, with a defined job, protecting them as they advanced into the teeth of the enemy.

He held the adjustable cheek-weld of the weapon in tight to his face, left hand in the crook of his right elbow, and put the red dot of his Aimpoint sight on the edges of the alleys the enemy were taking cover in – and let off controlled five-round bursts, assuring those guys either kept their heads down while the assaulters advanced…

Or else got shot when they stuck them out.

He was still on his first 100-round belt, and still smiling out loud, when he felt the first bewildering and sickening shock of pain low in the back of his thigh, just above the knee. He also had absolutely no idea what the hell was happening to him, and didn't even manage to react until he felt the second slash, in the other leg. The pain was sharp and raw, and he could feel his pants legs soaking with blood as he rolled onto his back – and then just had time to get both arms up to block the long evil blade coming straight down toward his neck.

He didn't have a lot of time to observe the guy swinging it, but he looked small, dark-haired, and mean, and faster than Kemp knew a man could be. The blade came down and thunked into the outside of both his forearms at once, and he shouted from the shock and pain of it – but then it took the guy a second to yank the blade free, from the ulna bone of his left arm. In that precious half-second, Kemp flashed his right hand down and got his pistol free, and even swept the safety up as he raised the weapon toward his attacker's face—

At which point the blade came free from his left arm and flashed toward the right, half-severing his right hand at the wrist.

Still attached by tendons, it flopped over, and Kemp started to black out from the pain. His vision stayed lit just long enough to see the man's chest erupt in a group of blood splashes. By the time he rocketed out of sight and fell over…

Kemp had lost consciousness.

\* \* \*

By the time Yaz reached him, Kemp was a bloody mess – worse than any casualty he'd ever had to deal with, in either combat or training. Mind overloaded and numb, Yaz let his weapon drop on its sling, whirled the med ruck off his back, and skidded to a halt on both knees beside the grievously wounded young Marine.

Everything outside his narrow cone of focus became a blur as he got out both CATs (combat application tourniquets) in his ruck, already knowing Kemp had two catastrophic bleeds – both popliteal arteries on the backs of his thighs pumping thick gouts of blood onto the ground – and also a severe bleed, the radial artery in his nearly severed wrist, blood pulsing out of it in regular spurts.

The first two were most urgent – a person can bleed out in 90 seconds from a severed femoral artery, and only a little slower from the popliteal, which branched off it – and Yaz knew if he fumbled the application of either of these tourniquets, for even a few seconds, that was it for Kemp.

He jammed his knee into one of the leg wounds while he got the tourniquet on the other one, twisting the windlass for everything he was worth. He could see the pool of dark red blood he squatted in already flowing out toward the edge of the dock. If Kemp had been face down, Yaz would have had to worry about him aspirating it and drowning.

With all the blood, panic, and tunnel vision, at first he wasn't even aware of the armed convoy that rolled out onto the dock behind him and started hosing the Marines' position with dozens of weapons, blanketing the area with skittering and snapping rounds, driving Marines under cover, unleashing hell.

Yaz's hell was right there in front of him.

* * *

Every Team 2 Marine was now either up on the line, or else actually out in front of it. The only exceptions were Coulson and Dunham, back holding the rear of the dock to the west – against a fast-growing crowd of surging dead guys, all of them suddenly very interested in the Marines' operation, now that it had gone not just noisy, but raucous.

The remaining 2/2 guys – SSG Cartwright, Meyer, and Graves – along with the LT, Fick, Blane, and even Chesney, were all hunkered down under cover of the pallet loaders, putting out withering fire to the front, trying to cover Gifford and the 2/1 veterans – Graybeard, Brady, and Reyes – as they hurtled back toward friendly lines, fleeing the advancing vehicle convoy and the heavily reinforced attack.

Every sailor, including those who'd been driving the transporters, had already cleared the fuck out, piling through the cargo doors of the warehouse and taking shelter there.

But even as 2/1, including the wounded but still very much combat-effective Gifford, skidded into cover behind the fat tires and steel bodies of the transporters, the tail end of the convoy finished skidding around the corner of that alley, fanned out, and accelerated hard.

It consisted of pick-ups, econo-boxes, and even two

motorcycles – every one with guys leaning out and firing weapons at the Marines' positions. Worst of all was the Singapore Police Force special tactics vehicle, an SUV with a mounted machine gun in its roof turret – the same weapon that had knocked Gifford down, but not out. All of these guns were bouncing and rocking, and the shooters still spraying and praying – but it was nonetheless a pummeling wall of lead hammering down the dock at them.

And it couldn't be long before the high-velocity hammering blew up something the Marines took cover behind.

Which would then blow up everything else.

Chain explosions, uncontrolled fires, and thousands of rounds spontaneously cooking off would really fuck up everyone's day. Unless something changed, soon, they were going to have to abandon this position.

Or else stay and perish.

# SEA OF BLOOD

When Yaz finally noticed the marauding convoy – which was only when an incoming round wounded Kemp again in the hip – he had to stop what he was doing and drag his bloody ragdoll of a patient into the cover of the transporters. It wasn't the source of the original injury Yaz had to get Kemp away from, but it was no less dangerous, to both of them.

Once out of the line of fire, Yaz got Kemp's own tourniquet off his vest, onto his half-severed wrist, and tightened it until the pulses of blood stopped. Now he had something like two seconds to look around – but, seeing there was no one else to do it, realized he was going to have to put out the medevac call himself.

Everyone else on this mission was either facing away and fighting, or else hiding in the warehouse. Smack in the middle of thirteen Marine Raiders fighting balls-out, and 30 sailors in support, Yaz was somehow completely on his own.

The only things that took priority over the medevac call were getting Kemp under cover, and getting those three tourniquets in place, which he'd done. But not before the limp, pale, and blood-soaked Marine had lost what Yaz estimated to be 30–40% of the volume of blood in his body. That made this a Class III Hemorrhage.

And there was only one class above that one.

"Seven-Nine Combat, from Reamer One Medical!" he

shouted into his chin mic. "Urgently requesting immediate dust-off of medevac bird! Repeat, require medevac, over!"

*"Copy that, Reamer, standing by for nine-line, over."*

Yaz took a second to get the two tightly wrapped rubber bands he kept there for the purpose onto his radio's PTT button, so it was hot-mic'd and he could talk with both hands free. In any kind of remotely ideal situation, he'd have someone like the RTO to make the medevac call, while he focused on his patient.

But the Marines fighting on the line were fully engaged. And a glance up ahead showed Coulson and Dunham firing steadily at lurching dead guys, now coming out of the woodwork of the base. Moreover, they were the team's rear security, and Yaz couldn't pull them from that duty.

So he made do, running through the fastest nine-line of his life, while also getting into the next phase of trauma care – namely keeping Kemp from going into circulatory system collapse from low blood volume. Hypovolemic shock was a foregone conclusion. Organ failure and death would be next.

"Line one – pick-up location same as mission insertion point! Line two – this freq and call sign! Line three – one Cat-B patient, urgent surgical…!'"

The rest passed in a blur, Yaz reciting on autopilot, as he hauled out the two bags of plasma in his ruck and tried to prep Kemp's arm to get a line in. But with so much blood loss, his veins had essentially collapsed, and Yaz couldn't make it happen. He was fumbling it. Once again, there was every chance seconds lost would mean a Marine lost.

He bitterly regretted not including a FAST1 in his load-out – an intraosseous infusion device, which would let him get blood or plasma directly into Kemp's bone marrow by jamming it in his sternum. But it was additional weight, and got discarded from the eternal need to not be too heavy or bulky to keep up with the men he was going to have to treat.

But then he blinked, sweat stinging his eyes, and yanked his mind back to the present. If he didn't manage to get this line in, there was no question in his mind Kemp was going to die – right here, and right now. If that happened, he'd have years to second-guess what he could have done differently, to indulge in regret and remorse for the things he'd done wrong. Right now, he had to focus on his task. And he so successfully tuned out all the chaos swirling around him…

That he didn't even notice the giant hovercraft that came blasting in from the other side of the harbor – with two mini-guns, a 50-cal machine-gun, and a full-auto grenade launcher, all of them manned by Team 1 Marines…

And unleashing nine different kinds of hell right back.

* * *

*"Yeah! Get some! WOOOOO!!!"*

At least half the Marines on the line were shouting this, though none stood up from behind cover just yet. And they were barely audible underneath the shrieking electric death-whine of the miniguns, the banging of the 50-cal, and the chain explosions of 40mm grenades – plus the explosions of fuel tanks and the vehicles themselves flipping end over end and rolling down the scorched concrete dock…

As a giant hovering landing craft of death came alongside the dock and atomized the ever-living shit out of them.

Fick, Blane, and the LT all just shook their heads and smiled as they peered around the tires of the transporters and watched the carnage on the dock ahead. It would have been nice if they could say they'd planned this, but the timing was largely down to luck. The LT had radioed news of the attack and ensuing battle to Team 1, and told them to light a fire. They did, but it was only because they'd just finished taking down their target, securing their own mission objective, and prepping it for launch, that they were able to ride out and come blasting in to save Team 2, instantly getting a whole lot more guns in the fight.

But the timing couldn't have been more perfect.

The last vehicle in the gang convoy had just turned the corner and lined up on the dock behind the others… when an 87-foot-long, 47-foot-wide 100-class LCAC (Landing Craft Air Cushion, pronounced *El-cack*) – a giant, heavily armed, latest-model U.S. Navy hovercraft and heavy transport landing craft – unexpectedly appeared on the scene. This was their sea-transport option, which they had gambled the mission on, and which Team 1 had just jacked from the belly of one of the U.S. Navy amphibious-well deck ships moored nearby – probably the dock landing ship, but none of the Team 2 Marines really gave a shit, and it didn't matter anyway.

What did matter was the 100-ton behemoth of a vessel came roaring in from the other side of the harbor on a wave of churning foam, its 16,000-horsepower gas-turbine engines powering the four lift fans below, and the two ducted propulsion fans at the rear, then pulled up alongside the dock, exactly paralleling the convoy on it…

With every single gun blazing.

The two small-boat pilots, who'd been dropped off in the second run of the shore launch, were a little out of their depth trying to pilot this strange giant beast, and banged the side of it against the dock, but the LCAC was pretty much designed for that, its superstructure surrounded by a rubber skirt inflated by the fans underneath.

It was like a gigantic floating bumper car. With miniguns.

And, this close, the four mounted heavy weapons on the vessel, along with the personal weapons of the dozen Marines not already manning the crew-served ones, basically couldn't miss – it was point-blank range, turkey-shoot time, and the biggest risk to the waterborne Raiders was splash-back damage from the exploding vehicles.

Side windows, windshields, and rear windows shattered, then disappeared entirely. Steel body panels erupted with dozens and then hundreds of ragged holes, hot rounds tearing through auto bodies. Engine blocks seized up. Drivers, passengers, guys leaning out windows, ones cowering in footwells, all got ripped to shreds, heads exploding, torsos peeling open and spilling their contents, limbs coming off entirely from hits with giant 50-cal slugs, or a hundred 7.62mm ones fired from a minigun in one second.

Both motorcycles, with a driver and passenger each, got dissolved into component steel, rubber, and meat, even before they could drop and skid along the concrete, as they were clearly the most hilarious targets in the eyes of the Marines doing the shooting.

High-explosive rounds from the Mk 47 Striker auto grenade launcher, 300 per minute, started to land as the grenadier found the range, immolating passenger compartments with fireballs, tearing and bending steel bodies, blowing out tires, and lifting cars and trucks off the ground, sending them flipping into the air and tumbling down the dock, carried by their forward momentum and super-heated expanding gases.

It was like the Highway of Death from Iraq all over again, except shorter and sharper, plus more close-up and personal.

And it was all over in seconds.

When the final gas tank had cooked off, and somebody put down the last flambéed gang member trying to drag himself across the charred concrete through the flames – either to get to a weapon, or just throw himself into the water – the Marines on the line stood up, and Blane was first to turn around and check on their six. His main concern was Coulson and Dunham in the rear action, which was still heating up even as the threat from the front stopped existing.

But then, much closer and a whole lot hell of a lot more shocking, he saw Kemp and Yaz down on the deck…

Trying to stay afloat in a sea of blood.

# EXTRACTION

*Changi Naval Base – Main Dock*

And this battle wasn't over, either.

The heavy weapons of the LCAC, and the return of Team 1, had decimated their human enemies – or rather rendered them into charred bone and steel skeletons, consigning them and their convoy to fiery and smoking nonexistence.

But the hellacious mayhem and racket of the LCAC attack was also drawing seemingly all the remaining dead from anywhere on the depopulated base. Coulson and Dunham were still holding the line to the west, and still dropping incoming undead a fair distance out.

A quick look over his shoulder told Blane the ones coming from the other direction liked their food barbecued – they were falling on the well-done remains of the local gangbangers, despite that flesh still being on the grill, and the licking flames cooking their own dead flesh at they walked heedlessly through it. Most then got dropped for good by Marines still on the line at the transporters.

So they had a little time here – not a lot, but a little.

Blane ignored the firing, shouting, moaning, and flames – plus the whipping sea-spray of the LCAC coming back around and docking nose-first against the dock – and squatted down in the lake of blood surrounding Kemp and Yaz.

"What do you need?"

"Get into his blowout kit, and stuff some Kerlix in those

bleeders." Yaz had finally managed to get the IV line in, thank God, and the entire first bag of plasma pumped into him, which was probably the only reason Kemp was still breathing.

As Blane got to work, he said, "Medevac inbound?"

"Affirmative," Yaz said, working to get the second bag of plasma hooked onto the line.

Kemp was still on his back, so Blane had to work by touch. The tourniquets had slowed the blood flow from the wounds on the backs of his legs to a steady seeping, but the highly absorbent gauze should stop even that. Blane jammed Kerlix into the wounds, giving thanks Kemp wasn't conscious.

If he were, he'd be screaming in pain from that alone.

This done, Blane stole a look over his shoulder, and saw the ramp of the LCAC already lowering down onto the dock, and the first of the pallet transporters driving up to it, then right out on it. Turning forward, he said, "ETA on medevac?"

"Unknown," Yaz said, moving to deal with the gunshot wound in Kemp's hip. He pointed out the slash wounds on his arms, bleeding lightly but steadily, and Blane started getting those wrapped up. "They were on cockpit standby, but I haven't exactly been in a position to hassle them for updates…"

Blane took a look around again, assessing the scene.

And the rest of the op turned into a race between the Seahawk winging its way there and the LCAC getting loaded.

The LCAC won.

\* \* \*

"Oh, God… what's his status?"

This was the LT, racing in with Fick close behind, both of them seeing the bloody mess that was Kemp for the first time.

Yaz realized he'd never put out the casualty on the team or local command nets. But he seriously couldn't do every damned thing, not left as he'd been entirely on his own.

Before he could answer, Master Sergeant Saunders came running up from behind, grabbed the LT's elbow – but then saw Kemp down on the deck. "Jesus. He gonna make it?"

The LT ignored the question. "Your guys all okay?"

"Fine," Saunders said.

"Good job," Fick said. "How'd it go?"

Saunders shrugged. "You've been on an LDS before."

"Crew still on board?" the LT asked.

"Some of them." He seemed inclined to leave it at that.

"Listen," Blane said to Yaz, leaning in and shouting over the other conversation, as well as the ambient noise of the raging fires and ongoing defense of their position. "I think we can get him back faster on the landing craft. That thing goes fifty knots, which means it can cover the three miles to the *Kennedy* in three minutes. And between the helo's round-trip flight time, plus landing and getting loaded up…"

Wiping sweat from his eyes, Yaz tried to think.

Looking back, he saw the pallet transporters rolling up the ramp in a line. From the briefing, he knew all six could drive right out onto the LCAC's main deck – which was most of the thing, the whole area between pilothouse, crew cabin, engines, and propulsion fans, which stretched in two rows down the outsides. As the boat was rated to transport 72 tons of cargo – including a dozen Humvees at 7,500lb each – the six pallet transporters, even fully loaded, were not a problem.

What was a problem was having a critically urgent casualty they had to get back to the hospital, yesterday. And while the LCAC was getting loaded fast, it wasn't fast enough.

"Fine," Yaz said. "But we've gotta go now. Shit-can the loading. We can come back for the ammo later."

The LT, looking physically pained, turned toward them and touched Yaz's shoulder. "Hey, Doc, we need to save our wounded Marine. But he's only one man — and that ammo means life for seventy-five hundred."

Yaz clenched his jaw. The rational part of him knew that's exactly why they had officers, and this was what they were trained to do – put the mission before the lives of the men. And then he felt eyes on him… belonging to someone who wasn't an officer, and who couldn't accept losing Kemp, no matter who else it meant sacrificing, and whatever the cost.

It was Meyer, slipping through the crowd until he could finally see the blood-drenched wreck of his buddy, down on the deck. His eyes were a foot wide, and his mouth obviously wouldn't work. He reached out…

"Somebody get him out of here," Yaz said, though he was just the one who got the words out first. It was obvious Meyer couldn't be there, and at best would make everything they had to do harder. Saunders grabbed him by the shoulder and elbow, spun him around, and got him moving away.

Moving instantly into the space they left, Doc Milam appeared, having leapt off the bow of the LCAC, last man out. Skidding in and unslinging his med ruck, as Yaz had a few minutes earlier, voice steady and expression composed, he said, "What's his status?"

Yaz opened his mouth to answer – but one of the sailors chose that moment to run up and say, "Has anybody seen Ensign Hayden? Nobody can find her…"

"Mother*fucker*," Yaz spat, finally losing his shit, totally overtasked and overwhelmed. He gestured at the mostly dead casualty at their feet, causing the sailor to pull up short. He'd obviously had some kind of panicked combat tunnel vision, and hadn't noticed what everyone was circling around.

But then something tickled at the corner of Yaz's mind.

Face slack, body going numb, he saw the face of Ensign Hayden, the earnest junior naval officer. And then he looked toward the security door she'd been heading to when he last saw her, but which he'd never actually seen her go out. Finally, his mind's eye replayed the attack on Flynn, and the only place his attacker could have come from.

Yaz nodded at the door. His voice affectless, he said:

"Check in there."

# SLIPPING AWAY

*Changi Naval Base – Main Dock, West End*

Sergeant Coulson's current problem was not keeping their torn-up junior Marine alive, nor finding the missing ensign, nor loading up the LCAC. His was that the glorious carnage Team 1 unleashed on the gang members was now drawing every remaining dead bastard on the base. To Coulson's mind, this factor already militated for them getting loaded up and getting everyone the hell out as quickly as possible.

But that was when word of Kemp getting hurt went out across the team net, along with the order to hold the perimeter while everyone speed-loaded the landing craft. Coulson stole a look behind him, just in time to see Kemp being loaded onto a folding combat litter, then carried toward the moored LCAC. He could also see reinforcements, 1/1 guys, pushing up to support him and Dunham in the rear.

That was the good news.

The bad news was that, by this point, most of the Marines were fighting on one side of the dock or the other, all retreating back into their shrinking perimeter. Coulson shot head, after head, after diseased head, making every shot count, dropping palsied body after body, more just stepping or tripping over the fallen ones. He stepped back smoothly as he fired, Dunham and now Sergeant Lovell doing the same on either side of him. When he went empty again, and paused to drop his mag out, he stole a another look behind him. They only held so much ground between the two lines, and it was the only place for the sailors, ammo, and loading op to be.

And it would be all used up in minutes.

Finishing his reload, Coulson's gaze was drawn to something to his right. Looking over, he saw four sailors carrying a second litter, their expressions at once terrified and heartbroken. On the litter lay a small limp figure, draped in a blood-soaked sheet.

*Shit*, he mouthed, facing forward and resuming firing. Things had gone even worse than he knew. Their thrilling escape from death at the hands of the marauding gang had been, well, thrilling. But it was no longer fun and games when their people started getting hurt, never mind killed.

KIAs just weren't funny.

As he went empty yet again, and reloaded while stepping backward, he suddenly realized he was standing in the biggest puddle of blood he'd ever seen. Lying nearby was one of those gang members, shot to death, a huge and exotic knife, with an elaborately carved handle, lying by his outstretched hand. Coulson was torn about whether to grab it – but then figured he could give it to Kemp.

When he recovered.

\* \* \*

"Ma–*rines!* We are *LEA-ving!*"

Somebody had to say it. Someone almost always said it.

The last Marines defending their shrinking perimeter didn't have to walk backward up the boat ramp firing as they went. But they did need to turn around and leg it pretty fast, as sailors scurried around the fighting withdrawal, getting the LCAC's lines untied and its ramp raised, while also trying to stay out of the Marines' fire lanes.

"Move your large ass," Fick shouted at one of the sailors.

"Hey!" the guy said, stopping and glaring. "Not nice."

"Life is like a box of chocolates, Chief. It lasts longer if you're not fat." Fick paused to fire his rifle over the man's head, dropping a dead guy lurching at him from behind. This didn't do much for the chief petty officer's hearing, but it did keep him alive.

Another sailor rushed by and tripped on a cleat, hurtling straight into Fick's chest, hugging him to stop himself. "Goddamn, Seaman," Fick said. "You smell like failure and corn chips. Kindly unfuck yourself and get on the boat ride!"

He did, along with the last of the others, but there was still some panic and confusion about making sure no one, Marines or sailors, got left behind. They had loaded up awfully fast, and were withdrawing under fire. But the LT decided they could do a more careful headcount once they were away from the dock, and so far everyone seemed accounted for.

Aside from getting Kemp's limp and blood-soaked form onto a litter and onto the landing craft, and briefing Milam on the medical actions he'd taken so far, Yaz was oblivious to the entire extraction. The front ramp got pulled up, the lines cast off, the engines revved back up, and the 160 tons of landing craft, crew, passengers, transporters, and gigantic haul of ammo and ordnance rose up on a cushion of air and pulled away from the blood-soaked dock. But by that time…

All Yaz could see was Kemp's life slipping away.

But he did hear and then see the Seahawk medevac flight buzzing in just as they floated out onto the harbor, which left him even less sure they'd called this one right, and already second-guessing himself. But it was done, and he needed to focus on what needed doing now.

He supervised as Kemp got carried off the deck and into the crew cabin, near the bow on the opposite side from the pilothouse. He and Milam then got back to work on him, Blane assisting, and Gifford – the only other one there was room for in the tiny compartment – kneeling nearby, just watching and breathing fast. He had a raw burn across one cheek and a bloody bandage wrapped around his arm wound, the type of combat buddy care anyone could have done for him. But, battling the lacerating thoughts that invaded his mind, Yaz wondered why it had to be Gifford in there.

Now he was going to have do the hardest and highest-stakes work of his life, not just with an audience, but a hostile one. As Milam hooked in their fourth and final bag of plasma, Yaz glanced up at Gifford and thought: *God, I hope it's really only three minutes back to the carrier...*

Soon the entire vessel and compartment were vibrating and bouncing around them. But, down on the deck of the tiny cabin, they couldn't see out, so had to imagine and hope they were tearing up as much ocean as it felt like.

"He's not breathing," Milam said, jerking Yaz back to the room, and into cold reality.

He took hold of Kemp's intact wrist, at the radial nerve. "Can't find a pulse."

Yaz moved into position to start chest compressions, while Milam got the kid's helmet off to make room for rescue breaths. When he did, the young Marine's trademark flop of hair fell out, lying against his paper-white forehead. Gifford leaned in from where he knelt on the deck – and, showing a tenderness that Yaz really didn't expect...

Reached out and stroked Kemp's hair.

# THE POINT OF YOU

Groundhog Day.

That's what their third go-round in quarantine felt like. For each of their first two stretches in here, they had just managed to fight themselves out of outrageously tight corners and back to safety. So they'd been giddy with adrenaline and the feeling of triumph, which had tided them over through the long hours in the bowels of the dingy oiler.

Last time, they'd also completed the mission with zero casualties – and with a haul of supplies that would keep them and everyone they knew alive for months.

But, this time… this time they'd taken losses.

And while everyone was happy to have ammo to shoot, they also started to wonder, in the privacy of their heads, and as the hours and days hung heavy, if they'd just be doing it on more and more dangerous missions – ones that would be necessary for the strike group's survival, but which would just keep whittling the Marines away.

Until there was no one left standing.

Also, in the dull silence of these sealed-off cabins and passageways, it was harder to forget there was no longer any world outside to go back to. No friends, no families. No loved ones, sweethearts, or old flames. There would be no shore leaves, none that weren't combat missions, and no three-day passes, vacations, or downtime between deployments.

The Marines were on their final operational tour – one that would last until they died. Or until they quit. Or the world ended for good. And now they were back in Groundhog Day all over again, with time dragging and stretching out into what felt like eons, unspooling down an endless dark road that stretched to a black horizon. And they couldn't help but feel they were losing energy, even as they were losing drive, motivation, and hope. Winding down.

Maybe even losing their ability to see the point.

Maybe it was just the death of Kemp. He'd been a good, happy kid, always with a kind word for everyone, who did his job capably and with good cheer. Everyone had mourned Flynn, when he died getting out of San Francisco. But Kemp's death just seemed wrong.

He had been so good. Too good for what befell him.

Also, grim and hopeless as quarantine was, it was hard not to realize this was basically life for everyone now. In a sense, the whole *JFK* strike group was a quarantine facility. They were all stuck in there together, and if they tried to leave they would die.

It probably didn't help that the Marines were jammed in with 30 sailors, persons other than grunts, non-Marines. Sure, they'd shared a common purpose at Changi. One team, one fight. But right now the Marines had lost another one of their own, a young man taken too soon, long before his time.

And they wanted to grieve in peace. And alone.

The sailors had their own hard loss to grieve, the brutally murdered Ensign Hayden. But it was as if each group inhabited a different dark cosmos of grief. There was no wormhole to transit between them, no radio telescopes sending or receiving alien transmissions to decode. These other people were just taking up space, and making noise, and getting in the way.

And they were all stuck in this purgatory together.

\* \* \*

Three days. That was how much time had passed so far.

But it felt like another eternity, all that time of not seeing the sun, maybe with the sun gone out for all they knew. And it felt like the world had ended all over again. They weren't even halfway through the mandated seven days of quarantine. It felt like the longest and worst Tuesday ever.

Three long days.

That was also how long Yaz had been hiding out by himself, sitting on a cushion in one corner of the compartment with the fewest Marines in it, resisting multiple efforts to console or engage him. Most but not all of these had been by Gunny Blane, who just kept coming back and checking on him, no matter how many times he was rebuffed.

Yaz had seen most of the other Marines come and go, as they moved around, trying to keep themselves from going shit-house crazy. But one he hadn't seen was Meyer, his former guardian and medical assistant. Yaz had intentionally stayed clear of him after the fight, during their extraction and move into quarantine, unable to look him in the face.

Meyer had been close with Kemp, battle buddies in both gaming and real life. And it wasn't just that Yaz had failed to save Kemp, or even arguably gotten him killed. No, worst of all was the horrific way Kemp died, and that Meyer had to see him like that. Among all the Marines in both teams, Meyer had been kinder to Yaz than anyone but Blane.

And in return Yaz had stolen his best friend.

Now, he guessed Meyer was probably hiding out in some other corner of this deck, nursing his grief and his loss, but at least consoled by his brothers among the Marines. Yaz counted this as a blessing, if a cold one. He still didn't know how he could look Meyer in the eye.

But three days was also how long it took Gifford...

To come right out and blame Yaz for Kemp's death.

*  *  *

"Why the fuck are you even here, man?"

Yaz looked up. Yep, it was Staff Sergeant Gifford.

Of course it was him – that rough-edged, flinty-eyed, and heavily stubbled NCO. Yaz knew he'd be coming for him. It had always just been a matter of time. Maybe the other Marines had kept him from doing it before now. Maybe Blane, or Fick, had kept Gifford at bay. Even now, a few of the other Marines stood in a ring behind him as he towered over Yaz in his corner, perhaps there to prevent actual bloodshed.

But, to Yaz, it just felt like he was surrounded.

He reflected again that they were on their own down here. Like inmates in a prison, with only a handful of guards, ones who would never come inside to quell a riot, or save a life, not for any reason, except to put down an outbreak.

Because they couldn't chance the infection risk.

Yaz remembered how Drake had come to him again before this second mission, reminding him his first duty was not to the Marines – but to everyone in the strike group. Yaz had asked him what it mattered if one of the Marines got infected, since they'd all be in quarantine. And Drake had said, "Yeah, it *does* matter. Because you'll all be in quarantine together. And what happens if one of you turns? We could lose every Marine on both teams. And what happens to the rest of us then?"

Yaz snorted to recall this, thinking it didn't much matter whether he let the team go down to infection or get taken out one at a time by survivors with machine-pistols and machetes. Either way, everyone was going to die eventually. And maybe the Marines were better off without him, always fucking things up, and failing in his job to take care of them.

Maybe it would be better if Gifford put him down.

Yaz knew the NSF guards outside the entrances wouldn't save him. They were there to keep the inmates inside. Not to keep order. And definitely not to protect anyone.

"I said, why the fuck are you here?" Gifford repeated. He prodded Yaz's curled-up form with the toe of his boot, trying to get a response out of him. It wasn't precisely a kick, but it wasn't exactly gentle either. His voice grew lower and meaner. "What are you good for? What's the fucking *point* of you?"

Yaz looked up numbly, just waiting for it. He wasn't going to resist, didn't want to give Gifford anything to push against. But Gifford didn't really need it. He squatted down and spoke quietly, his mouth a few inches from Yaz's face.

"I swear to Christ. You turning up here has been like three good men leaving." He squinted in thought. "In fact, three good men is how many we've lost since you turned up." He thought a little more, working up a head of steam. "Some help you are. Some fucking corpsman. You not only let good Marines die. You're also the son of a bitch who made Two-One killable. Not a scratch on any of the five of them. Never once. Totally untouchable. And now two of them are dead and in the ground. In a watery grave, rather. You motherfucker."

Something snapped inside of Yaz and he came back to life. Or, given what he chose to say, maybe he was actually trying to get himself killed. Holding Gifford's gaze, he said,

"Yeah, well, if you hadn't gone tear-assing around that corner, running straight at the attack… if you'd waited for intel about the vehicles with mounted weapons, and not gotten yourself shot… Kemp would be just fine right now."

Gifford's expression froze to black ice – and his hand went to the knife on his belt, opposite his pistol. The Marines had all surrendered their rifles, grenade launchers, and machine guns. But no one liked the idea of sitting around waiting for somebody to turn, and then not being able to do anything about it. But, right now, the presence of deadly weapons in quarantine was starting to look like a bad idea.

His voice a lethal whisper, Gifford put his left arm on the bulkhead behind Yaz's head, leaned in even closer, and squeezed the pommel of his knife until his knuckles were white. "I fucking told you to stay with Kemp before I went."

"I don't fucking work for you," Yaz said, shoving Gifford away from him, then standing up, all in one fast motion.

"Oh, yes, you fucking do," Gifford said, standing up as well, squaring up, and jamming his finger in Yaz's chest. "You work for every Marine on this team, or on any other team, or anywhere on this ship, or on any other fucking ship. You fucking work for *us*, motherfucker."

"You know what?" Yaz said. "Fuck you. Just fuck you, man." He looked past Gifford at the other Marines behind him, suddenly seeing them all as attackers, unable to imagine they were there to protect him. Some part of him knew how much he was going to regret this, but he said it anyway.

"Fuck all of you."

And, just like that, Yaz crossed the Rubicon. Another one.

And, once again, there'd be no going back.

# BLACK SWAN

*USS Rainier – Quarantine Deck*

"That's enough."

Gifford's reptilian eyes narrowed, as he'd just grabbed a fistful of Yaz's shirt, hauled his fist back, and opened his snarling mouth to speak – but got cut off by Gunny Blane, coming through the hatch, and wading into the fray.

Yaz just blinked slowly, wondering if Gifford had waited until Blane was off taking a shit or something before coming after him. In any case, Blane hauled Gifford around by the arm and said, "Find some other place to be, Staff Sergeant. Right now."

Not just Gifford, but all of them cleared out, and soon it was only Yaz and Blane in the small compartment. Yaz sat back down on his cushion and stared off at nothing. Blane sat down beside him, knees bent, hands on the deck, looking the same direction.

Finally, Yaz looked over, his expression bitter.

"Fuck Gifford," he said.

Blane sighed. "I know you already know this. But you can't afford to say fuck Gifford. Or fuck anyone on this team. It won't work. And it'll work out worse for you than anyone."

Yaz looked down at the deck.

Blane said, "One day you're going to need Gifford to save your life. Never mind that you're going to have to save his."

Yaz shook his head. "I know. You're right. I'm sorry."

Blane exhaled and leaned back against the bulkhead. "You did your best back there. Every combat medic loses guys – you know this. There's nothing else you could have done."

"I could have done as I was told. And stayed with Kemp."

Blane shrugged. "You were just trying to do your job, by getting to a wounded Marine, on the front line. Hell, way in front of the front line. That was pretty damned fearless."

Yaz snorted. "If only it had been smart."

"Nobody gets to second-guess what you did – not even you. Especially not you. Listen to me, Tom. You were in a combat situation, directly in the line of fire. And combat simply *is* making impossible decisions, in fractions of seconds, with lives hanging in the balance. Then living with it. You made a call."

"It was the wrong one."

"You can't judge the decision based on the outcome – only based on what you knew at the time. If we knew in advance how shit was going to work out, all our decisions would be perfect ones. And our intel and ISR totally failed to predict a large force of survivors, getting onto a secure military facility, with a convoy of vehicles and heavy weapons. None of us predicted that. It was a black swan event."

"Was it? Or is that going to be our new normal?"

Blane exhaled heavily again. "Yeah. I don't suppose they'll be the last survivors we have to deal with."

Yaz laughed.

"What's funny?"

"You were right, back in the mess. How we're all wired to be tribal. But, the thing is, tribes go to war. That's the downside of tribalism. And we just got it, good and hard."

"Hey, it still beats being off on your own."

Yaz laughed, but he wasn't mollified. "I should have known. And I should have made a better decision."

"You made a solid decision based on the information you had at the time. And I'm never going to blame you for that."

"Gifford sure as hell does." Yaz almost added that he also sure as hell blamed himself. But that much was obvious.

"Listen to me," Blane said. "You need to draw a line under it. You have to find a way to learn the lessons of the past – while letting the past go."

"Yeah. I've never been too good at that."

"Which part?"

"Either one. Both." He looked up and locked eyes with Blane. "So… what do I do about Gifford?"

"Just wait it out. He'll cool off."

"Will he?"

"Yeah. Right now he's torn up with grief. For guys wired like him, that manifests as anger. And anger needs an outlet, a target. He's just blaming you because you're here."

Yaz tried to make himself believe this.

"Though, after he does calm down…" Blane nodded at the hatch the others had exited through. "You're going to have some ground to make up with the others. Because you're really going to want them on your side, too."

"Yeah. Back on Wall Street, we would have called what I just did a CLM – a career-limiting maneuver."

Blane didn't laugh, and neither did Yaz. In fact, he realized he was tearing up and his breath was shallow.

Here he was fucking things up for himself again. Evidently bound and determined not to let himself belong, anywhere. He wiped his eyes, and laughed bitterly.

"What?" Blane said, looking over.

"Something my therapist told me once." He paused to look over and see how Blane would react to this.

"Hey, don't look at me to judge you. So you were a rich asshole with childhood trauma issues. You're not alone."

Yaz shook his head, surprised and relieved. Thank God there was one person here he could relate to totally.

"So what'd she tell you?" Blane asked.

"How do you know it was a woman?"

"Just a guess."

"She told me I push people away – before they can do it to me first. To protect myself from rejection. To pre-empt it."

"Yeah," Blane said. "That's a problem. You fix it yet?"

"Obviously not."

They both laughed.

But then Blane's smile faded. "That what happened in your last attachment? With DEVGRU?"

Now Yaz's smile bled away. "Depends who you ask."

"I'm asking you."

"Dave would definitely tell you a different story."

"Who was Dave?"

"Outgoing CMC of DEVGRU. Enjoying one last relaxing combat deployment off in the Hindu Kush."

Blane looked over. "Outgoing to where?"

"Retiring, after twenty. Got a chance to triple his salary."

"PMC?" Private military contractor.

"Yeah." Yaz put his head in his hands, remembering. "Man, things just never work out for me anywhere."

"Things never work out… until they do. You want to tell me what happened?" When Yaz didn't answer, Blane said, "You tell me when you're ready. Or never. Or years from now." He smiled. "We're gonna be stuck together a while."

"God," Yaz said, head still in hands. "I swear, a big part of me just wants to quit. Pack it in."

Blane nodded, staring ahead. "Of course you do. This shit's hard. It's always hard. Hell, I've quit many times – sometimes in deadly earnest."

Yaz looked over. "So what did you do then?"

"Then I dragged my ass back up, and back into it." And with this, Blane climbed to his feet, and offered a hand down for Yaz, who took it. "You know what Mary Pickford said."

"No, Gunny. I seriously do not."

Blane smiled. "She said, 'This thing that we call failure is not the falling down… but the staying down.'"

Blane pulled Yaz up beside him.

And now they were both back on their feet.

* * *

Seconds later, the hatch banged open again.

Behind it were the LT and Fick, the former with a laptop under his arm, both striding purposefully into the room.

"Ah," Fick said to Blane. "There you are."

"We need our Ops Sergeant," the LT said.

Blane nodded at the laptop. "Where'd you get that?"

"They shoved it under the door. Basically."

"Okay," Blane said. "What's up?"

"New mission," the LT said.

Blane squinted. "We already got them megatons of food and ammo. What they hell else could they possibly want from us?"

"Fuel," the LT said. "Only two ships in this strike group are nuclear powered – the rest all run on gas or diesel, and we've seriously brought down their stores by dragging all their asses out to Hawaii, and then Singapore."

Fick said, "And nobody rides for free, motherfucker."

Blane nodded at the laptop. "Let me guess – they want us planning the next caper while we're still here in lockdown."

"Yep," the LT said. "You want downtime, join the Army. Marines work."

"Can I help with the planning this time?" Yaz asked.

"You know how to use Powerpoint?"

"Afraid so."

"Then you're fully qualified. Welcome aboard."

Everyone moved to a table and took seats around it.

"Got an early-stage concept?" Blane asked.

"We've got let's call it the germ of an idea," the LT said.

"Two words," Fick said. "Motherfucking Dubai."

"Why there?" Blane asked, as they sat down and the LT got the laptop open and waking up.

"Because they've got all the petroleum products." The LT pointed at the screen, which showed a map view. "Port of Jebel Ali – previously the busiest port in the Middle East, and largest manmade harbor. Tons of port-side refueling facilities."

"Nice."

"Yeah, but it's a twofer for us. Because Dubai is just to the east of the largest offshore oil field, not just in the region, but in *the world* – the Safaniya field. And offshore oil fields mean—"

"Offshore drilling platforms," Blane said.

"And oil platforms mean…"

"Big-ass offshore desalination plants. Where we can find spare membranes for our own desal plants."

"Bingo. That's the hope, anyway."

Fick leaned his thick torso toward the laptop and said, "That's not even the best part, though. Check this out." He switched to satellite view and zoomed in. "Not just the world's largest manmade harbor, but definitely the coolest. I give you... Palm Jumeriah."

Onscreen, the others could see an archipelago, a group of clustered islands, just off the coast of Qatar and alongside the port facility. And it was definitely not a natural one – formed in the shape of a palm leaf, eight graceful fronds curving off a central stalk, all of it surrounded by a circle.

Fick grinned. "Also jammed full of entertainment and attractions – six marinas, a water theme park, something called a 'Sea Village', and boardwalks that circle the palm and spell out an Arabic poem. How freaking cool is that?"

The LT said, "We're not going to the water park, Fick."

"Hell, I can't think why not – the dead sure don't have any use for a Jurassic Park River Adventure. Or wave-pool surfing."

To his surprise, Yaz felt his phone buzz in his pocket, and pulled it out to find a text message from an unknown number. He hadn't gotten a text of any sort in weeks, and wondered if it was Singapore's telecoms staying on the grid longer. While Fick waxed rhapsodic about water rides and the LT tried to get him back on topic, Yaz checked the phone under the table. Reading the message, he had no idea how the sender had gotten his number. He sure hadn't given it to her.

```
Hey, Yaz. Looked pretty bloody down
there on that one. Good job keeping
yourself alive. Whenever you get out
of lockdown... come find me. - Rain
```

It occurred to him this might actually be the last text he ever got.

But, more importantly, just like that… suddenly he had something to live for.

Maybe they all did.

Slipping the phone back in his pocket, he tuned back in to the discussion, and checked out the various views of the Qatari port and flowering island formation. He said, "Looks nice. Aside from the inevitable undead population. It's definitely exotic."

"Yep," Fick said, tilting back in his chair, grinning. "It's just like your goddamned recruiter said. Join the Navy and see the world… The whole cocksucking depopulated post-Apocalyptic undead crapsack world…"

"Hey," Yaz said. "If it's got fuel, membranes, and water rides, it'd be churlish of us to complain."

"Yep," Fick said. "Like a sore dick – can't beat it!"

"Roger that, Master Guns," Blane said. "Roger that…"

# *MARSOC*

## will return in

*ARISEN: Raiders, Volume 3 – Dead Men Walking*

The Zulu Alpha, and the world's greatest military ZA adventure, start for real in:

*ARISEN, BOOK ONE – FORTRESS BRITAIN.*

Love this book? Share the love, support independent authors, and make me your best friend forever by posting a quick review on Amazon (michaelstephenfuchs.com/arisen-raiders-tribe-review). Thanks!

Want to be alerted when the next ARISEN book is released? Sign up for e-mail alerts at www.zulualpha.co.uk/alerts and we'll keep you updated. (And we'll never share your address or use it for anything else.)

You can also interact with other ARISEN readers, plus the author himself, by liking the ARISEN Facebook page (facebook.com/ZulaAlpha) – and/or joining the ARISEN Series Fan Community (facebook.com/groups/official. arisen.community).

And you can follow Michael on Facebook (facebook. com/michaelstephenfuchs), Twitter (@michaelstephenf), Instagram (@michaelstephenfuchs), or by e-mail (michael-stephenfuchs.com/alerts).

*With ENDGAME, the climax & conclusion of the ARISEN epic, the main series is complete. But...*

The story doesn't end here. Across the entire overrun world, two whole years of ZA remain to be explored, and many of your favorite heroes will return, in forthcoming prequels and spin-off mini-series, including:

### *ARISEN: RAIDERS*
and
### *ARISEN: OPERATORS*

To be alerted when these adventures are available sign up for e-mail alerts, like the *ARISEN* Facebook page, and follow @ theZuluAlpha on Twitter.

Meanwhile, come back and live through the beginning of the
end of the world in *ARISEN: Genesis*, the pulse-pounding
and bestselling first *ARISEN* prequel.

And then live through it again, except harder and faster, with the SF soldiers of Triple Nickel. ***ARISEN: Nemesis.***

*Salvation. Vengeance. Vanity.*
**NEMESIS**

# THANKS &
# ACKNOWLEDGEMENTS

Huge thanks and a gigantic fist-bump to the amazing Straight 8 Custom Photography (straight8photography.com) for the complete and total asskicking cover image for this one, too. Again. :)

Many thanks again to J. Wesley Johnson, Rob Griess, and other ARISEN readers, all of whom have served in uniform, for so many of the awesome new Fickisms. You still rock.

Most or all of the stuff about Tribe (and depression) come from Sebastian Junger's *Tribe: On Homecoming and Belonging* and/ or Johann Hari's *Lost Connections: Uncovering the Real Causes of Depression – and the Unexpected Solutions*. You should buy and read their books, most especially the first one.

Ginormous thanks to USMC Sergeant (ret.) Joshua Brooks – for the bit about how there are no black or Mexican Marines, just Marines, and the one about how Marines learn lessons, plus a bunch of stuff I'm sure I forgot, as well as answers to more real-time research questions about the Corps and life onboard ship than I could possibly remember. You should seriously buy the post-apocalyptic anthology (getbook.at/fragments-of-america) with his complete and total asskicking story in it, as well as the sequel when that comes out.

The dialogue between Yaz and Walker about him lying to maintain his operational status was stolen from *The Unit* – I think actually the second episode – and if you haven't already watched this stunningly great program (created by CSM Eric L.

Haney and David Mamet) then I don't even know what to do with you at this point. :)

"I lift. Cardio's for people who can't shoot" is also courtesy of Pual Trjeo, along with just-in-time pronunciation notes via WhatsApp voice message. Not that he's currently stationed anywhere I write about or anything...

"Hard to say? Hard to say, is it? I'll tell you what's hard to say, it's hard to say, Oh my God someone please help me there's a man in my office with a *flamethrower*, that's what's hard to say!" is from *Caddyshack II*, written by Harold Ramis and Peter Torokvei, line delivered pricelessly by Randy Quaid.

https://tvtropes.org/pmwiki/pmwiki.php/Main/MagicalNegro

"Howdy boys, anything I should know about?" is, of course, from *Real Genius*, via Alex Heublein.

"My operational authority supersedes your rank." and "We walk." are from two sides of one scene in the second-best film of all time, Michael Mann's *Heat*.

Fick's recitation about elephant crapping and lutes is from Philip José Farmer's *Riverworld* series, book three, *The Dark Design*, which, yeah, I read in seventh grade.

https://tvtropes.org/pmwiki/pmwiki.php/Main/MoreDakka

Much of the music this book and the prior one were written to was just various permutations of writing playlists for previous books. However, here's a Spotify playlist of the turbo-charged lineup (with also a few extra new entries from the main list) that I put together for when I was really dragging, not to mention languishing in quarantine, like most of the rest of us: michael-stephenfuchs.com/raiders-1-2-playlist. Tragically missing from Spotify, still, is Viks Sideburns, the greatest mash-up artist of all time, and one of the better musicians and producers. You should totally check out his Soundcloud page. (soundcloud. com/sideburnsofficial) Anyway, here's a YouTube playlist with the missing Sideburns and also diRTy WoRMz tracks: michael-stephenfuchs.com/raiders-1-2-sideburns.

# ARISEN

*Hope Never Dies.*

Fans call the bestselling and top-ranked ARISEN series: "thoroughly engrossing, taking you on a wild ride through utter devastation" … "the best post-apocalyptic military fiction there is" … "Wall to wall adrenaline – edge of your seat unputdownable until the very last page" … "the most amazing and intense battle scenes you've ever experienced" … "rolls along like an out of control freight train" … "They grab you on the first page and kick your ass through the entire series" … "insane propulsive storytelling" … "the most harrowing, sustained action sequences I think I've ever read" … "the wildest and best rollercoaster I've ever been on" …

"A one-of-a-kind ZA opus. The indomitable warrior spirit shines through from start to finish" … "You feel like the explosions are going off beside your head" … "you never know what the hell is coming at you next" … "Every time I think it cannot get any better, BAM!" … "Blows World War Z out of the water" … "The Game of Thrones of the Zombie Apocalypse" … "not only the best zombie apocalypse series in print, it's also better than any military classic written by Clancy, Coyle or Poyer" … "the new Gold Standard – by far the most thoughtful and intriguing zombie series ever written" … "Like a Michael Bay movie on steroids" … "by far the best-written most intense series I've encountered" … "like trying to ride a bronco in a tornado" … "roars out of the gate at 200mph and just keeps going" … "I DON'T KNOW WHAT TO SAY ANYMORE!!! I JUST DON'T – This is the best military fiction series ever written! Hands down" … "If you haven't read these you need to reevaluate your life" … "A work of art – a beautiful, smart, tension-filled experience that will leave you both exhausted and grateful, filled with such astonishing richness and depth" … "dials the volume to the point of annihilating the sound system" … "A superb ending to an absolutely mesmerizing and phenomenal series. This was an experience I'll never forget."

They are the most capable, committed, and indispensable counter-terrorist operators in the world.

They have no rivals for skill, speed, ferocity, intelligence, flexibility, and sheer resolve.

*Somewhere in the world, things are going horrifyingly wrong...*

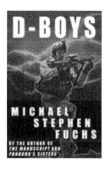 

Readers call the D-BOYS series "a high-octane adrenaline-fueled action thrill-ride", "one of the best action thrillers of the year (or any year for that matter)", "a riveting, fast paced classic!!", "pure action", "The Best Techno Military Thriller I have read!", "Awesome!", "Gripping", "Edge of your seat action", "Kick butt in the most serious of ways and a thrill to read", "What a wild ride!!! I simply could not put this book down", "has a real humanity and philosophical side as well", "a truly fast action, high octane book", "Up there with Clancy and W.E.B. Griffin", "one of the best Spec Ops reads I have run into", and "hi-tech and action in one well-rounded explosive thriller."

Printed in Great Britain
by Amazon